The
Taste
of
Ginger

The Taste of Ginger

A NOVEL

Mansi Shah

LAKE UNION PUBLISHING

Text copyright © 2022 by Mansi Shah
All rights reserved.

Published by Lake Union Publishing, Seattle
www.apub.com

Amazon, the Amazon logo, and Lake Union Publishing are trademarks of Amazon.com, Inc., or its affiliates.

ISBN-13: 9781542031905
ISBN-10: 1542031907

Cover design by Micaela Alcaino

Printed in the United States of America

For Mom and Dad, whose endless love, support, and sacrifices made this dream possible.

And for all immigrant parents: we see you and appreciate the path you have paved for us.

1

A gaggle of women, all speaking over each other in loud, animated voices, filled my parents' small living room. It was like watching a *National Geographic* special about social dominance, where pitch and decibel level determined the leader. They wandered around the room, grazing on homemade samosas and pakoras, careful not to get oily crumbs on the delicate fabric of their brightly colored saris.

I was sitting at the dining table near the front door so I could fulfill my assigned duty of greeting the guests as they arrived for my sister-in-law's baby shower. From across the room, I heard snippets of conversation from my mother's friends.

"Did you hear her son dropped out of medical school to be with that American girl?"

"I'm not surprised. I heard she walks like an elephant."

Without knowing whom they were talking about, I sympathized with the girl. My mother had often accused me of this great atrocity—walking like an elephant. I was around nine years old when I realized she wasn't calling me fat. She meant I wasn't demure and obedient—qualities every good Indian daughter should have.

Near me, a pile of presents had amassed over the last hour. Boxes wrapped in pastel paper with cute cartoon monkeys, turtles, or bunnies. They made most thirty-year-old women feel one of two things: a maternal pang and the gentle tick of her biological clock, or the desire to run screaming from the room. I glanced at the front door, leaning toward the latter response, but wasn't sure if it was because of the baby paraphernalia around me or the suffocating feeling I got whenever I went back to my parents' house near Devon Avenue—Chicago's very own Little India.

Across the room, my mother, dressed in an orange-and-gold sari that clung to her ample hips and chest, offered to bring my sister-in-law, Dipti, a plate of food. She'd been fawning over Dipti all day, telling her she needed to rest to keep the baby healthy.

"You are a mother now, beta," she'd say, shooting me a look of disappointment every time she referred to Dipti being a mother. I winced inwardly at hearing the term of affection she used to call me as a child. It had been a long time since I had been beta.

My mother's long hair, streaked with white, was pinned into a neat bun with dozens of bobby pins and adorned with small fragrant jasmine flowers. It opened her face and softened her sharp features. Until yesterday, we hadn't spoken in months. Not since she found out that my boyfriend—now *ex*-boyfriend—and I had been living together in Los Angeles. Cohabitating with a dhoriya was, in her opinion, the most shameful thing her daughter could have done. Living with a white boy was right up there with marrying someone from a lower caste or talking back to your elders.

It's not like I had made it my mission to disappoint her. Until then, I'd tried to convince myself that I'd end up with a caste-appropriate Indian even though I'd never met one that I'd been attracted to. But when Alex tilted my chin to meet his blue eyes before our lips touched for that first kiss, I knew I was in trouble. It wasn't long before he became my first love, and I was convinced we were destined to be together. Until one day we weren't. I'd just never imagined that *I'd* be the one letting *him* go. And so soon after I'd told my parents that if they couldn't accept Alex into their lives, it was the same as not accepting me. Timing could be a real bitch sometimes.

A group of aunties who were crowded around Dipti burst into laughter. She was only five and a half months pregnant, so I'd thought I'd have a few more weeks to mentally gear up for this trip back home, but my mother had insisted on having the shower before our family— well, everyone except me—went to India for my cousin's wedding later that week. She'd consulted a priest, who'd consulted the stars, and today, Sunday, November 25, was the only auspicious date that aligned with both the cosmic universe and her social calendar.

So there I was, back in the house I'd been desperate to leave after high school, standing guard over the ever-growing mountain of onesies, rattling plastic toys, and other tiny treasures.

A chilly breeze wafted in when the door opened again. Small bumps formed along my arms. I'd lived in Southern California for nearly a decade now and couldn't handle even a hint of the approaching Illinois winter.

"Miss Preeti!" Monali Auntie, my mom's best friend, called as she kicked off her champals outside the front door near the other jeweled and beaded sandals before scurrying into the house. She had always been like a second, cooler, more approachable mother to me and was one of the few people I had been looking forward to seeing at this party.

"Where is your sari?" Monali Auntie asked, eyeing the sapphire panjabi I wore instead of an intricate, elaborate sari like the rest of the women in the room were wearing. She clucked her tongue before spreading her arms wide and swaddling me in a warm, caring hug. I made sure my hands steered clear of her hair, which was pulled back into a tight chignon that she had probably spent hours perfecting, and I knew better than to be responsible for a hair falling out of place. The spicy smell of cinnamon and cloves lingered on her skin as if she had spent all day in the kitchen.

"The same place as your coat," I said, raising an eyebrow. She was the first person to arrive without a jacket.

"Oy, you! Do you know how much time I spent draping this sari around my body?" She put a hand on her slender hip and posed for effect. "You think I'm going to get wrinkles on it after all that work?" She flicked her hand, dismissing the thought.

I laughed, expecting nothing less. Monali Auntie had three sons and had always insisted that because she didn't have a daughter to pass her looks on to, she had a duty to maintain her style. Sacrificing comfort in the name of fashion was just one of those burdens.

Leaning closer to her, I whispered, "Well, I didn't want to say it too loudly, but your sari does look much neater than everyone else's." How any woman managed to wrap six meters of fabric around her body without a team of NASA engineers had always been a mystery to me, but Monali Auntie managed to pull it off solo. Anytime I'd been in a sari, it had taken my mother and at least one other person to wrangle me into it.

Her lips stretched into a satisfied smile as she smoothed the thick bundle of pleats cascading from her waist to the floor. Then she tugged the delicate dupatta draped around my neck like a scarf. "I suspect your mother was not very happy with this decision."

"Is she ever?" My clothes were still traditional Indian wear, but certainly less formal than the sari that was "expected of a respectable woman" my age, as my mother would say.

"Just because you're a lawyer doesn't mean you must always argue," Monali Auntie joked before turning to scan the room. "Now, where is the guest of honor?"

I gestured toward a group of women near the sofa. Dipti's fuchsia-and-parrot-green sari flattered her figure despite the mound protruding from her belly. The silk patterned border covered her stomach and left more of her back exposed, as was the customary style of Gujarat—the state in India where my family and the other women in the room were from. Despite living in America for over twenty years, my parents didn't have any friends who weren't Gujarati. Much to my chagrin as a teenager trying to fit into this new country, Devon Avenue gave my parents the option of living in the West without giving up the East, and expecting their children to do the same.

Monali Auntie said, "Come. I need to give her my wishes. And you need to mingle with the guests rather than sitting alone like a lazy peacock."

I dreaded having to listen to everyone ask me why I wasn't more like Dipti, why I was thirty and not married, a spinster by Indian standards. They'd whisper behind my back about the poor fate my mother had been dealt. An unwed daughter over the age of twenty-five reflected a failure of the parents. If only they had taught me to cook or clean properly, perhaps then I would have found a nice Gujarati boy by now. And if the fates were kind, might even have popped out a kid or two.

Monali Auntie stood poised to shoot down any excuse. Before I could utter a word, my cell phone vibrated, and my law firm's number popped up on the screen.

"Sorry, Auntie, it's work. I need to take this."

She shook her head and wagged her finger at me while I backed out of the noisy room and into the kitchen.

After closing the door, I whispered into the phone, "So glad it's you."

Carrie Bennett, my best friend and partner in crime at work, laughed. "Is your trip down memory lane that bad?"

I slumped against the counter. "It's as expected. Why are you at the office now?"

"Because being a lawyer sucks. The Warden forgot you were out of town this weekend, so I'm stuck working on some bullshit brief that needs to get filed tomorrow. I'm in your office—where's your file on the senator case?"

The Warden was the moniker Carrie and I had given our boss, Jared Greenberg. "Thanks for covering," I said before explaining where she should look to find the documents.

~

After we finished chatting, I lingered in the kitchen for a few moments, staring out the window at the little wooden swing hanging from the oak tree in our small fence-lined backyard. Burnt-orange and deep-red leaves littered the ground around it. The swing's chains were rusty from many years of harsh, wet winters. A year after we'd moved into this row house, my father had put it up to remind my mother of the hichko that sat in the garden outside her family's bungalow in India.

Whenever she received a pale-blue onionskin-thin letter from her family in India, she went straight to that swing and read it over and over until the paper nearly ripped apart at the delicate creases. The swing had been his attempt to make America feel more like home and was one of the only thoughtful gestures I remembered him showing her. Not surprisingly, an arranged marriage coupled with a culture that didn't accept divorce did not result in many romantic gestures between my parents.

The basement door opened, and my brother, Neel, came through dressed in jeans and a hoodie. He looked so much more comfortable than I felt. I'd have traded places with him in a second. He and my father had been relegated, willingly so, to the basement, where they could watch football while the party was underway.

"Just grabbing more snacks," he said. "How's the babyfest going?"

"Awesome," I said dryly. "I get to sit in a room and watch everyone fawn all over your perfect wife in her perfect sari with her perfect baby on the way."

Neel picked up a samosa and sank his teeth into the crunchy pastry shell. He had the metabolism of a hummingbird and could probably eat his weight in fried food without it affecting him in the slightest. "If it's

6

any consolation, she's less perfect when she's puking up water and bile in the middle of the night."

I scrunched my face. "Are you seriously eating while talking about puking bile?"

He shrugged and took another large bite. "Bile is nothing. I see way worse at the hospital. This kid came in on Friday with—"

I held up my palm. "Unless this story ends with the kid having a paper cut, you can stop."

Our mother walked into the kitchen with a full bag of trash. "What are you doing hiding in here?" she said to me. "People are asking about you."

After an hour of eavesdropping while I'd sat at the dining table greeting guests, I knew they weren't, but it wasn't worth arguing about. "I had to take a call from work."

It was technically true. But my mother's sour expression made clear she didn't approve. She thought I should be more focused on starting a family than on my career. When I had been born, my parents had followed the tradition of having an Indian priest write out my Janmakshar—a horoscope that mapped out my entire life. According to that, like my cousins, I should have married by twenty-five and had two kids by now. Shunning dirty diapers in favor of clean paychecks was only one of many deviations from my Janmakshar.

"Why doesn't Neel come out and say hi to everyone?" I said, casting him a mischievous grin. "I'm sure the aunties want to congratulate him too."

Neel dashed toward the basement. "Sorry, women only," he called over his shoulder. "I'll talk to them some other time!"

I had taken a step toward the living room when inspiration struck. "I'll be right there." I turned and ran up the stairs to my bedroom to get the one thing that would make this party more bearable while having the side effect of pleasing my mother.

~

With my Canon T90 SLR camera covering most of my face, people hardly noticed me. I couldn't believe I hadn't thought of bringing it down sooner. My parents had given it to me for my thirteenth birthday. Presents until that point had been academic workbooks so I could pull ahead of my peers in school. As an immigrant child of immigrant parents, I grew up knowing my future had to be their future. That meant getting the best grades, going to the best college, and getting the best job to ensure the sacrifices they had made for us were validated. Spending even a dollar on something that didn't further that agenda was unthinkable. When I got the camera, for the first time I understood how my American friends felt on their birthdays, focused more on having fun than being practical. But then the next year I'd started high school, and my birthday present had been the application packets for all the Ivy League colleges. "Never too early to start planning," my dad had said. It made me cherish the camera even more.

After high school, I'd wanted to become a photographer, but my parents had balked at the idea. "The only wedding photos a decent girl should be taking are the ones she is *in*!" my mother had said. My father had summed it up more succinctly: "It's a lower-caste job. Medicine is better." I could not live in Neel's shadow any longer than I already had, so medicine was not an option.

After college, I convinced my parents to let me spend a year pursuing photography. Confident I could earn a decent living at it, I pacified them by agreeing to go to law school if it didn't work out. I'd been twenty-two, full of passion and energy, and so very naive. After interning at a studio in downtown Chicago for what amounted to less than minimum wage, I wasn't any closer to being able to move out of my parents' house and support myself. I hated that my mother had been right. For years I hadn't been able to pick up the camera again, as if my failure was somehow its fault rather than my own. It wasn't until Alex had encouraged me to start again a year ago that I had. I began slowly, bringing it out when traveling or at the occasional family event I was guilted into attending. Like Dipti's baby shower. With the cold war between my mother and me in effect, I would never have come were it not for Neel. It was important to him, so no matter how uncomfortable it made me, I had to suck it up. Besides, even I knew not showing up would be crossing a line with my mother in a way that I couldn't take back. My family was no different from every other Indian family we knew, and putting on the pretense of being a happy family was more important than actually being one. There would have been no greater insult than the shame of her having to explain to her friends why I wasn't there.

I meandered through the room trying to find the best lighting. Gita Auntie, one of my mother's friends, animatedly spoke to some of the guests. She was short and slight, well under five feet and one hundred pounds. She looked up at her friends, her eyebrows scrunched, while she gestured wildly. Peering through my lens, I waited for a moment when she appeared calm and happy, her cheeks full of color and a smile on her face, before I clicked the button and released the shutter.

She turned toward the flash, startled. "Oh, Preeti. You must give me warning so I can check my hair. Now come. We take one with all of us." She put one arm around my mother's shoulder and beckoned for me with the other.

"Oh, no, no, Auntie. I'm fine behind the lens. Besides, this camera is old and hard to use."

"Oy, excuses! Keep your camera then. But at least be social."

It wasn't an ideal compromise, but I preferred it to pasting on a fake smile that would be preserved for years to come. As I moved closer, Gita Auntie continued her story about another friend's daughter. "You know, now she will never find a good Indian boy. She's *damaged*. What family will allow her to marry their son after she lived with that American boy, hah?"

They all nodded with that side-to-side bobble that to the untrained eye could have been *yes* or *no*, but they all understood what was meant by it.

A lump formed in my throat. My mother shifted her gaze toward the worn carpet, a light-tan color that had survived the last couple of decades remarkably well, but that was probably due to the strict no-shoes policy within our home. Her biggest fear was that her friends would find out I wasn't so different from the girl they were gossiping about, that once everyone knew the truth, I'd be destined to be alone forever. No good Indian family would let me marry their son.

Gita Auntie reached out and cupped my chin with her thumb and index finger and shook my face from side to side. "Our little Hollywood lawyer. When will it be your turn?"

I leaned back to politely break from her grasp. Gita Auntie didn't believe in personal space, preferring to communicate with her hands rather than her words.

"I work seventy hours a week," I offered as my excuse.

"You must think more seriously." She put her hand on my shoulder and then lowered her voice. "You are *thirty*, no? After that, you know, women lose their luster."

I bit back the urge to say I had just bought a fancy new moisturizer that promised to keep my "luster" intact for years to come. Instead, I forced out an empty laugh and found myself using Alex's old coping mechanism. He'd do it whenever he was agitated. It used to drive me crazy, but right now, counting slowly in my head was a better plan than causing a scene and making the day with my mother more uncomfortable than it already was. *One, two, three . . .*

Monali Auntie must have noticed the troubled look on my face, because she put down her plate and marched over to our group.

"Come. Let me take a photo of you with your family." She was the only person in the room I would have trusted with my cherished camera. And she knew it.

My mother and Dipti adjusted the pleats on their saris as we stood in a line with my mother in the center. After making sure her clothes were in order, she reached over and took each of our hands, her quintessential family-photo pose. Nothing to give away that she hadn't spoken to her only daughter in months. After all, what would people think if they knew?

As we stood waiting for the click of the shutter, I could focus on only one thing. It was small. Stupid. I knew that, especially given how the past year had gone. But I couldn't shake the feeling. She had reached for Dipti's hand first. Part of me was angry, but another part of me—the analytical side—didn't blame her. After a long day at the hospital, Dipti still could roll out a paper-thin rotli that puffed evenly when placed on the heat and could dance a flawless twelve-step garba routine. Even if I'd been given a week to prepare, I couldn't have done either of those things. And she never talked back to my mother. Ever.

I gritted my teeth. *Twelve, thirteen, fourteen . . .*

It seemed obvious that even though I was the daughter she had, Dipti was the one she wanted.

2

When the party began winding down, I volunteered to do the dishes just as a good obedient daughter should. Being in the room with my mother and pretending as though we were one big happy family had been suffocating, and I needed the escape. The calming sound of running water was a nice contrast to the loud, chirping voices I'd listened to all afternoon. Only a few more hours and I'd be on a plane back to LA.

Back to the apartment I'd dreaded going to since Alex moved out. It still hurt not to see his slightly crooked smile and dark-brown hair framing his pale skin when I came home after a twelve-hour day at the office. Even with Alex's stuff gone, I could feel him there. There was a black smudge in the hallway from when we moved in his dresser and my end had slipped. And a hard patch on the rug in the living room from when he knocked over a beer while waving his hands at the television during a baseball game. That apartment was full of happy memories as much as my parents' house was full of difficult ones.

The pain was even more acute because I had no one to blame but myself. Alex had asked me to go with him when he'd found out he had to move to New York for production of the independent film he had written. But I'd been too scared. Not of him or of us. But of the life he was proposing. Him working on his movie, me leaving my law firm job and pursuing photography. The bohemian-chic lifestyle he'd painted was romantic, and idealistic, and completely unstable.

I knew it wouldn't work out the way he envisioned. My family had been crammed into a three-bedroom town house with three other families when we first immigrated to America when I was seven years old. My parents had struggled from paycheck to paycheck. There was nothing romantic about it. I knew it wasn't smart for me to give up the security that came with my awful job without having a backup plan for after we burned through the money he'd been paid for the screenplay. My parents had taught me early in life that love wouldn't pay the bills. And it wasn't just my bills to worry about. Neel and I were our parents' greatest investment. Their financial struggles had put Neel and me in a place where we no longer had to worry. And in our culture, the "we" had to be the four of us. Five, when he married Dipti, and soon to be six.

My fingers brushed over a tiny chip on the edge of a plate. The thin white Corelle dishes with the blue flower pattern along the edges were the first ones my parents had bought in America. Over the years, my brother and I had bought our parents new dinnerware sets. Even though the gifts were prominently displayed in the china cabinet my parents had purchased at a garage sale twenty years earlier, they were never used. My mother said the old dishes were perfectly good, so why "waste" the new ones? My parents lived cautiously, assuming financial instability was always around the corner. During my childhood, they'd often been right. But now that it no longer threatened our family, they still couldn't let their apprehension go. It was as though the stress had become so much a part of them that it defined them.

I felt a tug on my ponytail.

Neel hoisted himself onto the counter, his long legs dangling almost to the floor. Like me, he was more legs than upper body. "Did we get some good loot?"

"A bunch of these." I handed him the stack of checks I had collected from the cards Dipti had opened earlier. Each was for twenty-one, fifty-one, or one hundred and one dollars.

He glanced through them and smiled wryly. "I'm sure Mom and Dad would be appalled if they knew when we give money to our friends we give them"—he paused for effect—"*even* amounts."

I laughed. We'd grown up hearing that gifts of money had to be in odd amounts. An even number meant bad luck. No one would dare take that risk. And people never dropped down a dollar. That would be cheap. But adding a dollar was generous. If I'd learned one thing from my mother, it was that perception was everything.

He placed the checks back on the counter. "The aunties try to marry you off to a nice Gujarati boy?"

"No. Turns out I lost my luster when I turned thirty."

Neel laughed and then pretended to study my face. "I thought there was something different about you."

I threw a towel at him. "I had to fly to Middle America to be at this party because you knocked up your wife. You can finish the dishes."

"But dishes aren't men's work." He imitated our mother's nagging tone while he grabbed a dirty bowl. "Seriously, I'm glad you're here. But I wish you were coming to India with us."

"I can't." My gaze shifted to the pale-green linoleum floor. "It's like being in a sea of brown people who all seem to be judging me for not being brown enough."

Another voice said, "What does that mean? India is home."

Neel and I spun around. It was just like our mother to sneak into the room and start eavesdropping. Her arms were laden with platters, but she somehow still moved as silently as a ninja. My expression was as sheepish as Neel's, both of us hoping she hadn't heard him making fun of her.

Her lips pressed together. She placed the trays on the counter and ripped off a large piece of aluminum foil.

"I was seven when we left India. Of course it's not home for me."

Neel wiped his hands on the towel as he headed for the door. "If you two are going to get into this again, that's my cue to check on Dipti."

The foil crackled as my mother wrapped samosas. "It's still your country."

"No, it's not! *This* is my country." I pointed my finger toward the ground. "I've got a passport to prove it."

"When people look at you, they see who you are, not your passport."

I cringed inwardly when she touched upon one of my biggest insecurities. Even though I felt American and wanted to be seen that way, with my brown skin and dark hair, I knew I didn't look the part. Everywhere I went, my Indian culture and appearance followed me. When I was fifteen, within months of getting my American citizenship, I'd been at the grocery store with my mother, and an older white man had cut in front of us in the checkout line. I looked at my mother, and her eyes told me to ignore it. But I thought it was a simple mistake. I got his attention and politely said he'd cut in front of us, assuming he'd apologize and take a step back. Instead, he glared at me and said words I'd heard both before and after that day, but the chill in his tone was something I never forgot: "Go back to your country." My passport had changed nothing of who I was. To this day, when someone cut in front of me, I remained quiet.

After several moments of strained silence, my mother said, "It's good you came for Dipti's baby shower."

I was taken aback by the change of subject and compliment. Varsha Desai wasn't big on thank-yous, so this was as close as it got. If she was trying, I guessed I should too.

Before I could open my mouth to say something polite in response, she continued. "But you should be coming to India to celebrate your cousin's wedding. I didn't raise you this way."

There it was. Her trademarked, patent-pending civil comment followed by an insult. Why should I think our first conversation after our falling-out would be any different from any of the ones before it?

I threw up my hands. "Four months ago you told me you wanted nothing to do with me because Alex didn't meet your biodata requirements. I assumed that included family weddings."

She stopped packing the leftovers and met my gaze. "I was trying to protect you. You need someone who shares your culture and values."

"I didn't ask for your protection. I can take care of myself." That last part was mostly true. She didn't need to know that even though I hated saris, the real reason I didn't wear one today was because I'd lost so much weight from the stress of the breakup that the form-fitted sari blouses I owned sagged off my shoulders in a way that no amount of safety pins could salvage. "Did you ever consider that if you had looked past the fact that he wasn't Indian, then maybe you would have liked him?"

"Preeti, start taking responsibility for your actions. I told you to do whatever you want."

"Oh, sure! And you also said if I stayed with him, I wouldn't be welcome in this house again." I put my hands on my hips. "So, which is it? If I were still dating Alex, would you have invited me to Dipti's baby shower today? Would you still want me to come to the wedding?"

My mother waved her hand as if shooing away a fly. "Why do you always have to talk back? I reached out. You are the one who did not respond."

I thought back to the birthday card she had mailed me last month. It remained unopened in the shoebox in which I stored all the birthday cards I'd received from my parents since we'd first moved to America. There were a couple voice mails before the card, but I'd ignored those too.

"You'd already said enough. I wasn't going to read whatever back-handed, gloating comment you put in some card too."

My mother wrinkled her brow. "What? You didn't . . ." Her voice trailed off, her expression shifting from confused to sullen. She nodded, more to herself than to anyone else. Maybe she was understanding for the first time that I had been so hurt, so infuriated, by what had happened between us that I couldn't even open her birthday card and see her familiar scrawl.

Neel walked back in, the kitchen towel slung over his shoulder. "You two still at it?" He swiped a pakora from the aluminum pack our mother was wrapping.

She and I both glared at him, but he seemed oblivious.

He said, "Maybe the best thing would be to start fresh and spend some time together as a family. Pree, we're not leaving till Friday. You can still get a ticket. It'll be fun."

Easy for him to say. He was going to India with his perfect Indian bride and new baby on the way. He wouldn't be branded a "failure."

Our mother said, "Neel is right. You are the only sister. It will look bad if you don't go. Who will do the duties you must perform?"

She still didn't get it. I dug my nails into my palm so deeply that I knew I'd leave moon-shaped marks. All she cared about was what people would think. It was all she had ever cared about.

"I'm sure someone else can fill in." I gestured toward the living room and plastered on an innocent smile. "Like Dipti."

"Come on, Pree. It's important to me," Neel said.

There was that word again. *Important.* The last time he'd used it was for this baby shower. When I knew something mattered to him, I rarely turned him down. But the thought of being in India, of dealing with my parents on their turf, amid the pollution and noise and assaulting smells, made my stomach churn.

"I'm sorry," I said to Neel. "I should head to the airport. I don't want to miss my flight."

Without a glance at my mother, I picked up my camera and marched up the stairs to my old bedroom and grabbed my packed suitcase. I had put in my time and was ready to get back to California. My mother and I got along much better with thousands of miles separating us.

3

Back home in Los Angeles, I managed to avoid thinking about my mother by relying on a familiar standby—work. Freedman, Lerner & Foster occupied five floors of ocean-view real estate in Santa Monica, but I rarely had the opportunity to appreciate the panoramic vista of the sun setting over the Pacific Ocean. Most days were like today, in which my fingers were glued to my keyboard, hammering out a summary judgment motion.

I'd billed over a hundred hours during the week and a half that I'd been back. This was, in part, because my mentor, Mike, whom the Warden had assured was a lock for partnership given his nine years of unwavering dedication to the firm, had been passed over and was told to leave. If partnership hadn't been attainable for a white male like Mike, then what chance did I have unless I worked harder than everyone around me? When I graduated from high school, my father had made sure I understood that I needed to work twice as hard to get half as far as a white peer, but I didn't want just half of what white people had, so I worked four times as hard. As the only Indian woman at my firm, I had always known I had to make up for not being white, and I was confident I would. I'd keep my head down, not make any waves, and continue being the top biller in my class so there would be no way they could turn me down for partnership when the time came to decide.

My office, no larger than a prison cell, was cluttered with binders, files, and a rainbow of highlighters and sticky notes. Having no plans for the upcoming holidays made it easy to focus on work. My entire family had left for India four days ago and would not be back for a month, so even if my parents and I weren't fighting, I couldn't have gone to Illinois. I hadn't received so much as a text from Alex since he'd moved to New York. I couldn't believe that after nearly two years together, it was so easy for him to make a clean break. There hadn't been a single day since our breakup that I hadn't wondered if I should have gone with him, but maybe that was because dwelling on the past felt easier than dealing with the present.

I allowed myself only a moment to take in the last of the vivid blues and purples streaking the sky that Tuesday evening. There were so many times I'd wished I could forget work and take my camera to the beach to catch the sunset. While I was crafting arguments for the brief that was due on Friday, my cell phone began belting out its melodic ringtone. My fingers fumbled around in my oversize purse trying to find it. A long string of unfamiliar numbers flashed on the screen. Only the first two mattered. Ninety-one. India's country code. I nearly dropped the phone in my haste to answer it.

"Something's happened," Neel said.

I jerked up. Neel's tone sent a shiver down my back. I pulled my cardigan tighter around my shoulders. Was it our parents? Cousins? Mama or Mami? I squeezed my eyes shut, bracing myself.

"Dipti. She's in the hospital." The line crackled as if it were strained by having to transmit Neel's voice across the globe. Damn cell reception!

I fell into the ergonomically correct mesh on the back of the chair. When I'd gone through the list of possible people he could be calling about, Dipti hadn't even entered my mind. I checked my watch, did some quick math, and figured it was about five in the morning in Ahmedabad right now.

"What happened?" I shouted into the phone the way my parents had done during the calls from India I remembered from my childhood. Calls that told us Nani had passed away, and then Nana, or that Fua had had a stroke.

There was a soft buzzing sound in the background. I pushed the phone closer to my ear. Was it static or was he crying? It had to be the connection. I couldn't remember the last time he'd shed a tear.

"She was in a ricksha . . . a truck hit it. She . . . the baby . . ."

I pictured one of those kerosene-powered, three-wheeled buggies that we used to take all over Ahmedabad because my mother didn't want to drive through the chaotic traffic. They could barely take on a goat, let alone a truck!

The line crackled again. "We . . . she . . ."

His voice trembled. I knew it was bad. He took after our mother, rarely losing his composure.

"Are you okay?" I pressed the phone closer to my ear.

"Me? Yeah. Just some abrasions that need to be stitched. But Dipti . . . she's . . ." He breathed in sharply. "They can't wake her up! I don't know what to do."

My eyes welled up at the angst in his voice. We had always been a package deal—if one got emotional, usually the other did too. Forcing myself to sound confident, I said, "She and the baby are going to be fine. If you need me, I'll get there as fast as I can."

A few moments of silence passed. I glanced back at the sun setting over the Pacific. A week ago, I'd been so relieved to return to my familiar California life.

"Neel, say something."

After a few more moments of silence, he said, "You don't have to."

Hearing the hesitation in his tone, I knew I did. He had always been my rock, especially lately while I'd been dealing with the situation with our parents and breaking up with Alex. Without hesitation, I closed the brief I'd been working on and navigated to a travel website.

"Hang in there. I'll get on the first flight I can."

"Thanks."

His relief was evident. I had no doubt I'd made the right decision and knew for the first time in a long while that he needed to lean on me more than I needed to lean on him.

4

The next flight to Ahmedabad left close to midnight. After booking it, I packed my things, ignored the new emails that had come in during the last couple minutes, shut down my computer, and headed toward the Warden's office.

The interior of the firm was as impressive as the view. I rushed through the hallway of frosted glass doors with brushed-nickel name-plates on them and then up the dizzying spiral staircase that connected the floors. Bright Warhols loomed over me as I maneuvered around the sterile white furniture.

The firm was emptier than usual. I could have heard a binder clip drop against the commercial-grade carpet. There wasn't the usual chaos of everyone moving around at lightning speed. There was no buzzing sound from so many people talking at once that it was impossible to follow a single conversation.

As expected, the Warden was pacing around the wide expanse of his corner office, headset secure atop dark-brown hair that was peppered with grays, and arguing with the person on the other end of the phone.

When he caught my eye, he held up a finger to let me know to wait. I could tell from his tone that he was in a foul mood. Leaning against the wall outside his office, I closed my eyes and tried to summon the strength to explain to him that I needed to leave work. Immediately. Absences were, at best, frowned upon.

"Come in, Preeti!" he bellowed after a few moments.

He said my name with the hard *t* sound that grated on my ears every time I heard it, but he'd never bothered to learn the correct pronunciation. He was shaking his head while he lowered himself onto his chair. My legs moved as if I were wading through molasses as I made my way to the chair across from him.

Jared's brows furrowed together. "People need to learn to step up to the plate around here. When I was rising up through the ranks, I knew I needed to knock it out of the park every single day. We're like athletes. We need to commit three hundred sixty-five days a year. Now, getting people to do work is like pulling teeth." He pounded his fist against the desk before forcing a smile. "Sorry, slugger, I know that you aren't part of the problem. I got your hours report for last week."

I gulped, wishing I could have caught him in one of his rare good moods.

Fingers clutching the armrests, I said, "Jared, I'm really sorry to trouble you with this, but I just got a call from my brother. My sister-in-law has been in an accident. I need to fly to India to be with my family."

Jared scowled and then quickly forced a neutral expression. "I'm sorry to hear that." His tone was measured. "How serious is it?"

"My brother wouldn't have called me unless it was bad. My sister-in-law is pregnant, so I'm sure that complicates things. Hopefully, she and the baby will be fine, and I'll be back in no time."

Jared clasped his fingers together and leaned back in his chair. "I'm sympathetic. Really, I am. But with Mike leaving the firm, you're my MVP. If you aren't back by Monday, I have to dip down into the second-string offense . . ."

He stared at me. Expecting what? That I'd promise to be back by Monday? That was the answer he wanted to hear. It was the answer he was *expecting* from me because during my time at the firm, I had made clear that my family and personal life fell second to this job. The same as his did for him. It was common knowledge around the firm that Jared hardly ever saw his attractive Korean wife or kids and that she seemed fine with the arrangement as long as nannies were employed, her credit card bills were paid, flights were in first class, and she didn't need to accompany him to law firm events. In exchange, she and the kids would pose for a holiday card each year, playing the part of the idyllic family so he could maintain appearances with his clients. If Jared didn't prioritize his own family over his work, he certainly didn't have sympathy for others who did.

My hands grew damp. I felt the four years and thousands of hours I'd put into this career slipping away. The travel time alone would make it nearly impossible for me to be back by Monday. "Jared, you don't have to do that. I'll finish the summary judgment motion on the plane and send it to you by email. The time difference might be challenging, but I'm sure we can make it work. I'll have internet access and check my email as often as I do here."

Internet access hadn't been readily available in India during my last trip, but that was fifteen years ago, and surely it had to be by now. I could make this work. I *had* to make this work, or I would end up like Mike. Besides, I'd told Alex I couldn't go to New York with him because I needed this damn job. I had to make this work; otherwise I had given him up for nothing.

He sighed. "Look, Preeti, I like you. You know that. I've been trying to groom you for partnership since you started here. But it's what I was just talking about. Teamwork. Obviously, you should be there for your family. Within reason. After that, you have to decide whether a personal sacrifice may help our team win the game."

"I'll be back in no time. You won't even notice I'm gone," I said, hating myself for letting him minimize what was going on with my family but feeling like I had to assuage his concerns.

As I left his office, he said, "I'll cover for you as long as I can, but everyone is overstretched, so the bench isn't that deep right now."

5

Back at my apartment, I only had an hour to pack before Carrie would arrive to pick me up and drive me to the airport. I flung my normal daily wear—tops, shorts, and skirts—into a carry-on bag. It had been fifteen years since I had packed for India, and every trip before that had been a struggle, resulting in several arguments with my mother because I'd wanted to stay in Illinois and spend the summer with my friends.

I grew anxious knowing I would have to see her again, and on her turf, no less. But I pushed the feeling aside. This trip was about Neel and Dipti. Not about my mother. And not about me.

As I was about to zip the suitcase, I focused on the thin bright-orange straps of a tank top. I pulled it out and held the soft cotton close to my chest, remembering my prior trips to Ahmedabad.

Before we left, my mother would micromanage every item of clothing I packed. As a girl, it was important that I dress in a modest and respectful way so I didn't draw unwanted gossip toward our family. It had been like when we visited my parents' friends' homes in Chicago—Neel was able to wear jeans and T-shirts, while she demanded I put on panjabis. I'd felt like an imposter parading around in traditional Indian outfits after I'd spent so much time becoming—and wanting to be—American.

She would pull out tank tops and dresses that were bare shouldered, admonishing me to "take something sober."

She didn't understand that those clothes were a large part of my new American identity. They were the armor that helped me hide among my classmates at school. Our house fell just outside the city line of the public school that most of the Indian kids who lived near Devon Avenue attended, so we kept to ourselves or the few other Indian immigrant kids who also attended our public school. Those first few months after we moved to Chicago had been rough. Neel and I were teased and harassed about our accents, our clothing, and the fact that we didn't fall into either the black or white racial category that most of the other kids did. I couldn't understand why our parents had moved us halfway around the world, away from Nani and Nana, who spoiled us and always took our side against our parents, to experience all these negative things that we had never experienced in India. In Ahmedabad, I had never questioned whether I belonged in the community in which we lived. Now, in addition to doing work we had never done before like laundry, cleaning, and cooking, I was constantly reminded by kids at school that we did not belong. That we were "other." That we were foreign. I quickly learned that being foreign was the worst thing you could be in America.

One day Neel wasn't in the usual place where we would meet after school. I heard some rustling by the bushes and found him curled up with his hands over his stomach, like he'd been punched repeatedly. On his back, some schoolkids had taped a sign that said, *Go Home Towelhead.* I didn't understand. We didn't wear turbans. Neel didn't say one word to me when we walked home, and I knew not to ask. That night, he told me we needed to learn to act like the other American kids when we were outside our home. No more lunches packed with Indian food, no more shiny gold earrings, and no more Indian clothes. Survival required blending in.

First, I studied American television shows after school, trying to mimic the accents. Our parents only spoke Gujarati to us in the home when we first arrived, so Neel and I would practice our American accents with each other in hushed whispers out of their earshot. Having been born into India's upper caste, we could easily tell which students were America's equivalent of upper caste—the white ones—and we found ways to connect to those students. Neel began helping them with their math homework, using that time to befriend them by showing them that he liked the same TV shows, sports, and foods as them. Convincing them that even though he looked different on the outside, he was the same as them on the inside. Once we'd transitioned, we avoided the other Indian immigrants who came through the school, remaining quiet and avoiding eye contact when the other kids teased them. To come to their aid would have meant giving up some of the ground we had gained. They would have to find their own way to be American, just as Neel and I had found ours.

My mother's need to preserve our Indian heritage by interacting only with the immigrant Gujarati community outside of our schooling undid all the hard work we'd put into fitting in. It infuriated me, but I'd never had the courage to tell her, because on some level, I was still that little girl in India who had been taught at an early age never to challenge her parents.

Now, as I stood in my bedroom clutching my orange tank top to my chest—something that was bare shouldered and far from sober—I winced, thinking about how many fights she and I had had over clothing, knowing none of them had been about the clothes. There was no need to add another argument to the list.

I turned my small suitcase upside down, the contents falling into a pile on my bed. I pulled out everything sleeveless, replacing the items with simple cotton long-sleeved shirts and modest dresses that fell below my knees.

Satisfied that the new contents of the suitcase would have passed my mother's scrutiny, I zipped it shut.

Pausing with one hand on the cold doorknob of my bedroom and the other hauling my bag behind me, I checked my watch. Carrie was supposed to be here in five minutes, which really meant twenty. I couldn't shake my mother's reaction upon learning I hadn't opened her birthday card. I let go of the suitcase and knelt on the floor by my bed, dropping my head until I felt the scratchy carpet fibers brushing against my cheek. Peering into the darkness beneath, I saw the old shoebox.

I lifted the lid with the care of an archaeologist unearthing a centuries-old artifact. Lying on top was the unopened pale-green card. Every birthday, I received a card from my parents with a check or cash inside. During those childhood years when money was tight, it would be eleven dollars. When things got better, it jumped up to fifty-one, and at its peak it hit two hundred and fifty-one, an amount that represented a tiny fortune to my parents. Knowing I could earn that money in a couple hours, whereas they would work for days, I told them they didn't need to send me anything, but they insisted.

I started at the bottom of the pile and reread the twenty-two cards already stacked in the order in which I'd received them. Each had a similar handwritten note: *Happy Birthday, Preeti. You are a good daughter. We love you. Dad and Mom.*

I smiled as my fingers glided over the embossed tennis racket on the front of the card from my fourteenth birthday. That year I had earned a spot on the varsity tennis team. My seventeenth year I graduated from high school, and all my parents' friends had come to the ceremony to stand in place of our relatives in India. At twenty-eight I met Alex at the firm's annual holiday party, where he had been part of the waitstaff. The card from that year was a simple one with a basket of flowers on the front and a poem about daughters inside.

After reading through the old cards, I held the pale-green one that had arrived on the morning of my thirtieth birthday last month. I'd convinced myself that whatever was written in the card would make me feel worse, so I'd tossed it into the box, unopened.

The cool paper of the envelope felt smooth against my fingertips. Concerned with preserving the card in as pristine a state as the others, I used the very edge of my fingernail and ripped a slit into the top, one millimeter at a time, until there was a clean opening. I pulled out the card, and a check fluttered to the carpet beside me. Two hundred fifty-one dollars with *Happy Birthday* written on the memo line.

This time in addition to the standard message from my dad, there was a separate note from my mother.

Preeti,
I know how you feel, but this is for the best. You'll see. Trust me.
Mom

Trust her? I squinted, angered by her last sentence. As I sat on the floor leaning against my smooth bed linens, I wondered how my mother—the woman who focused more on her traditions than her daughter's happiness—could possibly have understood how I had felt after Alex and I had broken up. The suffocating feeling of wanting to be the dreamer who could throw caution to the wind and follow her heart, but knowing deep down that I was the practical, steady person my parents had raised me to be. At the end of the day, no matter how much I fought against my nature, the fear of instability they had raised me with had prevailed. I had been right not to open her card before.

～

"Sorry I'm late," Carrie said as she pulled her red hair into a ponytail, revealing the small gold hoop on the top of her ear, a remnant from her punk days at boarding school. She smoothed her thick bangs onto her forehead. They were cut in a severe straight line falling just above her eyebrows, giving her an edgier look than the average attorney.

"I built that time in," I said, slipping my carry-on into the back seat.

Carrie was what I called "punctually late." She always turned up fifteen minutes after the agreed-upon time. Fifteen minutes. On the dot.

As I slid into the passenger seat, I detected the faint smell of cigarette smoke that always clung to her skin and clothes.

She paused with her hand on the gearshift. "I'm sorry about what's going on with your family."

"Thanks," I said, focusing on the empty sour-candy wrapper that crinkled as she nudged it while switching gears. "It's a lot to process, but I know they will be fine." My jaw stiffened in determination.

She pulled away from the curb and drove toward the highway. Given the late evening hour, there wasn't much traffic on the southbound 405. She swerved in and out of lanes, passing cars like a taxi driver in Manhattan, sometimes tailgating so closely that my foot pumped an invisible brake.

"When do you think you'll be back?" she asked.

"As soon as humanly possible. Once I know Neel and Dipti will be okay, I'm on the first flight back. The Warden's probably going to fire me if I'm not."

"Don't worry about him. The billable hours will still be here when you get back." She pounded on the horn when another car tried to cut her off.

It was easy for her to say, but I'd always worried about my place at the firm more than she had. I'd never expected to be given the same latitude as my white peers. I chewed on my bottom lip as I stared out the window at the familiar street names on the exit signs. I could recite every exit on the 405 between the 101 and 10. In thirty-six hours, I'd be in a city where I wouldn't be able to drive because the streets were chaotic with the animals roaming through them and the lack of any city planning. The handy GPS application on my phone would be useless because there weren't official street names or addresses, and it would be pointless to type in *the pink house next to the tea cart at the Jodhpur intersection.*

"I always wondered what it would take to get me back to India. I guess now I know," I said wryly. "I haven't been since I was a teenager, and I didn't like going then. It's dirty and loud. Everyone expects me to be some doting, obedient girl who never expresses any opinions and never contradicts her parents. I don't know how to be that girl."

"None of us do. It's why we became lawyers."

I offered up a smile to show her I appreciated her attempts at levity. "You should have heard his voice. He sounded scared and panicked. The last time I heard him sound like that, he'd gotten the crap kicked out of him in junior high," I said.

We continued down the freeway, zipping in and out of lanes.

In a soft voice, I said to her, "I thought about calling Alex. He was pretty close to Neel. Maybe he'd want to know what's going on . . ."

She cast me a disapproving look. "It's been over three months, Pree. He's in New York, and you're here. Let him go."

I wondered how long Carrie had been waiting to say that. A lump formed in my throat while the slow burn of loneliness swept over me. I longed for the day when he wouldn't still infiltrate all my thoughts.

"My brain knows it's over. It's just hard when there are so many reminders."

"I'm just saying you have enough to worry about when you get to India. Maybe leave the Alex depression here in California and start fresh."

She had a point. I would arrive in India and walk straight into a situation no one in my family had ever prepared for. I didn't have room for Alex anymore.

6

The international terminal at LAX was crowded with parents carting around children, couples asleep on each other's shoulders, and travelers having animated conversations. Even though moments earlier in the car I had resolved to let Alex go, I couldn't help but remember that the last time I had been here was with him, and we'd been one of those couples sitting next to each other excitedly talking about our vacation to Australia after having spent Christmas with his family. It was the only vacation I had taken during my four years at the firm, and I'd timed it for the end of the year, when the Warden wouldn't frown upon it as much.

Carrie might have been right, and I should stay away, but nerves got the better of me as I sat in a sea of strangers. I picked up my phone and dialed the first number in my favorites.

He picked up on the third ring. Hearing the familiar way he said "hey" and the low baritone of his voice gave me the same feeling I'd had when he used to pull me in to his chest and hold me.

"Where are you?" he asked, likely hearing the screaming kids and airline announcements in the background.

"The airport."

"Oh?" I thought I could detect a small smile in the way he said the word, and I realized that he might have thought I was coming to New

York to see him! When we'd left things between us, we'd said we were both better off with a clean break. It only made sense to keep talking if we planned on being together. Maybe he thought that was why I was calling him now.

"I'm going to India," I said quickly.

"Oh," he said again, sounding deflated. This time I definitely heard his disappointment.

"I know it's been a while." I lowered my voice, the closest thing to privacy in the crowded terminal. "There's some stuff going on with my family, and I didn't know who else to call."

I could picture the way his chocolate-brown hair curled over his forehead, contrasting with his glacier-blue eyes. He was terrible about getting haircuts, and without me to remind him, I had no doubt he'd let it grow out since moving to New York. He thought the curls in his overgrown hair made him look like a weed, but I'd always thought they made him look younger and more carefree, a refreshing change from the corporate types in suits at my firm.

"What's wrong?" he asked, his concern evident.

I pressed the phone closer to my ear, wishing there weren't thousands of miles between us. "Dipti and Neel were in a car accident in India."

"Are they okay?" He knew better than anyone else how close I was to Neel.

"Neel's okay. Or at least he was okay enough to call me and tell me Dipti and the baby suffered the worst of it." I felt my voice falter. "I've never heard Neel sound so upset. It was bad, Sheep." Without thinking, I used my familiar pet name for him. When we'd first met and he'd asked about my job, I'd joked that I was just another corporate monkey. He'd laughed and said he was a sheep, no different from every other lost soul in Los Angeles flocking to the entertainment industry. He started calling me "Monkey," and I began calling him "Sheep." We rarely used each other's real names unless we were fighting.

35

I heard him sigh and could envision the serious look on his face. His small dimples hidden because they only revealed themselves when he smiled.

"Pree, I'm sorry to hear that, and I hope they're okay."

"Me too."

"Is there something you need me to do?"

It was nice that he still cared. I was glad I'd ignored Carrie's advice and called him. Maybe he and I had been wrong, and we were strong enough to be friends.

"I'm not sure there's much that can be done, but thanks. I'll have to see what the situation is like when I get there." I glanced at the young family sitting in the seats across from me. The mother was leaning over, rifling through a carry-on bag, trying to locate something for her toddler while her husband casually rubbed her back. They had the familiarity of two people who knew the other was there without having to acknowledge each other. I missed that.

"It's really good to hear your voice." I closed my eyes and whispered into the phone.

He was silent, and I wished I knew what he was thinking.

"Sheep? You there?" I asked.

He cleared his throat. "Yeah, Monkey, I'm here."

I smiled at hearing him use our pet names too.

After a few moments, he said, "I guess it's stupid, but I thought you were calling from the airport because you were coming to New York."

I wished I could be that spontaneous girl he believed I was. "I'm sorry," I said. "I should have realized how that would look."

"Pree, it took me a long time to get used to not seeing and talking to you every day."

"I know."

"We were together for a long time. You know I care for you and your family." He sighed, and I could hear the conflict in his voice. "But the only way we can move on is if we let each other go. I think we were right when we said it was too early for us to be friends. I care too much to be the person you lean on now that we're not together."

My eyes misted. I'd tried desperately to convince Alex that we could make long distance work. I was certain we could make the best of any situation. But he had known he would not be happy with flying back and forth across the country every other weekend. He'd tried it with a past girlfriend and seen so many of his colleagues try that and knew it usually ended with someone feeling alienated and alone. He didn't want us to drag things out like that. His feelings hadn't changed since we'd been apart.

"You're right." I choked out the words. "I'm sorry if I did anything to upset you. I just didn't know who else to call."

"Maybe Carrie can be that person for you now."

I knew he was trying to be helpful, to solve a problem that needed a solution, but the words stung. There was such finality to them, but I couldn't blame him. He'd been clear from the start that he didn't believe in long-distance relationships.

A tear slid down my cheek, and I swatted it away, checking to see if anyone had noticed. I caught the eye of the mother sitting across from me, and she offered me a sympathetic smile. Embarrassed, I turned away from her.

"I'm sorry I called. And I hope your movie is going well. You deserve it."

"Thanks. I don't mean to upset you, Monk—"

"I know. It's not you. It's just all this stuff with Neel and Dipti. I'll be okay, though. You're right. I've got Carrie if things get rough. Bye, Alex."

I hung up before he could say another word. He had been my first relationship and, consequently, my first breakup, and my inexperience combined with the emotional weight had left me feeling totally inse-cure. I'd deferred to him on what made sense when two people who'd once loved each other were letting each other go, and his choices had been no friendship, no conversations to unpack why things had fallen apart, and no continued contact. While I was generally good at putting on blinders to the world around me, having someone I had cared about so deeply exit my life so swiftly had been hard to comprehend. I'd been sure we could salvage the friendship that had underlain our romantic relationship if we just worked hard enough at it. It turned out that desire was one sided. Carrie had been right. Hearing him be so sweet, while still being firm on the decision to not even be friends, had been crushing.

~

When I took my seat on the crowded flight full of Indians, I could tell from the black socks with open-toed sandals and T-shirt tucked into the slacks of the man sitting next to me that, unlike me, my seatmate was actually *from* India—born and raised. If there was any doubt, it was erased when I sat down and breathed in the overpowering scent of Cool Water cologne. It immediately reminded me of Virag Mama. I couldn't believe I'd be seeing him tomorrow for the first time in fifteen years.

My seatmate looked like he was anxious to chat. I forced a yawn and popped in my earbuds, warding off any conversation. Small talk with a stranger wasn't something I was up to.

Despite the steady stream of cool air blowing on me from the overhead vent, my skin felt hot as I thought back to Neel's call. The trip from LA to Ahmedabad, Gujarat, was a grueling thirty-hour journey, spanning over nine thousand miles. I had no idea what state Dipti would be in by the time I landed. Maybe she would be fine and already be discharged from the hospital! Or maybe . . . I stopped myself. I couldn't think about the other extreme. If there was ever a time in life to put my plan-for-the-worst attitude aside and focus on the positive, this was it.

As the plane began to taxi away from the gate, a man across the aisle pulled out his wallet and flipped it open to a photo of the god Shreenathji. The man touched the feet in the photo and closed his eyes. Dad went through this same ritual every time he boarded a plane or sat in a car. I had been raised to do it as well, but after a white childhood friend saw me doing it and yanked the laminated photo of the god from my hand and crinkled her nose at it, I'd stopped doing it around my friends and eventually stopped doing it at all. My parents noticed. Especially because Neel continued the ritual, but it was just another thing on the growing list of things Neel did right compared to those I did wrong. Still, despite my complicated relationship with God—or the gods—today I closed my eyes, too, praying for the first time in at least a decade. I silently pleaded that Dipti would be okay by the time I landed in India.

The plane took flight over the cool azure waters of the Pacific Ocean. Feeling like it might be longer than I wanted before I would see it again, I leaned forward to get a better view out of my neighbor's window, but it was too dark to see anything.

The loud hum of the jet engines filled the cabin and drowned out the voices around me. I leaned back, trying to think of happier things, trying to remember some good moments from the summers my family had spent in India. Neel, my cousins, and I would light fireworks every night, nothing major like rockets, but the small spinning tops that shot out pink and yellow confetti or volcanoes that erupted streamers. Fireworks were everywhere, and it made missing the Fourth of July with our friends back in America more palatable. During the scorching days, Virag Mama would take me to the Vadilal ice cream shop on his scooter. Sometimes we would pick up channa batura for dinner. The batura so fresh that oil still dripped off them, soaking into the newspaper they were wrapped in. I'd rip apart pieces to mop up the spicy chickpeas and gravy.

I was lost in my daydreams when I felt the pressure of another human body close to me—too close. The hairy arm of the man next to me was nestled up against mine on the armrest.

He was watching a Bollywood movie, unaware that his arm had crossed the unspoken seat barrier. I jerked my arm away and mumbled an "I'm sorry" even though I wasn't the one who had touched him. He didn't seem to hear me through his headphones. He was so fixated on the screen that he didn't even notice the touch of a stranger.

He crossed his legs, his knee now jutting into my thigh. Again, he seemed not to notice. He was used to a world where throngs of people boarded buses and trains, some of them dangling off the sides, barely hanging on. Restaurants packing in as many customers as possible and people bumping into each other on streets were a way of life. I would never win a personal space war against this man, and it was futile to try. It had once been my way of life, too, but becoming an outsider had made me a keen observer. Personal space was one of the first behavioral changes I'd made when we moved to Chicago. I saw how white people kept each other at arm's length, and I learned never to cross that barrier, and to make sure people never crossed that barrier with me. Eventually, I realized the distance kept people from getting too close emotionally as well and helped me hide any other cultural insecurities I had. Fitting in meant letting go of who I was and becoming someone new.

I folded my arms tightly across my chest and sank low into my seat, bracing for the journey ahead.

7

The hot sunlight on my face revived me from the long journey as I wove through the throngs of people outside the Ahmedabad airport. Using my fingers to shield my eyes from the blazing sun, I scanned the crowd. Every single face was Indian. Growing up in America and working in a predominately white law firm, I was used to being the one who stood out. I hadn't been to India in so long that I'd forgotten what it was like to blend in. Yet despite looking the same as those around me, I felt exposed, like an imposter who would be caught at any moment.

Eventually, I spotted Virag Uncle, or Virag Mama, as my mother used to correct me whenever I slipped into the English word *uncle*. He looked just as he did fifteen years ago: tall, lean, oversize glasses covering most of his gaunt face, and unruly hair tamed by almond oil.

All around me, people murmured their namastes and bent to touch the feet of their friends and families. It was the respectful way to greet an older family member, and I leaned forward to touch Virag Mama's toes with my fingertips. It felt odd, performing this ritual after so many years, but I could tell he was pleased I had remembered the convention.

"So little luggage?" he asked in Gujarati while taking my bag.

It took me a second to process my first language, the one I had once known better than English. I was not feeling confident enough to string

Gujarati words together. "I had very little time," I responded in English, grateful that my relatives in India were fluent in my second language.

He handed the bag to his driver, a young man with an emaciated build who could not have been more than twenty years old. The driver placed the luggage in the passenger seat while Virag Mama and I climbed into the back. His car, like most in India, didn't have a trunk. People around us were squatting on hoods, tying suitcases to the tops of the cars with thick yellow rope, but we could fortunately forgo that ritual and not waste more time at the airport.

~

Ahmedabad was familiarly foreign. While I had heard my parents speak of the country's progress during the last decade, as we maneuvered through streets packed with people using nearly every mode of transportation that had existed over the past century, that progress wasn't obvious to me. Camels and oxen pulled squeaky lorries piled high with perishables and clay pottery. Wheeled transportation of all forms was present and accounted for: cars, buses, motorcycles, rickshas, bicycles, and scooters, all tooting their high-pitched horns. Cows wove through the traffic with careless abandon, almost as if they knew they were sacred. The animals, people, and vehicles on the roads moved in whichever direction they chose. Traffic signals and lane markers were suggestions rather than law. In comparison, LA traffic was a perfectly orchestrated symphony.

My stomach churned at the thought of Neel and Dipti in a car accident in this chaos.

"How is she?" I forced the words out of my mouth, knowing that anything could have changed during my lengthy flight across the globe.

Virag Mama patted my knee and said, "Don't worry, beta. Everything will be fine."

I could tell from his tone that he still saw me as the little girl who had run around the house chasing after Neel.

"I'm old enough to know the truth."

He let out a heavy sigh. "Old habits are hard to break. You're like my daughter too." He took off his glasses and rubbed his eyes before placing them back on his nose.

A ricksha whizzed past us carrying a dozen children in school uniforms: boys in light-blue short-sleeved button-down shirts and brown shorts, girls in white cap-sleeved button-down shirts beneath blue dresses. Neel and I had worn similar uniforms before our family moved to America. The older kids stood in the openings and clung to nothing more than the roof of the open buggy. Other vehicles drove mere inches away from them. The children laughed and called out to each other, oblivious to the dangers of the way in which they were traveling. Neel and I had done the same thing when we used to live here, carefree and impervious to risk, but I now clutched the door handle and wished for seat belts and traffic laws.

"How is she?" I repeated.

"She's been in a coma for many hours straight now. We'll know more when we go to the hospital."

A weight settled on my chest. I began to feel hot and rolled down the window.

As visually frenetic as the city was, it had always been the smells that struck me most. When I was a kid, I had cracked the same bad joke every time we stepped off the plane: "Smells like we're in India!" The odors were unique—the aroma of poverty mixed with the smell of progress. The cleansing scents of citrus fruits, jasmine, and sandalwood coexisted with the stench of garbage, body odor, and pollution. A smell many people might find offensive but for me was oddly comforting.

A tired smile crept onto my face when we pulled into the driveway of my mama's house. Lakshmi. Naming a house was as important as naming a child. Lakshmi was the goddess of prosperity, wisdom, and light. It was the house my mother had grown up in. And the one my family had lived in until we'd left for America. It was customary for married couples to live with the husband's family, but my father's parents had passed away during his college years, so my parents had lived in Lakshmi.

The two-story white walls were grayed with pollution and the passage of time. The windows that had once opened directly to the world were now covered with a mesh screen to keep out insects. Maybe this was the progress my parents had been talking about.

On the left was the garden where I had seen my first peacock. I had been terrified that the large bird was close enough to touch. They ambled to the bungalow each morning, and my nana would toss them grains after his morning prayers, yoga, and meditation. He held my hand while I fed them. It was the only way I felt safe around them. He had passed away seven years ago, and it felt strange knowing that when I walked into the house, he would not be sitting in his favorite chair by the window, drinking his chai and reading the newspaper. Neel and my parents had come back to India for Nana's funeral, but I'd told them if I took a break from law school, I'd fall behind. In hindsight, a couple extra days dodging the Socratic method probably wouldn't have affected my professional future, and now I regretted the trade-off.

In the garden was the bench swing where I had once run to show my parents my new champals only to feel a warm, squishy patty of fresh cow dung seeping between my toes, destroying the new sandals. In America, the worst thing I had to worry about was a Westside housewife leaving a dropping from her poodle on the sidewalk and relying on the street cleaners to pick it up by the next morning.

While I saw improvements to the house and garden area, I was relieved that the bench swing itself, the hichko, was untouched. It was the same one I had spent countless hours on and had seen in photos of my mother as a little girl. It held generations of stories hidden among the rusting metal and splintered wood.

The inside of the house was just as I remembered, except for the new upholstery on the living room furniture; it used to be a soft coral but was now a pale green. As I glanced around, every corner of the house harbored memories. The dining table where we'd had countless family dinners was covered with red and gold wedding decorations. The same small, old-fashioned television set with antennae sticking out at odd angles still rested on the wooden table where I had skinned my elbow when Neel and I were fighting over the channel, as we always had. The glass top of the coffee table had a chip from when I had seen a gecko lizard creeping along the wall and dropped a mug of hot rose milk. I thought I hadn't missed India at all, but the nostalgia of being in this house again washed over me, and for a second, it felt like home again.

On the main floor, the smell of fresh roses, jasmine, and marigolds filled the air. On the couch was a large steel thali holding flowers that Indira Mami was using to thread garlands for her son's wedding. She beamed when she saw me and then rushed to greet me, nearly knocking over the thali. Virag Mama and she had always made a funny pair because she was as curvy and plump as Virag Mama was narrow and lean.

"Kem cho, Indira Mami," I said, bending to touch her feet, just as I had done with Virag Mama at the airport. She guided me to the place on the couch where I used to sit as a little girl, the space right across from the window that looked onto the garden swing. She remembered so much about me even though it had been so many years since I had set foot in this house.

After going through the general pleasantries of whether I was hungry or thirsty, we got to the subject of my visit.

"If you are not too tired, you can go to the hospital. Neel and your parents are there," Virag Mama said.

I seized at hearing I'd have to confront my mother, but no amount of jet lag or apprehension would keep me from going to the hospital and seeing Neel.

"I'm ready now," I said, heading back toward the door.

"Good. It is best if you go," Indira Mami said in English. Her accent was strong, but her message was clear. Dipti was not good.

I wanted to ask them for more details but bit my tongue, remembering I wasn't in America anymore. An elder had given me a suggestion, which in this country was tantamount to an order, and that was not to be questioned.

~

The ancient fluorescent bulbs cast an eerie yellow light in the hallway, tinting everything with a jaundiced glow. I hated hospitals. I'd never understood how Neel and Dipti could work in them. To me, they reeked of despair and sadness.

Indian hospitals were especially bad. The smell of antiseptic was overwhelming, but it could not mask the lingering stench of stale urine. The uniforms of the nurses and doctors were drab. There was no sign of the pretty pastel scrubs and sterile white walls from the hospitals Neel and Dipti worked in back in Chicago. Neel was probably distraught knowing that these were the best conditions he could give his wife right now.

When Virag Mama and I entered Dipti's room, she was lying on a flimsy bed with her eyes closed. An IV kept her hydrated, and two machines beeped steadily—one monitoring Dipti's heart rate, and the other, the baby's. Neel kept vigil in a green plastic chair. I crossed the room and put my hand on his shoulder. He bolted upright. His eyes were bloodshot, his face gaunt. His cheeks and chin were scratchy with stubble.

He gave me a fierce hug. Without me asking, Neel answered, "I don't know. She's been in and out of consciousness. Mostly out for the past half day or so. She lost a lot of blood."

"She's going to be okay. Both of them are." I tried to sound reassuring but didn't know if I'd been successful.

"I don't know, Pree—it's bad." As he shook his head, the premature gray hairs that had once made him look distinguished caught the light. In this setting, they made him look old.

"Don't think about that." I touched the edge of Dipti's bed. "Can she hear us?" Her eyeballs twitched underneath her closed eyelids. The movement was unsettling.

"She can't respond," Neel said.

I nodded. "What do you need from me? I can sit with her while you get some food or take a walk."

"The way people drive here . . . there was . . . a truck." Neel shook his head. "It slammed into the side of our ricksha. Not even an accident. It just kept honking and going against the traffic like all the other cars do but . . . dammit. Those stupid rickshas fold like accordions. If I had switched seats with her . . ." His eyes misted.

The last time I'd seen my brother cry was the day those kids in school had beaten him up when we first immigrated. We'd come a long way from that day, but seeing him so unglued again worried me.

After some persuading, Neel agreed to leave Dipti's side but only to go find the doctor to discuss the next steps. Not being in charge was killing him. Virag Mama put his arm around Neel's shoulders and led him out of the room. I sat in the chair Neel had vacated, the plastic still warm.

Dipti's body was still. Her hair was pulled back into a loose ponytail, exposing her expressionless face. The familiar mound protruded from her stomach. I wondered if she could sense the people around her. I had no idea what to say to her. She and I had never been close. I'd never understood how she could be born and raised in America and still cling to dated Indian customs, like eating only after her husband had finished his meal to make sure he had piping hot rotlis. We came from two completely different worldviews. I wouldn't know what to say if mine was the first face she saw.

Still, I willed her to wake up. The longer she was out, the worse her chances of recovery. And the less likely it was that the baby would survive. I thought back to how I'd felt when Neel first told me about the baby. He could hardly contain himself. I said and did the right things to match his excitement. But while I was happy for him, I was sad for me. Things were changing again. They had started when he met Dipti. The dynamic had shifted from Neel and me being a team to Neel and Dipti, leaving me on my own. With a baby, that divide would only grow deeper, and I'd fall even lower on the priority ladder.

Even though Neel and I had adjusted to America differently—he being able to adopt the right facade in social interactions but keeping Indian traditions at his core, while I internalized the new American customs as I adopted them—we had always remained close. We were the only two people in this world who shared the exact same experiences, and our bond was both resilient and forgiving.

When he met Dipti, I didn't blame him. It wasn't his fault that his life was moving forward while mine was standing still. A few years later, I met Alex. I had been a late bloomer, given that my parents had forbidden me from dating all through high school. By the time I got to college, I was still awkward and shy around boys, and my parents still insisted that I focus on my studies until I was ready for marriage. So it wasn't until I was twenty-eight that I met Alex, my first real boyfriend, and he quickly grew into someone I loved as much as Neel. I began to understand why Neel had to shift priorities when Dipti entered his life.

Now, the thought of losing the baby was devastating. During the past few months I'd accepted the inevitable change that was coming and was happy to be its only foi. Between Neel, Dipti, and me, the baby would have the stable, loving, and financially secure American childhood that Neel and I hadn't. I could only imagine that losing a child would be close to the way I would feel if something ever happened to Neel. I shuddered at the thought.

Dipti had to wake up. She just had to.

I tentatively reached for her hand. It was colder than I expected. "You have to get through this," I said, hoping she and the baby could hear me.

The sterile room was surprisingly quiet, given the number of people rushing back and forth in the hallway. The only sounds were the beeping of the monitors and compression from the machine her breathing tube was hooked up to. I stared at everything my brother held dear, afraid he might lose it all. A framed photo of Krishna Bhagwan hung above Dipti's bed. I clasped my hands together and found myself praying for the second time in days. I prayed that Dipti and her baby would pull through this and go on to lead long, healthy, happy lives. The alternative was unthinkable.

My stomach began to churn. My parents had to be nearby. Seeing them, particularly under these circumstances, would be difficult. Not enough time had passed for the anger, resentment, and guilt to fizzle. If I was still bothered by it, I had no doubt that my mother was too. If there was one thing I knew, it was that Varsha Desai could hold a grudge.

Despite my best efforts, the exhaustion of traveling was catching up to me. I found myself drifting off. The melodic beeping of the heart rate monitors lulled me into a hypnotic state. My head became heavy and fell toward my chest, forcing me to jerk it back to wake myself.

"It's okay to sleep," Neel said when he returned and found me nodding off. "I'm going to be up anyway. I need to monitor what the staff is doing to make sure nothing slips through the cracks."

Virag Mama retrieved a hospital-grade blanket from the nurses' station. It had the same scratchy consistency as the blanket I had used as a barrier to prevent direct contact with the man next to me on my flight.

I pulled it over my shoulders and fell into the comforting darkness that was waiting to catch me.

~

I'm not sure how much time had passed when I awoke to nurses rushing into the room, flinging me away from Dipti's bedside. The heart rate monitors belted out an alarming sound. The numbers on one machine were declining. 68. 64. 57. 49. 40. 37.

There was a whirl of activity in the once-peaceful room. Neel's eyes were as wide and shiny as the thali Indira Mami had been using to hold the flowers for the garlands. Nurses speaking rapid Gujarati pushed him back. They were talking too quickly for Neel and me to understand what was being said. Neel resisted, trying to force himself forward. One of the nurses injected a clear liquid into Dipti's IV line.

"How many cc's did you give her?" he barked in English.

No one responded to him, but the numbers began to creep up. 43. 45. 49.

Medical staff called out orders. Virag Mama forced Neel from the room, presumably at the direction of one of the nurses. I was hazy from sleep but tried to extricate myself from the mayhem in the room. Seeing an opening, I stumbled past a nurse and made it to the hallway. The noises from inside the room faded as she closed the door. I fixed my gaze on the floor and steadied myself by resting my hand against the textured yellow-tinged wall. It was rough against my palm. Eyes downcast, I slid my fingertips along the cool plaster, taking only two steps before I smacked into someone rushing toward the room.

"I'm so sor—" I stopped cold when I realized I was looking into my mother's dark-brown eyes.

8

Shocked from the chaos, I mumbled a quick hello. I had no idea what else to say to her, so I turned back to find Neel. He was leaning against the wall, breathing sharply. Water. I would get him some water. From over my shoulder, I saw my mother put her hand on Neel's back. She told him to be strong. No matter what happened, whether someone had died or whether as kids we were too scared to stay home alone, she always told us to be strong. Maybe sometimes it was okay to let go and allow someone else to take care of you, okay to be vulnerable. That was something I'd learned from Alex.

We had been dating for about five months and had entered that comfortable period where we could sit with each other in our pajamas and eyeglasses without any pretenses. After a long week at the office, we'd polished off a bottle and a half of wine, and he'd been teasing me about how guarded I was about my past and family, joking that I must be hiding some big secret, something horrifying like underwear with holes in it or a messy closet! I never talked about growing up in a dingy row house near Chicago's version of Little India. Or about how my parents had trouble holding down jobs after they had immigrated, and we often struggled to pay bills. It was a far cry from the life I had now, and it was a life I wanted to forget.

But my alcohol-induced state mixed with his sultry "I want to know everything about you" blue eyes made me share more than I ordinarily would have, including a story from junior high I had never told anyone.

~

Back when I was in eighth grade, my teacher had announced the annual field trip and passed out the permission slips, and I braced myself for the cost. Dad had lost his job again a few months earlier, and there was nothing new on the horizon. Seventeen dollars. I did the math. That was sixty-eight cans of vegetables at the discount grocery store where my mother had started shopping. My heart sank.

It took until the day before the permission slip and fee were due for me to work up the nerve to ask my mother for the money. The paper was now creased and worn from being carried in my pocket for two weeks, waiting for the right opportunity to approach her. Before emerging from my room, I sat cross-legged, head bent, palms together before the photo of Krishna Bhagwan that hung over my pink-and-white bed. Ever since arriving in America, I'd stopped doing my daily prayers, turning to Bhagwan only when things were bad, so I didn't expect them to be answered.

I passed by my parents' bedroom. Dad was lying in bed, underneath the sheets, watching TV. Ever since he'd lost his job, I rarely saw him doing anything else.

My mother was in the kitchen, sitting at the table with a notebook, calculator, and set of bills spread before her. Her brow was furrowed as she tapped out numbers. She had permanent bags underneath her eyes and constantly appeared exhausted. The familiar smells of roasted cumin and mustard seeds wafted from the kitchen and got stronger as I approached her.

I handed her the paper.

"Is it the same place you went last year?" she asked after scanning it.

"Yeah."

She paused. "Do you need to go again this year?"

Even at the age of thirteen, I understood how difficult it was for her to ask this question. It was the first time she had ever suggested I not participate in a school activity. To my parents, school and education were sacrosanct because they were the way to live a life independent of obligation.

Putting on my most nonchalant face, I said, "No, it wasn't that fun last year."

I climbed off the barstool and ran to my room, all the while hoping she would yell after me that I could go. But there was nothing other than silence. My body started to shake, and I slid down the closed bedroom door. It was one of the rare instances when I allowed myself to cry.

Anger swept through me because I wished my parents would stop being so damn proud and just ask our family in India for help. They had money and fancy houses and servants. But my mother refused to tell them the truth about our life in Chicago. We were supposed to be living the American dream, and they would worry if they knew we weren't. And even if we did tell them, my dad's pride and fear of obligations would never have allowed him to accept help.

I knew it was silly to cry over a field trip, but this was the one thing I would not be able to explain away to my friends when they asked why I wasn't going. None of them knew about my dad's job problems. I was too afraid of them looking at me differently. Of them knowing that in addition to being Indian and vegetarian and having parents who spoke with a funny accent, I couldn't afford a few dollars for a field trip. I cried knowing all my efforts to fit in would vanish in an instant. I cried because life was unfair. Or maybe it was because I was thirteen and didn't know how else to deal with it.

Startled by a knock on the door, I wiped the tears away and frantically rubbed my eyes. I jumped up and used the camera my parents had given me on my last birthday to cover my blotchy, tearstained face, pretending to check if the lens was clean.

My dad walked into my bedroom and placed something on my dresser. "Here."

I peeked out from behind the camera and recognized the crumpled piece of paper along with seventeen dollars in cash.

A few weeks after I'd told Alex that story, I had to fly to Seattle for depositions. When he dropped me off at the airport, he handed me an envelope. It was plain, letter size. We stood outside the busy terminal at LAX, frazzled people milling around us. He told me not to open it until I was through security. As soon as I saw him exit the sliding doors, I slipped my index finger under the seal. Inside was seventeen dollars in cash—a ten, a five, and two one-dollar bills. On each of the bills was a single word written in red marker: *I, Love, You, Preeti.*

I looked up, searching for him, but he had already been swallowed by the others weaving in and out of the terminal. My heart pounded as I finally understood what it meant to love someone and *be* loved by someone. He moved into my place the next month.

After we broke up, this was the memory I played over and over in my head like a movie reel, questioning how we could have gone from that moment to eventually parting ways. We'd had a plan. I blamed myself for not sticking to it. During our first year as a couple, we went through the highs and lows of Alex writing what he hoped would be a production-worthy screenplay only to have his agent tell him to try again. Then this past January, he got a different call. The one that began with, "Alex, old boy, I sold your movie." We were so giddy with excitement over that call, having no idea it would set us on a trajectory that would eventually pull us away from each other.

~

But none of that mattered now, and that moment seemed like a lifetime ago rather than earlier this year. I could not have imagined then that instead of being in New York living a bohemian-chic lifestyle with Alex, I'd be in a hospital in Ahmedabad praying that my sister-in-law and her baby would make a speedy recovery. At this moment, the only thing I should have been focused on was a way to comfort Neel.

After I'd trolled the halls for a couple minutes, it became clear that this was no American hospital, and my search for a vending machine dispensing bottled water had been in vain. I forced myself to return to the waiting room where I'd seen my mother enter a few minutes earlier. When I'd fought with her in Chicago last month, I had not expected to see her again so soon, let alone in a hospital halfway around the world.

Like me, my mother was five feet four, but she seemed shorter with her shoulders hunched forward in the same way she'd scolded me for doing as a child. "A woman must always stand with dignity," she would say. I guess even she had her limits. Taking a deep breath, I approached her.

The sparse waiting room was full of mismatched chairs made of plastic and wood. The walls were the same faded yellow as the hallways. A few strangers sat clustered among their relatives.

I was surprised my mother was outfitted in a maroon-and-cream panjabi, the top falling to her knees, covering most of the billowy pants that tapered at her ankles. It was the same style she had disapproved of me wearing at Dipti's baby shower. And now she was one of the only women in the room who wasn't wearing a sari.

"Hi," I said.

She spun around. "Preeti." The bags underneath her eyes carried more weight than usual.

We sat across from each other, avoiding eye contact.

At last, I broke the heavy silence. "Where's Dad?"

"He's gone for water."

Hopefully he'd have better luck than I'd had. I stared at a red-and-white placard that hung on the wall behind her. The words were written in Gujarati. After moving to America, I had had no need to read or write it anymore, so those skills had long since faded, but I tried to sound out the letters in my head the way a child would.

Finally, I said wryly, "This wasn't what I had in mind for my next trip to India."

Ignoring my tone, she said, "It is good you are here."

The forced conversation felt stifling, so I stood and crossed the waiting room. Peering down the hallway, I saw Neel and the doctor heading toward us. The doctor had a chart in his hand, and Neel was gesturing wildly, pointing to things on it. I went back to my chair and waited.

When Neel and the doctor walked in, Virag Mama and other relatives and friends gathered to hear the news. Every chair was taken, and people were standing in clusters along the walls. I was taken aback by the number of people who appeared in an instant. I did not remember them arriving, and although they looked familiar with the characteristic rounded Desai nose and high cheekbones, I could not identify them all. Some were dressed in suits, like they had rushed from their jobs to be here. Word traveled quickly in this city of eight million where, unlike in Los Angeles, everyone seemed to know each other. My parents looked around the room and acknowledged each person with a small nod or modest smile.

"She's stable, but they don't know if they can save the baby," Neel said, an edge to his voice. "I'm going to call a colleague back in Chicago. There has to be something more we can do." He shot the doctor a cutting look.

The doctor refrained from reacting. "As you wish," he said.

This country was so damned polite, people never expressing what they really felt.

Virag Mama gave Neel a cell phone. While on the phone, Neel stood more erect and cupped his chin with his left hand—he was shifting into doctor mode. The emotion and vulnerability I'd first seen in him were gone. He looked as though he were having a routine consult with another physician about a random patient. He looked somewhat comfortable for the first time since I had arrived.

But then after conferring with his colleague, Neel sank into the chair next to me. My father handed him a steel cup of water.

In the past couple of years, my father seemed to have aged immensely. My mother used to help him dye his white hair black with a bottle of at-home color treatment. At some point most of his hair had fallen away, only sparse patches remaining. He still dyed those the deep black that was now shockingly dark against the yellowed walls.

No longer looking like a composed physician, Neel bent over, placing his head between his knees as if the room were spinning. Surprisingly, Dad put a hand on his back. Physical affection wasn't his forte. It was subtle, but I saw Neel flinch for a moment—instinctively. Our parents had never been big on physical contact, so it was an unfamiliar feeling.

"You and Preeti were both born in this hospital," he said with tenderness that I'd never heard. "Have some faith in Bhagwan."

Neel's head jerked up. "Bhagwan isn't going to help! Only science will, but I'm stuck here with no way of getting my wife and child back to modern medicine in the United States!"

Dad's hand fell away. Neel rarely lost his cool. And never talked back to our parents. Even I was caught off guard.

I knelt in front of my brother. "This situation fucking sucks. It does," I said, not worrying about my language. This was about Neel, and I had to be as real and straight with him as I always was. "I'm here. Whatever happens. We are a team," I said, repeating to him the same words he'd said to me on our first day of school in Chicago.

There was no point saying everything would be okay. If they lost the baby, we both knew it wouldn't be.

9

The afternoon had crept into dusk. Most of the relatives had filtered out and gone home, promising to pray for our family that night and return the next day. They offered to have their servants bring food.

"It's not necessary." My parents delivered the expected response as though reading from a script.

But we all knew people would send food anyway. It was custom. Not adhering to it would have been unfathomable, like giving a cash gift in an even amount.

With everyone gone, the room was quiet. Dad and Neel had gone to Dipti's room. Virag Mama and Indira Mami were speaking with the hospital director. It was just my mother and me. She dropped into the chair across from me and rubbed her temples.

"What did your job say about coming here?" she asked.

"They were understanding," I lied, wondering what the Warden thought of the brief I had emailed him before landing in Ahmedabad. If he needed changes, I wasn't sure how I would find time to revise it with everything going on.

"How long will you stay?"

"As long as Neel needs me." I hoped that Dipti and the baby would be back to normal as soon as possible. The longer I stayed, the more tenuous my hold on my job would be.

My mother nodded while her lips curled into a small smile. "It is good for him to have you here. You two have always been close."

I slumped low enough in my wooden chair to rest my neck on the hard back. "I only wish I'd been here when it happened."

"These things are up to Bhagwan," she said, gesturing toward the skies. "We cannot control it."

While I appreciated her attempt to absolve me of any blame, I wasn't quite ready to let myself off the hook. "If I had come with you guys for Hari's wedding, I'd have been here when this happened."

I'd have gotten to speak to Dipti before she fell into a coma—tell her how much Neel needed his new family even though he pretended not to need anyone. He and I were the same in that regard. The combination of our Indian parents teaching us to never show "weakness" and us feeling like outsiders when we immigrated caused us both to develop hard exteriors—with everyone. But once we let people in, it was hard to let go and imagine a life without them. I'd felt that way about Alex and was certain Neel felt the same toward Dipti even though he'd never be able to express it openly.

Fatigue swept over me while my mother and I continued to sit in silence. I pondered our conversation. Something was different about the dynamic between us. The edge I'd come to expect from her had dulled. Maybe she felt calmer in India—the place she'd always considered home. Or maybe she was just too damned tired to fight.

"Did you open your birthday card?" she asked in Gujarati a few moments later.

I opened my eyes when I heard her voice, once again aware of the dingy surroundings in the hospital waiting room.

I shifted in the hard-backed wooden chair, afraid she was going to bring up the dreaded topic of Alex.

Her plastic chair creaked as she readjusted.

"I should check on Neel," I said in English, thinking back to the message in my birthday card, not ready to delve into those issues, whatever they might be.

~

In the hallway, I noticed a tall, lean figure striding toward me. My face broke into a huge smile. Relief washed over me, and I dashed to meet her halfway.

"Thank God you're here!" I said, giving Monali Auntie a huge hug and inhaling the familiar smell of cinnamon and cloves.

"Look at you! You must be exhausted." She held me at arm's length, examining me as if it had been years rather than weeks since she'd last seen me.

I'd forgotten I was still wearing the baggy jeans and wrinkled sweatshirt I'd worn on the plane. "I came straight here."

"I can see that."

She'd come over with my family for Hari's wedding, and I knew that as a de facto member of our family, she wouldn't be far from the hospital during this time. She had always been there for me, helping me cope with everything from a scraped knee to fights with my parents to my breakup with Alex. Seeing her was enough to calm some of the anxiety.

"Have you seen your mother?" she asked.

"Yeah," I mumbled.

She looked at me sternly. "This is not the time for any unnecessary drama."

I met her eyes. "I know."

She scanned the hallway behind me. "Oh, have you met your friend yet?"

"Which friend?"

"You know, Biren."

I creased my forehead, trying to place the name.

She slapped me on the back. "Come now. His father is the president of the electric company in Ahmedabad. You remember. They do lots of charity work. Anandbhai has a foundation and helps women and children in India get out of abusive living conditions by finding families in the West to look after them."

Nothing registered, and the charity work sounded like something I would have remembered had I known it.

"Oy, you! You have a memory like a goldfish!" She flicked her hand. "You used to play together as children when you lived here. My God, trying to separate you two was like trying to part the sea! I saw his mother here earlier. Maybe they went home."

The more I thought about it, I did have vague memories of a tall, scrawny boy I used to play cricket with on our lawn outside Lakshmi. I hadn't seen him during our last few visits to India. I recalled my mother telling me his family had moved to Mumbai.

10

That night Neel stayed behind at the hospital, and I went back to Lakshmi with Virag Mama and my parents. I was too emotionally and physically drained to have a substantive conversation with my parents. Other than the short exchanges in the waiting room, we had all been relying on our old family standby: avoidance. While we had dinner with Virag Mama and his family, we avoided talking about my parents walking out on me when they found out I was shacking up with a dhoriya. As we unpacked my luggage, we avoided the fact that he and I had broken up. Then when we discussed sleeping arrangements, we avoided the fight with my mother last month.

I was thankful that Indira Mami suggested I sleep in the small room they used as an office but could pull a cot into. It allowed my parents and me to have separate spaces and continue to practice the avoidance we had adopted as a religion—the one aspect of Indian culture we could all agree upon.

As I sat on the bed my cousins Hari and Bharat had prepared for me, I thanked them. On previous trips, the firmness of the mattress and pillows had jolted me, but this time I didn't care. I was grateful for the chance to lie down, undisturbed, for the first time in two days.

"Sorry this happened before your wedding," I said when Hari handed me a clean towel. His hair was styled the same way as his father's, the unruly, thick waves tamed with almond oil.

"It cannot be helped. We very much hope everything will be fine." Despite spending a year in America while earning his master's degree, Hari still had a strong Indian accent. But his skinny frame had filled out and become more muscular while he had been abroad, and our relatives joked that the added weight was evidence that America had been very "prosperous."

"Hopefully."

"I am sorry that it is under these circumstances, but we are very glad you were able to come," Bharat said, pushing his thick, black-rimmed glasses back into place.

Hari nodded. "Laila is very excited to meet her didi."

I opened my mouth to ask who Laila was and then snapped it shut. How could I have forgotten the name of his fiancée, my soon-to-be cousin? Their elaborate wedding invitation had sat on my front table for months, and I hadn't bothered to learn a key piece of information from it? I had no doubt memorized the holdings of several useless cases during that amount of time.

"When is the wedding?" I asked.

"In twelve days' time for the wedding itself, but the events start in just one week," Hari responded. "But of course, we will change if it is necessary."

"Whatever happens with my family shouldn't affect your wedding." I smiled at them. "I can't believe how grown up you both are. It's been so long since I've seen you."

"It is okay. We know how busy you are being such a high-powered lawyer," Hari said with admiration in his voice.

I made a mental note to check in with the Warden about the brief I had emailed him earlier.

Pulling my legs onto the bed, I said, "I should go to sleep. Tomorrow's going to be a long day."

As I rested my head against the dense cloth brick that served as my pillow, I thought about how Hari had called me didi. I barely knew my cousins. Hari had been a toddler when we left, and Bharat hadn't even been born. I'd spent summers with them when we were kids, but they were so much younger than Neel and me that it was hard to form any lasting relationship with them. I couldn't help thinking that family was a feeling more than genetics. I would move mountains if something ever happened to Carrie, but would I really change something as important as my wedding date for cousins I hadn't seen in fifteen years?

Certainly, my relationship with Hari and Bharat was nothing like the one I had with Neel. When Neel had called to tell me about an accident in India, if it had been Laila or Hari or Bharat, I would have felt bad. Of course. But I couldn't guarantee I would have jumped on a plane. Today I realized that if something had happened to Neel or me in America, our family in India would have raced to be with us, even though we hadn't spent time together in over a decade. In India, family trumped all else even if there wasn't an emotional closeness in addition to the bloodline.

I pulled a heavy rajai over my body. The weight and warmth of the blanket were soothing and felt so different from the feather-light, fluffy down comforter I used in America.

Despite being exhausted, I tossed and turned, unable to sleep. After what felt like an hour, I picked up my phone, my finger poised over Alex's number. With one move, it would be calling him. I wanted so desperately to hear his voice again, to update him on what was going on. But he'd made clear I shouldn't call him again. As difficult as it was, I had to respect that. I tucked the phone into my bag and closed my eyes.

My sleep was restless. Several times during the night, I heard two packs of stray dogs in the vacant lot behind the house barking with all their might, the all-too-familiar sound of a turf war. I covered my ears with my hands but couldn't drown out the noise. It felt like I had just closed my eyes and fallen asleep when my nose twitched, and I awoke to the aromatic smell of khari biscuits and chai. It was still dark outside. My eyes adjusted to the moonlight. I tiptoed past Hari and Bharat's open door; they were sound asleep. Years of living in India must have made them immune to the cries of animals. I, on the other hand, was out of practice.

I crept down the cold marble stairs and found my parents, Virag Mama, and Indira Mami sitting at the dining table with steaming mugs in front of them. The white-and-blue Corelle dishware had been a gift that my family had brought to India over twenty years ago. My parents used the same set at home.

"Are you hungry?" Dad asked.

"Starved." I plopped down into a chair at the table, using jet lag as an excuse to eat in the middle of the night.

Indira Mami shuffled to her feet to pour me a cup of tea. She was wearing a full-length, zippered pink robe, another item I recognized. My mother wore a similar one in white with paisleys on it. Both were from the Sears outlet store. I imagined Indira Mami had mended hers several times over the years, just as I had seen my mother do to hers. My parents believed that their relatives in India should have the same American comforts we had, so whenever they purchased something for themselves, they would purchase a second to bring to India.

"What time is it?" I asked, scanning the room for a clock. "Why is everyone awake?"

"Four fifteen," Dad said.

"Neel called from the hospital," Virag Mama said. "We should go there soon."

I sipped the tea, basking in the warmth as it traveled from my mouth to my stomach. I broke off a piece of a khari biscuit, and the warm, salty, buttery flakes clung to my fingertips until I licked them off. There was something about the texture of khari biscuits in India that had never been replicated back home. It instantly brought me back to my early childhood in this house.

~

It was eerily quiet when we arrived at the hospital. The dimly lit hallways had only a few nurses shuffling back and forth, checking on patients. Those who passed us nodded, seeming to know that our family had special permission to be in the hospital beyond the standard hours. Virag Mama knew the hospital director, so we could come and go without question.

Neel was angrily gesturing to the doctor outside Dipti's room. We stood back to give them privacy. After he finished, Neel marched toward us. He combed his fingers through his messy hair. As expected, he hadn't slept well.

"It was a rough night," he said, shoulders slumped. "But she's fighting."

"Dipti's tough," I said.

"Yeah, she is. But I meant the baby." There was a small glimmer in the back of Neel's eyes: pride. His mouth curled into a rueful smile. "It's a girl."

A girl. Neel's daughter. My niece. Dipti had been adamant about the gender being a surprise, so none of us had known. Hearing that made the situation more real. It was no longer about a baby we couldn't picture. It was about a little girl who would twirl around in frilly dresses until she made herself so dizzy she tumbled over. It was about a teenager who would beg to wear makeup and go on a first date. A perfect angel whose every milestone I would capture through my lens so none of us would forget.

"Girls are strong," our mother said, taking a step forward. She took Neel by the elbow and guided him to the waiting room. "Come and sit. You need some rest."

Once in the waiting room, Neel took a deep breath and continued, "Dipti's had a severe placental abruption." He leaned forward and placed his head in his hands.

We waited until he was ready to continue. Dad rubbed his back, like he had the day before. This time Neel didn't flinch at the contact.

Eventually Neel spoke again. "The accident caused a large amount of her placenta to separate from the uterus. The baby is losing oxygen, and Dipti doesn't have enough blood or strength to sustain her and the baby." His chair creaked as he leaned back. "All of her energy is going toward keeping the baby alive . . . the doctors think the best way to save Dipti is to"—he choked on the next words—"deliver the baby, which would effectively terminate the pregnancy."

No one spoke as we processed the news. I clutched the armrests of my chair, afraid to move. A clock ticked in the background, the sound seeming to get louder and louder. My stomach swirled with nausea. I looked at our mother, and her expression was as disconsolate as I felt. I could only imagine Neel's pain.

"Is there nothing else that can be done?" Dad asked.

Neel shook his head. "If it were a little later in the pregnancy, she would be viable, and we could try to keep her alive in the NICU. They'll do what they can, but I know it's too early for that. And I could lose them both if we wait much longer. They can keep Dipti hooked up to the ventilator and keep giving her blood transfusions until the baby is strong enough to be removed in a few weeks . . . but by that point, Dipti won't survive on her own." He choked back a sob, swallowing hard. "I can't lose her." He looked at me, eyes glistening with pain and fear.

I didn't know which "her" he meant. I looked at the painting of Bhagwan that hung in the room and gritted my teeth. So much for hearing our prayers. I felt like Bhagwan was taunting us.

I knelt on the floor in front of Neel. "How much time until you have to decide?"

His gaze had never looked so hollow. "Not long."

Mansi Shah

"Remember, we are a team. No matter what," I said.

Neel looked helpless, like a small child. His eyes seemed to plead that someone else make this decision for him. Seeing the desperation on his face made my heart ache.

We couldn't both fall apart, so I summoned the courage he would have shown me had our situations been reversed. With a steady, confident voice, I said, "We'll support whatever choice you make."

He nodded absentmindedly, as if he'd heard the words but wasn't sure what they meant. "She would want me to save the baby. She loves that baby so much . . ." Tears clung precariously to his lower eyelashes, poised to spill onto his cheeks without warning.

I rose to give him a hug. "It's not her decision to make. Whatever you do, she'll understand. We all will."

Neel rubbed his eyes. Tiny red veins wove their way through the whites. He fidgeted, unable to stay in one position for more than a few seconds. He clearly wanted to save them both. Neel saved other people's babies every day. It was cruel that when faced with saving his own, he was powerless.

~

I emerged from the hospital room in search of coffee for Neel. He had been awake for countless hours straight, and caffeine was the only thing sustaining him. At the end of the hallway, I saw Monali Auntie standing with a tall man, around my age, with trendy black-rimmed glasses and a button-down shirt with cuffed sleeves. He stuck out in the hospital because he had the same Western look as Neel and me and, to a certain extent, even our parents. Monali Auntie pointed in my direction, and he nodded. Then she frantically waved me over. I wasn't sure what she was up to. This was India. For all I knew, she had brokered my arranged marriage in those two seconds!

Grabbing my hand, she said, "This is Biren. You remember?"

68

I glanced up at him, and I do mean up, because he must have been around six feet three and was the tallest person I'd seen since arriving in India. Somewhat shyly, I said, "Yeah, Monali Auntie reminded me that we used to play together as kids."

"Yes, it was a very long time ago." Biren spoke perfect English but with a slight accent I couldn't place.

"My parents said your family moved to Mumbai."

"Yes, we were there for a year, and then we moved to Australia. I went through most of my schooling in Sydney."

I smiled, now able to identify the lilt in his voice. "Thank you for coming during this time. Monali Auntie said your family has been stopping by the hospital and bringing us food and tea," I said in the same way I'd heard my mother thank the other visitors who had come earlier.

"Of course," he said. "Your family would do the same for us."

I nodded. He was right. Regardless of whether days, weeks, or decades had passed since my parents had last seen his, they would have jumped to help in any way they could. As much as I didn't connect with most of my parents' friends, I respected that they were always there for each other. With obligation came loyalty. And while I didn't feel any obligation to my friends, I couldn't say that I had that same level of unquestioned loyalty either.

"Do you still live in Australia?" I asked.

He shook his head. "We moved back to Ahmedabad after I finished my pharmacy degree."

"That must have been quite an adjustment."

"We always knew we'd come back home, so it wasn't too much of a shock to the system."

We saw my parents and Neel walking from Dipti's room to the waiting room. Neel's head hung low, as if he were about to face his executioner.

Monali Auntie put her hand on my back. "Go. Be with your family."

I offered an apologetic smile and said, "Thanks for understanding. I was just on my way to find some coffee for Neel."

"No worries on that," Biren said. "I'll find a couple steaming cups and bring them over to you."

"Thank you," I said, grateful for the kind gesture.

After the initial shock had worn off, Neel approached the decision the way he approached every major decision: by being pragmatic. He and Dipti could have another baby, but there was only one Dipti. He couldn't imagine his life without her in it.

"I'm so sorry, Neel," I said, throwing my arms around him in a fierce hug. "We'll get through this."

His forehead dropped to my shoulder, and I felt his tears soak into my shirt. "She'll never forgive me for this," he mumbled.

I shook my head. "Don't say that. She will. You had to do what was best for her."

"You don't understand how much this baby meant to her."

"No, I don't. But I know how much you mean to each other. She won't forget that, even with something this awful."

Once the decision was made, the four of us sat in a circle, cross-legged on the floor of the waiting room. We bowed our heads, closed our eyes, placed our palms together, and prayed while tears slid down our cheeks and sobs escaped from our throats. The four of us had been in that prayer formation many times during my childhood when we got calls from India that someone had passed away. Monali Auntie, Biren, and the other relatives and friends made a ring around us. Dad led us through the hymns, his impassioned voice reverberating through the room. I had long forgotten the words, so I mumbled under my breath, feeling a bit like a phony. But then with each round of prayers, I started recalling more words, and my voice became louder, bolder. We prayed that Dipti would survive and, by some miracle and against all odds, the baby would too. Our prayers had to be answered. They just had to.

11

The next day when Dipti finally awoke from her procedure and was coherent, my parents and I stood silently outside the room while Neel broke the news to her. None of us could make eye contact while we thought about how Dipti would react upon learning the baby growing inside of her was gone. The doctors had done everything they could after delivering the baby girl, but the trauma of the accident was too much for her. She'd lasted less than an hour.

Dipti's gut-wrenching wail said it all.

I jumped when I heard it, about to rush into the room to help, but my mother put a hand on my shoulder to stop me.

"Let them have time," she said.

I hesitated, so used to being there for Neel that having him go through this alone was unthinkable. But then I realized my mother was right. Neel wasn't alone. He had Dipti, and I had to let them deal with this in their own way.

The wails and shrieks felt like they went on for days rather than minutes. Each one felt like a physical blow. I sank to the floor, bringing my legs to my chest and curling into a tight ball. It didn't seem right to ignore a person in pain, but I had to trust that my mother knew best about this. She could relate to Dipti in a way I could not—as a mother.

Eventually, there was silence, and Neel opened the door. His eyes were red and watery. It broke my heart to see him looking so defeated.

"Is there anything you need me to do? Anyone you need to call back home?" I asked him, desperate to find a way to help them through this.

"Later," he said, crestfallen. "Right now, she needs people, and I don't seem to be the one she wants." He stepped aside to let us filter in with him trailing at the back of the pack.

The already small room felt claustrophobic once we all entered. Dipti lay on the bed, her head propped up by dense pillows like the ones at Lakshmi. There was a chair next to her bed and two others against the wall by a small window that cast the only natural light into the room. The fluorescent lighting overhead hummed gently, audible only when none of us spoke.

Dipti appeared small and frail in the white cotton hospital gown that fell loosely around her. The first thing I noticed was her stomach, now missing the taut bump I'd come to expect. If it broke my heart to see her like that, I could only imagine what she had felt when she awoke from her surgery. The second was that her eyes were vacant, distant. As I stepped closer, I heard her whispering to herself.

"I'm sorry I failed you as a mother."

"I wasn't there to protect you when you needed me most."

"I would have chosen you."

Neel moved toward her and reached out to comfort her, but she flinched when he touched her shoulder. She glared at him in a way that made clear she blamed him. I cringed when I saw the hurt register on his face. Our parents had raised us to be tough and mask our feelings, regardless of the situation. I'd never seen him need someone in the way he needed her now. He'd lost his baby too. And it seemed there was nothing I could do to help either of them.

"Dipti, I'm so sorry," I said. "We're here for you. Whatever you need."

"You did this," she seethed at Neel. "You decided. Not me."

"I couldn't lose you," Neel whispered to her.

"Where's Dad?" she asked, turning away from him.

My father stepped forward, holding both tissues and water, ready to offer both.

"Sorry, Chetan," she said in a faint but kind voice. It was the first time since she and Neel had married that she'd referred to my dad by his first name. "But I need *my* dad."

"He's trying to get here," Dad said, trying not to look wounded. "His flight was delayed, so he missed the connecting flight in Europe. He should arrive tomorrow."

She wasn't trying to hurt my father, but I could tell she had. It had been just her and her father after her mom passed away when she was nine years old, so they had learned to lean on each other. Her eyes welled up, and I wondered if she felt as alone as she looked, surrounded by people who loved her but who weren't the family she'd grown up with.

As I stood next to my mother, it was not lost on me that Dipti was probably overwhelmed with missing her own mother right now. Even given my problems with my mother, I imagined she'd be the one I'd look to for guidance if I were ever in this situation. It was easy to dwell on the little things when you didn't think about there being a time when you no longer could. I wondered if Dipti ever recalled the small things she used to fight about with her mother.

"Uma," Dipti said softly, her eyes blinking as if she was struggling to keep them open. "That's her name. It means *tranquility*, which is what she deserves in her next life."

There was no need to use the formal convention of letting my mother name the baby the way my grandmother had named me and Dipti's had named her.

My mother stood in the corner, trying to collect herself, the occasional soft sob escaping. She'd no doubt picked several names for the baby, all of them in line with the traditions based on the alignment of the stars at the exact second of birth. When she'd first found out she would be a grandmother, her face had lit up with pure joy. Neel would have a family, and to her, there was no greater success. But that had all changed when the truck slammed into their ricksha.

Dipti demanded the hospital bring the baby to her.

"She's not fully formed," Neel said. "Please don't do this to yourself."

"Of course I know that," she snapped back. "I'm a doctor too. I know just as well as you do that her brain wasn't fully developed yet, or her eyes, or her . . ." Her face fell, like she would succumb to those inconsolable screams we'd heard through the door, but then she focused on Neel. She choked out her next words. "She was in pain, and she was alone. I couldn't comfort her then, but I'm sure as hell not going to let you take that chance away from me now."

I knew Dipti was in pain but couldn't believe she was saying such hurtful things to him! Neel became robotic, his eyes registering defeat. It seemed impossible to weather the barrage of insults being hurled at him while avoiding saying something he would regret. Instead of fighting, Neel motioned for the nurse to bring the baby.

"In a covered cloth," he said sternly.

With tears streaming down her cheeks, Dipti took the small package wrapped in a thick white cloth from the nurse and rocked a lifeless Uma in her arms. When Neel signaled to the nurse to take the baby away, Dipti stretched out her hands trying to reclaim her child, murmuring the name over and over.

"Uma, Uma, Uma." Dipti wailed for hours after the baby was gone.

~

That evening, my parents, Virag Mama, Indira Mami, Bharat, Hari, Monali Auntie, Neel, and I all crammed into Dipti's hospital room to listen to the Brahman who had come to advise us about plans for Uma's funeral. This was the only infant death our family had experienced, so we were unfamiliar with the customs, and the Hindu tradition had a custom for everything, no matter how obscure.

Dressed in a simple white cloth covering his frail body and adorned with a large vermilion dot between his eyebrows, the Brahman said, "Because she was younger than twenty-seven months, Uma should be dressed in red and buried."

"No," Dipti said.

Everyone turned to her, shocked she had spoken with such force in the presence of so many elders and a priest.

"No," she repeated after she had our attention.

The Brahman spoke in a soft, soothing, yet still authoritative voice. "It is the right way."

"No."

My mother sat on the edge of her bed. "I know this is hard . . ."

"I'm not burying my baby. Her remains will not be left to rot in the earth." She shuddered. She turned toward Neel, her eyes begging for his support. He came to her side, and she let him take her hand for the first time since she'd woken after the surgery. "Uma will be cremated. It's the only type of funeral I have ever seen, and the only way I know how to say goodbye. It's how I let my mother go and is what I want for my daughter."

The Brahman tried again. "Cremation is what we use for those who are older, less pure than Uma. It burns the body of the life's sins before we move to the next life. But she is pure."

My mother shifted her gaze to the side, collecting herself. Placing a hand on Dipti's forearm, she said, "This is our trad—"

"None of us even knew this custom until five minutes ago," Dipti said sharply.

She stared down the elders in the room, who seemed horrified at the thought of breaking time-honored rules, even if we were now learning of them for the first time. Dipti was traditional in many ways, but I was proud of my sister-in-law for fighting against it in this instance, for standing up for herself and Uma.

"She will be cremated, and she will wear white." Dipti folded her arms across her chest.

A mother had decided what was best for her child. Nothing would change her mind.

~

While my parents, Neel, and Dipti finalized the funeral plans, I retreated to the waiting room with Monali Auntie. Several other relatives and friends had gathered there already. People carried on quiet conversations about work and family and took turns offering me their sympathies for our family.

Monali Auntie put her arm across my shoulders and gave me a quick squeeze. "Everyone will get through this."

A tall, skinny elderly man with thinning white hair and glasses that were too large for his face made his way toward us.

"Kem cho, Anandbhai?" Monali Auntie asked him how he was.

He put his hands together and bowed. "Namaste. Very sorry for your loss."

She returned the greeting, and I followed suit.

He smiled at me, a caring, open expression. "She's grown now." He nodded his approval to Monali Auntie. "I remember when you were just a little girl, Preeti." He held his hand by his side, indicating how tall I had been back then. "I hear you are a lawyer now."

I nodded but didn't feel the same sense of pride he seemed to have in my profession. How could I when despite the tragedy going on with my family, my boss kept checking in to see if I'd had a chance to input his notes into a brief or find some additional case law? And all those emails ended with him asking when I'd be returning to work. My law firm life seemed so insignificant and far away from what mattered now.

Monali Auntie turned to me. "You may not remember, but this is Anand Uncle. He's Biren's father."

"Oh! I see the resemblance now," I said, thinking back to the tall boy with the Australian accent whom I'd met earlier. His father had the same large, kind eyes as Biren, a lighter tint of brown than most people in India had.

Someone across the room motioned for Monali Auntie, so she excused herself and left me with Anand Uncle.

"I saw Biren yesterday." Not recalling too much about Anand Uncle but knowing that jobs were a safe topic of conversation in India, I started there. "He said he's doing pharmacy now. It must be busy for you to run the family business on your own. And Monali Auntie said you are doing so much charity work as well."

Anand Uncle slowly bobbled his head from side to side. "We are lucky the business is doing well, and we are in a fortunate position to help those in need. But now is not the time to discuss those types of matters. Is there anything I can do to be of service to you or your family?"

"That's very kind of you to ask," I said, instantly liking him and thinking that his calm yet distinguished demeanor reminded me of Nana when he had been alive.

I was both surprised and intrigued that Anand Uncle was the first person in India who didn't want to talk about work. For everyone else, it seemed to be the topic most squarely in their comfort zone, myself included. His eyes were inviting, making it easy to be honest with him. "The only thing I really want is some kind of distraction from all of this—even if just for a minute—but now isn't the time for that either."

He nodded solemnly. "Maybe not. But if you can find a moment to be happy or to laugh, it is worth taking."

I mulled over his words. It was good advice. And it was nice to think that some of those moments would come again, because for the past few days, it hadn't seemed like they would. I gave him a timid smile. "Thank you, Uncle."

He offered his condolences again before he left the waiting room. I watched him leave, thinking that Biren was lucky. When dealing with my own parents, I'd always known to use a filter. But Anand Uncle seemed like someone his kids could easily open up to and approach when seeking advice about major decisions in life like careers, or family, or love. He seemed like the kind of parent Neel and Dipti would have been.

~

Uma's funeral was two days later. Dipti's father, Raj Uncle, had arrived the day before and had hardly left Dipti's side. I didn't blame either of them, but I could tell Neel felt even more shut out than he had before his father-in-law arrived.

In a caravan of cars, we made our way to the banks of the Sabarmati River. The pyre was already being built by the Brahman and his helpers. The tiny coffin rested at the center.

I, like the others, wore simple white clothing. White represented purity and was the traditional color of death in Hindu culture. My hair fell loosely down my back. An elaborate hairstyle would have been inappropriate. The breeze near the banks of the river blew through my hair, gently lifting and lowering the strands. The sand near the banks was a darker brown than the light grains on the beaches in Los Angeles.

Branches were organized around the tiny coffin. The baby's body faced south, which I remembered was convention. The Brahman began chanting prayers in Sanskrit, his voice soothing and powerful.

Occasionally, I heard him say *Bhagwan* and knew he was praying that God take care of Uma. My niece. My bhatriji.

This funeral was different from any other I'd been to. I'd never gotten a chance to know Uma, to hear her laugh, to spoil her with presents, to capture her smile through my lens. Still, the sense of loss weighed fully on me. It made me wonder whether the things I'd learned as a kid, like reincarnation, could exist. Maybe Uma was already in a better place, living a better life. Maybe Dipti's mother had found Uma and was looking after her in another life. When faced with a situation such as this, I had to believe there would be more to her short life. And I looked at my own life and wondered whether I had done enough with it. The gift of life felt so precious, and I could not stop myself from feeling like I should be doing more with mine than writing briefs for the Warden. I was, after all, one of the lucky ones who got to live.

The pyre was built next to the riverbank, and we gathered around it, forming a semicircle away from the water. Thick logs of wood were interspersed with thinner branches, now totally covering the coffin.

The priest handed Dipti's father a flaming branch and directed him to light the pyre to begin the cremation. I felt the heat graze my skin as the fire began to spread through the outer layer of wood. My knees went weak at the thought of a baby's—not just any baby's, but *my niece's*—body being burned to ash. I wobbled before regaining my balance.

The priest chanted a mantra as the flames continued to spread to other segments. My mind flitted to the memories we'd never get to share. Uma learning to walk, trying her first bite of dal, her eyes lighting up when she saw fireworks, me teaching her how to make chocolate chip cookies. I'd been determined to make her feel protected and comfortable—ensure that if there was something she couldn't talk to her parents about, then she could speak to me. Teach her that she didn't always have to be strong—that sometimes it was okay to be vulnerable.

I'd never get to say or do any of those things. More importantly, neither would Neel or Dipti.

The fire burned, spreading until each of the other branches and logs was fully consumed by the flames. The temperature around us had risen. Wind whipped through the air, not allowing the burnt smell to linger for long.

Neel covered his mouth, and when I saw tears stream down his cheeks and disappear under his hand, I couldn't hold back my sadness either. A sob escaped from my lips, and I buried my face in the end of the dupatta that hung around my neck. I felt a soft cloth brush against my shoulder and looked up to find my dad handing me a handkerchief, his own eyes red.

Dipti, who had been standing stoically during the funeral, almost as if she weren't in her own body, began to sway back and forth, like a shaft of wheat succumbing to the wind. She turned toward the skies, searching it, her expression hopeful.

"Mom," I heard her whisper, "please take care of my little girl."

Her dad squeezed her hard. "She will," he said, his voice choked with emotion. "They are together now."

Hearing Dipti's pleas to her mother was too much to bear, and I had to turn away to collect myself again. Even my mother's reserved expression cracked. She looked as though if she let herself cry for a second, she'd never be able to stop. She looked so human, so vulnerable, more than I could ever remember seeing her. The gravity of the situation weighed on me. I wanted to reach out to her, to offer her some sort of comfort, but couldn't bring myself to move. We had never had that type of relationship in which we acknowledged each other's vulnerable moments, but I had often wished we did. Before I could convince myself to make the gesture, she gathered herself, put one palm against Dipti's lower back and the other on her forearm to offer her support. The moment had passed.

"We must be strong," my mother said to her, barely moving her lips.

I wondered why. Why was my mother so insistent that we always be strong? If there was ever a time to lose control and be emotional, this had to be it. Dipti did not respond, but she did manage to stay erect by leaning against her father, his arm firmly around her waist, while the fire consumed the body of the baby whose cry she would never hear. Not knowing what to say and suspecting no words could provide any comfort, I gently placed my hand on Neel's shoulder. Another tear slid down my cheek. I brushed it away, the moisture warm on my fingertip. We stood very still as the fire raged on. The crackling of the branches as they broke under the pressure of the flames pierced the silence before being swallowed by the wind.

When it was over, the ashes were scattered into the river, engulfed by the flowing waters. Each ember now on a journey separate and apart from the others.

"We should go back. It's getting dark." Dad put an arm around Neel's shoulders.

Neel nodded and turned to Dipti. Her eyes were shiny and glistening. When Neel looked at her, his face revealed that he had lost more than his daughter.

"Virag Mama, I wish this wasn't happening during a time that should be happy for your family," Neel said.

"Such is life, Neel. We cannot plan it." Virag Mama patted him gently on the back. "Right now, you must focus on *your* family."

As we walked toward our cars, I saw an elderly woman begging to passersby near the riverbanks. A dalit. The lowest rung of Indian society—people who did not even have a ranking in the Indian caste system. As we approached with our somber faces and flowing white clothing, she stared at us, hunched over, using a large stick to support her weight. She began to back away.

But as we neared her, she hobbled forward, one hand open, and began crowing to Virag Mama in a low and raspy voice. I couldn't understand the dialect she was speaking, but she kept repeating the same message over and over to him while he shooed her away.

"Bhen, we have lost a family member. Leave us in peace," he said.

The woman persisted but could not keep up with his long strides.

My mother and I were walking behind Neel, Dipti, her father, and mine. Neel used Dad's handkerchief to dab at his eyes. The beggar shuffled toward him.

"Oh, Sahib. Oh, Sahib," she said over and over, her wrinkled hand extended before Neel.

His eyes welled again at the sight of her, and since arriving in India, I had now seen my brother cry for the third time, two more times than I had ever seen him cry before this trip.

I wanted to protect Neel and not have this stranger disturb him, but before I could utter a word, a hand rested on my shoulder, and I spun around to face my dad. His eyes were soft, looking at me like all he wanted to do was protect me. "Beta, it's not her fault."

"I know," I said, my voice flat.

I moved past the woman, telling myself that her circumstances were such that she had no choice but to approach a funeral procession.

When I looked back toward her, I saw Dipti hand her some crisp, colorful rupees. The woman put her dirt-crusted palms together in the prayer position and bowed before backing away.

"It's rude to stare," my mother whispered as she grabbed my arm. My mother glanced at the old woman hobbling away with the rupees clutched to her chest. "Any good we do today will give Uma peace in her next life."

As we drove away from the river, I saw the woman squatting by the riverbank, gliding a stick over the sand, her movements somehow both casual and with purpose. I caught my mother glancing back at the area where the pyre had been. Smoke still rose from the burnt logs. She swiped her cheek, as I had done earlier.

Virag Mama's words rang in my ears. *Such is life.*

That simple sentence resounded in my mind as we drove home, me in the back seat with Dipti and Neel.

"I'm so sorry," I said to them, wishing words could somehow change how they felt.

Dipti stared out the window, lost in thought. Neel tried to take her hand. Dipti pulled it away.

12

After the funeral, many people came by Lakshmi to give us their condolences. Dipti had retired to the bedroom upstairs, but Neel stayed on
the main floor with the guests.

In the past week, I'd stopped looking at Neel as my nerdy older
brother, the guy who played video games in the basement or chased
me around the house if I changed the channel when he was watching
television. He was an adult. I saw the man he'd become. He was a father
who'd lost his daughter. A man who had to control his grief because his
wife couldn't manage hers, and he knew one of them had to hold things
together. He and Dipti were a team. They had to balance each other,
and it was his unspoken responsibility to carry more weight right now.

For the first time, I considered that his relationship with Dipti
might be the type I wanted for myself. Watching them go through this
experience made me realize they worked together in a way Alex and I
never had. We had supported each other, but we were both focused on
our careers. So focused that we didn't realize those careers were taking
us in different directions, ones that didn't overlap. We never managed
to put *us* before ourselves. Watching Neel and Dipti, I realized why love
wasn't enough to make a relationship work and how much more was
needed. I still wasn't convinced the other extreme of arranged marriages

was the answer, but I did feel I could understand better why so many cultures were based on them.

I'd been meandering around the first level of the house seeing what I could do to help. Indira Mami was carrying a tray with small mugs of hot chai and serving it to the guests. Virag Mama was walking around encouraging people to take second helpings of the nasta that had been laid out on the large dining table. In our culture, there was no greater showing of respect than to tend to a guest's food and tea needs.

Neel had assumed his post of standing near the front door to greet people as they arrived and exited. The elders and my father had gathered near the Brahman, chanting prayers, their eyes closed and their voices strong. I found my mother in the kitchen squeezing lemons to make another batch of nimbu pani for those who didn't want tea.

"Do you need help?" I asked her.

She whirled around, startled. Once she saw me, she quickly dabbed her eyes with a towel. "I rubbed my eye after juicing all these lemons for the pani. It's so stupid."

I nodded, letting her have the lie.

"Let me help." I moved closer.

She sprinkled salt into the pitcher with the lemon juice, sugar, and water. "It's all done now."

Glancing around the kitchen, I asked, "Is there anything I can do?"

"Why don't you mingle with the guests? See if anyone wants more food or chai?"

It seemed both of those jobs were already covered, but I roamed around the living room, trying to figure out a way to be of some use. People were chatting in small groups. The only loud voices were those of the younger kids playing cricket in the yard. For a second, I wished I could trade places with them. Be young enough not to realize what had happened today, why everyone was gathered with solemn expressions. And be able to wake up tomorrow barely remembering today.

Eventually, I found a quiet spot in the corner of the dining room. Whenever people passed by me on their way to the bathroom, they cast me a reserved smile. To avoid that uncomfortable situation, I pulled my phone out of my purse, more out of habit than anything else. As soon as I saw there were six unread messages, in an almost Pavlovian response, I needed to find out what was happening back at the office. There were several messages from Jared, and I began scrolling through them. He needed me to draft a motion, and I was already mentally constructing the arguments before reading through the rest of the emails.

"You look rather deep in thought," someone said to me.

I looked up and saw Biren, the guy Monali Auntie had briefly introduced me to at the hospital. His tall, lean frame loomed over me while he stood.

"I guess I was."

He sat in the chair next to me. "Days like this are something you can't prepare for." He gestured to my phone. "It's good to have your mates on hand."

Sheepishly, I said, "Oh, this is for work."

He raised his eyebrows. "Really? You can't possibly be thinking of work with all of this going on."

I probably shouldn't have been, but I was. And from the look on his face, I could tell he thought that was ridiculous. Biren wore the same expression Alex used to don when I checked my emails while he was bouncing script ideas off me or when I was on the phone with my parents. Alex was all about living in the present, and it seemed Biren might be as well.

"What kind of work can't wait until after a wake?"

"My boss needs me to write a brief. He says court deadlines don't wait for family emergencies." I knew how cold the words sounded before I'd even uttered them out loud. I wished I could pull them back.

"Forgive me, mate, but that's just crap. People can't be expected to live that way."

Biren was right. Just as Alex had been when he'd said similar things to me for almost two years. On the day of my niece's funeral, I shouldn't be thinking about court deadlines. It was that simple. My priorities had shifted very far from the way my parents had tried to raise me. When I was growing up, my dad always said, "In life, the priorities should be Bhagwan, family, health, and then job." Sitting here, I realized that my work had jumped to the top of that list. And I had let it.

"You know what? You're right. Will you please excuse me for a minute?" I said, as I stood and headed toward the stairs with my phone in hand.

I closed my bedroom door and leaned against it. Sunlight trickled in through the window. It was cracked open so the cacophony of noises from the street came through unfiltered: dogs barking, the occasional mooing of a cow, the pop of fireworks, high-pitched horns on scooters and rickshas. With everything going on around me, it was amazing I could think straight, but my thoughts felt clear for the first time in months.

Seeing Neel and Dipti suffer through losing their child made evident how short life could be. I took a deep breath and picked up my phone. With the time difference, it was just before six in the morning in Los Angeles, but given the number of emails I'd received during the past hour, I knew the Warden was already in the office. It would probably be the last time I dialed the phone number that had become as familiar to me as my own. He answered on the third ring.

"Preeti, good to hear from you. I was beginning to think we were going to have to retire your jersey. Are you back in town?" His nonchalant tone irked me.

"No, I'm at my niece's wake in India," I said dryly.

"Yeah, I'm sorry to hear about all of that. I suppose you'll be heading back to Los Angeles now that the situation is . . . resolved. We're ready to have you back on the team."

Resolved? Had I been standing in his office, I might have punched him in the gut, but I remained calm. His reaction shouldn't have surprised me, given the transactional nature of his relationships with his family. I couldn't believe I had looked up to this guy for the past four years, that I'd put him above everything else in my life.

"No. I actually need to stay here for a few more weeks. My cousin's wedding is next week, and it doesn't make sense for me to leave before that now that I've come all this way."

Jared let out a low whistle. "Preeti, we talked about this before you left. I can't afford to have you riding the bench indefinitely. You're my star player. We need you at the ready."

Through his tone, I could practically see the smirk on his face. I wished I had the appropriate sports metaphor to lob back at him. I heard the clickety-clack of his fingers on his keyboard.

"I wasn't calling to ask your permission to stay, Jared." I stared out the window at the crowded streets outside our subdivision. Lorries and cars crawled by, avoiding pedestrians crossing at will. "I called to tell you I'm not coming back to the firm."

The typing stopped. "Preeti, don't throw away what you've built here. I can't imagine that's what you want after putting in all these hours to work toward partnership."

"That's why I'm getting out now. I can't keep devoting my life to something I'll never get at the end of the day."

"How do you know you won't get partner? If you work hard like you have been, you'll get there."

I laughed to myself. His promises of partnership were empty, suddenly sounding more like threats than anything else. I had seen countless senior associates ahead of me try and fail, and those were white attorneys like Mike who were part of the "club" in a way that I could never be. I'd never recount childhood vacations in which we flew first class, or use *summer* as a verb, or automatically assume a dark-skinned woman in the office was a secretary before thinking she could be an attorney.

"In the firm's hundred-plus-year history, there has not been a single Indian partner. And we have offices in Delhi and Mumbai." Feeling my resolve solidifying, I said, "It's a decision I should have made earlier."

"So, you'll be the first. Isn't that more impressive than being the fiftieth one?"

I shook my head. He didn't get it, and it was clear he never would. It wasn't much of a carrot to say that somehow, against all odds, I would break a ceiling that had been in place for generations because those in power—people like *him*—wanted it there. I had wanted to believe I belonged at the firm so badly that I'd ignored the cold, hard facts that had been there all along. Belonging was something you were born into. It wasn't something that could be earned. It had taken me far too long to recognize that.

I said, "Look, I appreciate the years I've spent developing my career with you. It's just not the right fit for me anymore."

"Well, suit yourself. We'll work on getting your replacement."

And then he was gone. In a matter of seconds, he'd gone from wanting me back to moving on to my replacement. He'd never even asked how Neel and Dipti were doing. He didn't care. His lack of empathy and compassion made clear to me that I should never have been working for him or seen him as a mentor. That I should never have wanted to belong to that institution in the first place.

When I hung up the phone, I laughed. I had just done the thing Alex had begged me to do months ago—quit my job so I could go with him—but I had been so scared of the unstable picture ahead of us, worried that it would look more like the childhood I'd vowed never to repeat than the romantic future he envisioned. I no longer had Alex or a job, but I felt like I was finally moving in the right direction. It had just taken me a few detours to get there.

~

Even though the mood in the living room was heavy, my step was lighter after having stood up for myself with Jared. A huge weight had been lifted from my shoulders. I had taken back control of my life. It was exhilarating. And terrifying. But mostly exhilarating. And still terrifying.

Biren came up to me and handed me a cold nimbu pani. "Decided to leave your work upstairs, did you?" he asked, motioning that I no longer had my phone.

"You could say that," I said, a small smile creeping onto my lips.

He took a sip of his drink. "You seem very coy. I might think you wrote the world's fastest brief while you were up there."

Feeling emboldened by what I had done, I'd lowered my defenses, and I was more comfortable with this stranger than I would normally have been. "Can you keep a secret?" I whispered, ensuring no one could hear us.

"You wouldn't believe how well," he said, a twinkle in his eyes.

The words were burning inside of me, and I had to let them out. "I just quit my job."

His eyes grew wide. "Seriously? I hope it wasn't something I said."

"It was. Sort of. It was more something someone else has been saying to me for a long time, and you helped me see he was right. But don't worry. This is a good thing, or at least someday, I'm pretty sure I'll look back and think it was."

"Are you certain?" His kind eyes showed concern.

I paused for a moment, thinking about what it might feel like to not worry about what I would write on my time sheet for every six-minute increment of my day and start living them instead.

I knew it would be difficult to explain to my parents what I'd done, but the adrenaline was still pulsing through me, and I said, "Yeah, I'm sure."

And I was. Or at least I would be after I called Carrie. That phone call would be difficult because we had been each other's rock for our entire time at the firm. I couldn't imagine ever being there without her, and I knew she felt the same way.

"You're in no rush to head back, then?" he asked.

"I suppose not," I said.

I glanced around the room and saw my mother passing out chai from a serving tray, her stoic face masking the pain I knew was simmering beneath the surface. I saw my father chanting prayers in a circle with the other men, looking like he belonged in a way he never had back in America. Dipti had come downstairs, and Neel was now seated next to her at the end of the large L-shaped sofa. Their body language was distant despite their proximity. It was subtle, something that would go unnoticed by everyone else in the room, but the photographer in me had always been an active observer, and I could tell there was an unspoken barrier between them. In this crowded house, it was difficult to find private time, but I'd have to make sure to pull Neel aside at some point because, while he was putting on an award-winning performance, I wasn't buying it. And now I could focus on him without any distraction from Jared.

13

After returning from a long walk the following morning, I anxiously bounced my foot while I waited for the countless pixels to conjure up the image of my best friend.

"Is this thing working?" Carrie said as she tapped the screen, her red hair swinging forward as she leaned in.

"Can you see me?" I asked.

"There you are. Finally, a fun use for this fancy video-conferencing software the firm installed." She leaned toward the screen, close enough for me to spot the faint freckles on her nose and cheeks. "So, *what* is going on? I haven't heard from you since I dropped you off at the airport. The Warden is losing his mind."

Hearing her voice and being able to see her through the computer screen was so comforting. "I know. This has been the most intense week of my life." My voice caught in my throat, and I couldn't get out any more words.

Carrie twirled a pen in her fingers like a tiny baton. "Jared was asking me when you're coming back. I covered and said it was a huge family emergency and there was no internet access where you were. I've been dodging him the last couple days so he can't keep asking."

I exhaled slowly. "I don't think he'll be asking you anymore."

"What do you mean?"

I wasn't sure how to break it to her. In many ways, I felt like I was abandoning her. We'd been in the trenches together since we started as summer associates all those years ago and had been inseparable since.

"Jared and I spoke yesterday. I'm not coming back."

Carrie's jaw fell slack. "*Ever?* Did that asshole fire you over this? There are laws to prevent this type—"

"He didn't fire me," I said. "I quit. Yesterday was my niece's funeral, and I was sitting in a room full of grieving people, and this guy caught me checking emails on my phone. I was thinking about a brief and hoping I could write it as soon as everyone left. The look on his face said it all. I don't want to be that person anymore."

"Niece's funeral?" Carrie said softly, putting the pen down. "So that means . . ."

I nodded. "They lost the baby. That's why I haven't been able to reach out sooner. Between being at the hospital and then making arrangements, there hasn't been a moment of privacy."

"But Neel and Dipti are okay?"

Again, I nodded. "Thankfully." I cocked my head. "Well, physically anyway. It's been awful watching them go through this and seeing what it is doing to them." I filled her in on the events since I had arrived, including Neel's choice to save Dipti and her reaction after the fact. Carrie leaned forward, rapt with attention, and let out a low whistle afterward.

"I don't know how a person emotionally recovers from something like this. It makes everything I've been worried about for the past few months seem insignificant," I said.

Carrie nodded. "Agreed, but doesn't quitting seem a little extreme? You're going to need a job when you get back, and this one isn't perfect, but at least it pays the bills."

"My cousin's wedding starts in a few days and will last a week, so I'm staying through that. He asked me to be the family photographer for the ceremonies leading up to the day, so I kind of have to." I paused for a moment and fiddled with the lens cap on my camera, excited to be using it again and hoping I wouldn't let Hari down. "I'll head back after that. After all, I need to dust off my résumé and find a job!"

"Look, it's fine if you want to leave the firm. Let's be honest—we all do. But you're not going to prove anything to anyone by taking the moral high ground. People like Jared are so stuck on themselves that they won't even notice you did that. And you know better than anyone that it's easier to find a job with a job. Unless you somehow inherited a trust fund that will outlive you . . . this just seems totally unlike you."

"Of course I don't have a trust fund," I said, thinking of the savings I had spent the last four years building. It was enough to live on for six months but not for a lifetime, which was the same concern I'd had when Alex wanted me to move to New York with him. *Maybe she's right. Maybe I should call Jared back.* Even if I'd hit glass ceilings, I'd get paid while doing it.

I took a deep breath. "I'll figure it out before I run out of money . . ."

Suddenly, Carrie's expression changed, and her face lit up as if she had solved a puzzle. "This isn't about money! You really think this is how you're going to win him back, don't you?"

She'd been my best friend for years and could probably predict my actions better than I could. Other than Neel, she probably knew me better than anyone else. I'd be lying if I said that I hadn't wondered if pursuing passion instead of paychecks would lead Alex back into my life. Prove to him that I could give him what he'd wanted. Our conversation at the airport had made me miss him terribly, and with all the heightened emotion of the past few days, I found myself craving the closeness he and I had once had.

"That's not why I'm doing this," I said boldly, my voice not revealing that I wondered if she was right.

"I know you've been through a lot in a short period of time, but it is crazy to be making such life-altering decisions in this state." She threw up her hands. "It just seems like you're running away."

"I'm not running away," I said.

I couldn't understand why she was so bothered. For years, we'd fantasized about what we would do if our hefty loans didn't require us to practice law. Open a patisserie, become a diplomat, figure out if we had what it took to write a novel. The possibilities seemed endless. It was one of our favorite pastimes while working late at the office, yet now that I was actually stepping away from big-firm life, she could not muster even a modicum of support.

Even with an entire hemisphere separating us, it still felt like she was in the room sitting across from me. We both stared at each other on the screen, unsure of what to say next.

Finally, she said, "Just make sure you think about this. I'm certain whatever you said to Jared can still be undone. Narcissists love a good crawl back. But the longer you wait, the harder it will be."

"I'll think about it."

And I would. Leaving my job was the opposite of being practical, which was what I'd done for my entire life. A conservative financial nature was one of the few attributes in life that my parents and I shared. "Save for a rainy day," they'd always said. And up until now, I had acted accordingly, believing that was the right way. Hearing Carrie's reaction made me further doubt myself. I hadn't been willing to make this decision a few months ago when my heart was also on the line, so what was different now?

To help her understand, and maybe even to convince myself, I said, "Even if I wanted to come back now, I couldn't. With everything that has happened with Neel and Dipti, I need to be here." After a long pause, I said, "With my family. And Jared made clear that staying any longer wasn't an option."

Saying the words aloud, putting my family before my job, was new ground for me. In some ways, Carrie was right that I should go back to the life I knew. Even if I started prioritizing my family above my job, there was no guarantee that they were ready to accept that from me. People fell into patterns, and they had gotten used to limited contact with me as much as I had with them.

She sighed. "It's probably good for you to sort out whatever you need to with your family. Just remember you have family here too."

Her words made me smile. Carrie was my family in the way I'd often wished my parents had been. Open, honest, not afraid of disagreeing with my decisions, but still always supportive. Like she was doing right now. Both of us knew that regardless of those choices, we were still there for each other.

"Don't worry. I'll be back right after the wedding. Job hunting, so I don't burn through all of my savings!" I sipped from the cold bottle of Limca I had brought up with me before the call.

"Okay. I'll talk some sense into you then." She glanced down at her watch. "Crap. I have a conference call starting. I'll tell Jared you've been going through hell and need some space to sort things out . . . temporary insanity, or whatever. Just in case you change your mind."

I managed a small laugh. "Thanks. But I think it's done."

The conversation ended on a more lighthearted note than it had begun, but I couldn't stop my thoughts from wandering to the last weekend my parents had visited LA. They had come seven months ago to meet Alex for the first time. And I hadn't known that the weekend would be the beginning of the end for my relationship with Alex and my parents.

I didn't realize my mother was standing in the doorway to my bedroom at Lakshmi until she moved her arm and the jingling of her bangles caught my attention.

"What's wrong?" she asked.

I'm not sure if it was the stress of the past few days or the jet lag, but I answered her honestly, something I rarely did because it wasn't worth the fight. Today, I didn't care.

"I was just thinking about how hurt I was when you left my apartment in LA."

Her jaw set into a hard line. "Not this again."

"What do you mean, 'again'?" I said. "We never talked through this. You stormed off, and it was done."

My mother stared back at me. "You made your decision. You knew how we felt. What was there to talk about?"

I threw my hands up. "Everything! Normal families don't act that way."

"Who exactly do you think is this 'normal' family?"

We both knew that by *normal* I meant American families. White families. Families like Carrie's. Families that wore shoes in the house, ate turkey and gravy on Thanksgiving, always had dessert after a meal, had pets, and had parents who kissed each other in front of their children. Since we had arrived in America, I had been pushing my family to be more American so that we could fit in, and my parents had pushed back just as hard, always saying that we didn't want to be like American families.

I cast my eyes downward. "I'm just saying this, what we are doing, can't be normal."

She shook her head. "It's not always about what you think, Preeti."

"No shit. I—"

"Watch your language!" Her eyes grew wide. "I didn't raise you to speak that way to your mother."

This was not an argument worth having, so I started again. "Mom, when you and Dad stormed out of my apartment, I stared at that closed door for over an hour, hoping you would come back and we could talk things through."

She sighed. "You know how our culture feels about damaged girls. You weren't even trying to hide it to protect yourself! Living with that boy before marriage and for the entire world to see. The only people you kept it from were me and your father, taking us for fools."

"I didn't tell you because I know you feel that way. But I don't. There's nothing wrong with what Alex and I were doing. I thought if you could see we were happy together, you could understand that sometimes the right people can find each other even if the biodatas don't match."

"How can you say that? I was protecting you. So you didn't end up hurt by that American boy. And that is exactly what happened, no?"

I flinched inwardly, but then looked her squarely in the eyes. "No. The person who hurt me was you."

As soon as the words were out, just like yesterday when I'd told Jared I was quitting, I felt both exhilarated and terrified. I'd never been that direct with her. We didn't openly share our feelings, even though I'd often wished we could. In the months that followed my parents' storming out of my apartment, I'd tried to keep some semblance of a relationship with them, but whenever I tried to bring up Alex, my mother would shut down. It was draining to pretend that the most significant person in my life did not exist. When she'd given me the ultimatum several months ago to choose between her and Alex, while it was difficult, I'd known I had to prioritize my future with him. She would not even hear my arguments about why there was room for both in my life and I should not have to pick one. Now, like she had after that conversation, instead of wanting to sit down and have a chat about what I had just said, she did exactly what I expected, what any Indian mother would have done. She stared at me silently, no emotion registering on her face. Coldness cut deeper than any angry outburst ever could.

"Think what you want. But someday you will learn it is childish to believe that love is all you need in a marriage," she said before leaving the room.

Screw it. I was tired of letting her end these fights on her terms. If she had wanted me to be an obedient Indian daughter, then she should have kept me in India for my entire life instead of moving me away from it.

"Wait," I called after her, not caring that everyone else in the house could probably now hear us. "We need to talk about this."

She spun back around. In a low but stern voice she said, "I tried to talk to you months ago. Remember? Hah? I called you twice. It was *you* who did not respond. You didn't want to talk about it then, so why should I talk about it now?"

Guilt was a powerful weapon. It was rare for her to show even this much emotion, and seeing it revealed just how injured she had been. Maybe even as much as me.

In a small voice, I said, "I didn't call you back because I was mad. Not because I wanted you to stop trying."

"You can't have it both ways."

Her words hung in the air as I realized Carrie had been right. Even if I hadn't been ready to admit it, part of the reason I'd immediately felt lighter after quitting was because it had freed me to go back to Alex. To move to New York and find a job there. The city had countless law firms, and what had seemed so daunting a few months ago now seemed possible. Not just possible, but the decision I always should have made. When Alex moved, he had taken a part of me with him, and to feel whole again I needed to go back to him.

I thought back to the moments in India when I had seen my mother's vulnerability. Like when she had been in the kitchen making nimbu pani and let tears fall when she thought she was alone. My heart ached to think of her reaction if I told her I had quit my job and was going back to Alex. I knew that from that moment onward we would have a series of interactions like the fight we'd just had. That is, of course, if we had any interactions at all. I'd never see her vulnerable side because it would harden like it had that weekend when she met Alex and stormed out of our apartment. The last time it had been easy to choose Alex. If anything, it was unthinkable not to, so it wasn't a choice. But now it felt like one. I was never going to be happy without Alex, my mother was never going to be happy with him, but I wasn't prepared to lose either.

Dipti had been floating through the house as if in a trance, so I was surprised when she stopped in the doorway to my bedroom soon after my mother had marched downstairs.

"Are you okay? Do you want me to get you something?" I asked her, desperate to ease her pain and push mine aside.

"I heard you and Mom fighting."

"Sorry. We didn't mean to be so loud. I hope we didn't wake you."

Mom felt like a label that only Neel and I should be using, and it sounded strange every time I heard Dipti say it, almost as if she were an outsider trying to fit in. Or worse, maybe it bothered me because she was the one who *did* fit in and I was the outsider.

Dipti was no longer wearing the white sari she'd had on for the past few days to signify that she was in mourning and was now wearing Western lounge pants and a cotton T-shirt. She sat on the bed next to me and stared out of the window. It was slightly ajar, and the smell of burnt paper from fireworks wafted in, likely from a neighbor's wedding event.

"What were you fighting about?"

"Oh, um, nothing important," I lied, in part because I didn't want to burden her with any of my problems, and also because I didn't feel like my relationship with my mother was her business.

After a long pause, she said, "Your mother is a proud woman. I imagine all mothers are." Her voice trailed off.

"When the time is right, you'll be a great mom," I said.

She nodded absently. "You are lucky."

It was my turn to nod. Disagreeing with her about anything was unthinkable given what she'd been through. My mother and I had spent a complex thirty years together, and Dipti had only been witness to a handful of them. She'd lost her own mother so young that I didn't think she could relate to the shifting dynamic I had with my mother as I became an adult. We all idolized our mothers as children, so hers was frozen in time on that pedestal.

"I'll go lie down in the other room again." She rose from the bed.

"Okay. We'll be quieter. Let me know if you need anything."

Without responding, she began to make her way toward the bedroom across the hall.

"Oh, Dipti." I jumped to my feet and called after her. She turned around. "I saw you give the beggar money at the funeral yesterday. I was wondering why you did it."

"She spoke the same dialect the servants used in my father's family's home in Mumbai."

"Oh," I said noncommittally, not sure why that mattered.

"When she approached Virag Mama, she told him she needed money to feed her grandchildren." Dipti then disappeared into the bedroom.

Her compassion humbled me. She had never had a moment with her daughter living outside of the womb, but she had become a mother nonetheless.

During this trip to India, I'd witnessed many different sides of Dipti that I hadn't expected to see. When she and Neel first married, I didn't understand his decision. His bringing home a doting Indian bride seemed to go against our unspoken childhood pact that we would not end up in marriages like our parents'. We'd vowed to have equal partnerships with our spouses, like we saw with the parents of our American friends or on television shows. That's what I thought I had found with Alex because if we had to fight through that many obstacles to be together and we still wanted each other, then that had to be love, right?

But then Neel brought Dipti home, and she was the least controversial wife he could have picked from our parents' perspective. A perfect biodata match. Complete with the mannerisms. Just like our mother had done when we were kids, Dipti would stay back in the kitchen, serving the rest of us a hot meal, and then she and my mother ate only after we had finished.

She seemed so traditional and so opposite from the type of person I could relate to, so I hadn't bothered to spend much time with her apart from family events. And she had taken Neel from me, converted him back into a more traditional Indian role after he and I had put so much time and energy into assimilating. Now I realized the Dipti I saw around my parents wasn't all of the person Neel married, and maybe their marriage wasn't so far off from what I wanted as well.

14

Virag Mama offered to push back Hari and Laila's wedding, but Neel insisted the preparations continue as scheduled. He reminded us that Nana had always said, "When faced with tragedy, we must celebrate the good."

So we did. My unexpected arrival necessitated some changes in the plans. Because Hari had no direct sisters, as the next-closest female relative, I would now be able to fulfill those duties. Mistakenly, I assumed my role would be similar to what I'd done at Neel's wedding. As we sat together in the living room the next day, I quickly learned that Neel and Dipti's wedding had been the American abridged version of the traditional Hindu ceremony. Dipti was more modern than I had given her credit for and had cut out several days of events that she thought were extraneous, like the baithak, which, from what I could gather, was nothing more than the wedding guests getting together for dinner on each of the three nights before the main days of ceremonies began.

When I asked the point of everyone being obligated to come to dinner for the days before the wedding, Indira Mami told me, "It used to be for the family to prepare invitations for hand delivery and assign the wedding tasks, but now we contract those activities outside of the family." With a shrug, she said, "Still, people expect the baithak, so we do the baithak. It's easier than having the gossip and seeming cheap if we don't do it."

That warm December morning, I also learned it was fortunate the wedding could go on as planned because it already was scheduled for the last possible day before the unholy period began. If the naming of children was done according to the stars, it was no surprise that marriage was also. Had the wedding not continued, Hari and Laila would have had to wait at least two months for the next "auspicious" period in February at the earliest.

"This is ridiculous," I said to Neel after we had both sat through another discussion about what time of day, down to the minute, would be most propitious to hold certain ceremonies. He was the only person in our family with whom I could share these views, and these conversations gave me a sense of normalcy, even if only for a few moments.

"Yeah," he mumbled. He had been understandably distant since Uma's funeral, but I still tried to engage him where I could and offer whatever help I thought would ease his suffering.

"Seriously, getting married at the right times hasn't really made anyone in this family very happy. Maybe the trick is to get married during *non*auspicious times!"

"I've been happy," Neel said. I'd forgotten he and Dipti had abided by the auspicious times when planning their wedding.

"Sorry. I meant everyone other than you guys." I immediately felt guilty for suggesting that anything was wrong with their marriage, especially because lately, it seemed clear something was.

I played with a stray thread coming loose from a seam on the couch cushion. "So, how are you and Dipti doing?"

Neel's shoulders were already slumped. He opened his arms in a gesture of defeat. "I don't know how to help her."

"Maybe it's better to just give her space right now until she's ready for help."

He didn't react, but I could tell he was pondering my words. I reached out and touched his arm. "I'm here if you need someone to lean on."

He gave me a rueful smile. "That's always been my job with you. And with Dipti."

"I know. And you've always done it well. But you also taught me well." I leaned close to him. "You are doing the best that you can with her right now. And I know she's your top priority, but you lost your baby too. You have to heal yourself as much as you have to help her heal. You always want to fix everyone else, but lean on us while you grieve your loss too."

"I've seen so many parents go through this when I've had to deliver them bad news at the hospital. It's completely different when it happens to you," he said.

"I can't even imagine. But it doesn't mean I can't listen."

He nodded. He wasn't ready, and I could see that, but I hoped that my words had gotten through to him.

My bond with Neel had been the most consistent relationship in my life. While we fought often, in large part due to him being more obedient and thus our parent's favorite while I felt like the black sheep, we had a shared history that kept us close. I couldn't blame him for how our parents responded to us. My parents gave him more leeway because he was a boy. As a girl, and a headstrong one at that, I was always under a microscope. It wasn't fair, but it was tradition.

~

The next week of wedding festivities passed by like a blur. While we were happy for Hari and Laila and their good fortune, it was still hard for my immediate family to distance from the great loss we had just suffered. Dipti had skipped the entire affair, and while my mother worried about what people would think about Dipti's absence, even she knew not to push further. While attending was hard for Neel, it also seemed like he and Dipti having some space apart was what they needed to process their own feelings about their loss.

By the time we got to the day of the actual wedding, I felt like I had nothing left in my tank. The sun beat down on me, causing me to sweat as if I were running a race. The elaborate sari I was wearing grew heavier on my body as the fabric collected the moisture sliding down my skin. I tried not to squirm while kneeling on the mandap as the maharaj, dressed in simple white cotton clothing that was in stark contrast to our elaborate formal wear, chanted mantras and took items from the steel bowls full of red powders, grains of rice, flower petals, and sticks and tossed them into the ceremonial fire in the center.

A young, lanky photographer in faded navy slacks and a white button-down shirt with the sleeves rolled up was scurrying around capturing photos of the wedding. Back at my law firm, the cuffed sleeves would have been trendy, but in this setting, I could tell the lack of formality in his attire signified he was working the event rather than attending as a guest. His camera clicked rapidly as he adjusted and snapped from different angles.

I ignored the sound and concentrated on tossing grains of rice into the fire when instructed by the maharaj, dotting Hari's forehead with vermilion, and carrying a coconut that had been blessed with a vermilion Hindu swastik for good luck.

It had been nearly a decade since a rough, hairy coconut rested in my palms. My parents had helped me move into my apartment in Los Angeles when I started law school and insisted on doing a religious ceremony to protect my home, including leaving a similar coconut outside the front door. The minute they left, I had pulled it inside, fearing that neighbors walking by in my heavily Jewish neighborhood might mistake the Hindu swastik for a hate symbol.

The photographer smiled at me as I descended from the mandap when directed by the maharaj. Before I could return his kind gesture, he leaned in to take a close-up of my face, leaving me disoriented, seeing dots from the harshness of the flash, so I couldn't check out what type of camera he was using.

"Just one photo, madam," the photographer said to me as he readjusted himself for a different angle. "Yes, please."

Madam? I associated the word with old ladies, and this guy didn't look much older than me.

The shutter clicked again. The dots returned.

"We can take it later, Tushar," Indira Mami answered for me, ushering me out of the way. "Focus at the couple, yaar!" She motioned a flat hand in the direction of Hari and Laila, who were sitting patiently with the maharaj.

Without argument, Tushar took a step back. His camera was digital. He furiously snapped away while guests mingled about the wedding venue, chatting and sipping chai and hardly paying any attention to the wedding rituals being performed on the mandap. Despite all the noise around me, I focused on the repetitive clicking of his shutter and wished I were in his place. For the days before this, I'd enjoyed being the designated family photographer for the wedding events, but Indira Mami and Virag Mama insisted that someone else needed to handle the actual wedding and reception. "You must be part of the ceremonies, or no one will even know you were here!" they said.

Seeing the world through my lens for the past few days reignited something in me that had been dormant. I remembered the way it felt to concentrate on one subject and ignore everything else around me. I felt the chaos and noise fade away, replaced by the laser focus of centering on a single thing and appreciating the nuances of it. I picked up details that I'd never have noticed had I just been a guest, like the way the light refracted and reflected off objects and people as they moved. I felt like through the lens, I was able to see India anew. Distill the truth from my childhood memories. I was able to notice more of the progress that my parents had spoken about over the years, because that progress was in the people and the way they behaved, rather than the storefronts and physical objects.

Relieved that my front-of-camera wedding duties were officially over, I sank onto a cushioned bench on our family's side of the plot. Like most weddings I'd seen in India, Hari's took place in a spacious grassy lot. It would have been difficult to find an indoor area large enough to accommodate the more than eight hundred guests who were in attendance. In the center was the mandap where Hari and Laila would be married. It had a minaret at each corner with garlands of marigolds strung between them. On three sides around the mandap were cushioned benches for the guests. Fans faced them, whirring at high speeds, but were no match for the heat. Bright-red and shiny gold paper decorations hung from strings stretched across the expansive plot and swung haphazardly with the movement of the fans. Garlands of marigolds, roses, and jasmine flowers dangled from the strings above.

I sat in the second row of benches on the groom's side and took a glass of filtered water from one of the waiters passing out drinks and snacks during the ceremony. It was a huge contrast to American weddings I had attended, in which people would sit with perfect posture in quiet churches, eyes locked on the couple standing with whomever was officiating the ceremony. For all the fanfare associated with Hari's wedding, the ceremony itself was rather informal. Children ran around playing in the grass. Guests munched away on samosas, pakoras, and other fried treats. Hardly anyone paid attention to the actual wedding, including Hari's parents. Indira Mami sat on a bench in the first row a couple seats over from me. She spooned pistachio ice cream into her mouth while chatting with my mother. It was the most relaxed I'd seen her since I had arrived.

With all the noise around us, I couldn't really follow one conversation.

"Lovely couple. Such good height-body, no?" I heard some aunties behind me murmur.

"The flowers here are quite lovely, but don't you think the Patels did a better job with the food last week?" said an auntie to my left, her cohort nodding.

"Your job is done for one child. Now only Bharat is left," I heard my mother say to Indira Mami and focused on their conversation.

"The same is true for you," Indira Mami said.

"Children in America watch so many movies. Preeti wants this love she sees in these films," Mom said, resigned.

"Bharat knows when it will be his time. We have already started making contacts for him. Children here understand their duties," Indira Mami said.

Marriage shouldn't be a duty. My gaze remained fixed on the mandap, as if I were engrossed in the ceremony, but out of the corner of my eye, I saw Mom nodding slowly. She had a distant look on her face.

Bharat was only twenty-one, and they were searching for his bride. Most guys I'd known at that age had been looking to score a keg and meet their next hookup.

Indira Mami said, "Once they grow up, they realize this American love is not lasting. Maybe she just needs more time to see that. You see how many NRIs come here to get married after all their dating. Maybe she needs your help like we helped Hari. It is good when we can introduce someone."

My eyes widened. *They'd better not!* I was here to be with my family during a difficult time. Not to find an arranged or "suggested" husband. Certainly not one who was *from* India! Even though the locals saw my Non-Resident Indian status as a demotion, I had worked hard on my assimilation into Western culture after we moved, and I was proud of the progress I had made. I was not about to have that work undone by some archaic Indian traditions. Besides, the only person I could see in that role was Alex, and he had been close to my thoughts while in India. Seeing this wedding unfold over the past week made it hard not to think about the plans Alex and I had once made. And with my job out of the way, there were no longer any barriers, and maybe he and I could still have that future we had talked about.

"We have tried in the past," Mom said.

Her tone made me cringe, because despite my earlier hope, I knew renewing my relationship with Alex was choosing him over my mother. She pictured a life for me that was like the one Hari and Laila were entering, and even though I loved my parents, that was more than I could give them.

"You must try harder then," Indira Mami said. "Does she know your nasib?"

I snuck a peek at Mom when I heard that unfamiliar word. Her jaw set into a hard line. Her eyes narrowed and shifted away from Indira Mami, making clear the conversation was over.

Nasib? I repeated the word in my head, trying to conjure up its meaning but unsure whether I'd ever heard it before.

Before I could think too much about what I had heard, I saw Hari and Laila on the mandap beginning their seven walks around the fire, signifying they were near the end of the wedding ceremony. I hoped they would have more in common than my parents did and end up finding real love instead of one born out of obligation. They deserved that. Everyone did. To me, the alternative would have been a prison sentence, especially after having felt love in the past. Even while Alex and I were broken up, I knew if I ever settled for something less, then I'd always remember what I was missing. I dabbed at the corners of my eyes with the end of my sari, praying that Hari and Laila would love each other with the passion and fervor that I knew was possible between two people. The love that I needed to get back.

15

The day after the reception, I found Neel sitting at the computer in Hari and Bharat's sparse room. As in all the other bedrooms in the house, the only photo that hung on the wall was one of Krishna Bhagwan, the god most revered by my family. There were no personal touches like I had back in my apartment in Los Angeles. The room consisted of two beds, two nightstands, a table for the computer, a locked closet, and the air-conditioning unit that spewed out much-needed cold air.

"What are you doing?" I asked, plopping myself onto one of the beds, wincing when I met the concrete-like density. I lay on my stomach, facing him.

"Canceling plane tickets."

He and Dipti had originally planned on spending a week in Goa after the wedding to have their babymoon before heading home and getting ready for parenthood. That trip didn't make any sense now.

"When will you two go back to Chicago?" I asked.

Neel swiveled away from the computer and faced me. "I'm not sure. Dipti is still so emotional. But I think it's best to go back home and get some sense of normalcy back in our lives." He buried his head in his hands and groaned. "We were so proactive about setting up the nursery before this trip! It will crush her to see it."

"Is there anything I can do? What if I fly ahead of you guys to get rid of everything?"

He looked like he was going to shake his head, probably out of instinct. He and I both had a hard time letting people help us. Probably part of our parents' "take care of yourself and never have any obligation to others" philosophy. But then he paused and looked at the floor.

"You know what," he said, finally looking up. "I think it's not a bad idea for someone to do that. But it doesn't have to be you. You probably have to get back to work too, right?"

I turned my gaze away from him, but he knew me too well.

"What happened?" he asked.

"Oh, it's nothing," I said, not wanting to burden him.

He rolled the rickety chair he sat on across the white marble floor, one of the loose wheels squeaking as he glided closer to me. "What's wrong?"

Pulling myself up so I was sitting on my heels, I glanced at the open door and said in a low voice, "I quit my job."

Neel's eyes grew wide. He, too, glanced over to make sure no one could overhear us. "You did? When?"

"I'm not really sure when the technical date is. But I said some things to my boss before the wedding started . . ."

"Pree, why?" He pulled back for a minute, the color draining from his cheeks. "Is it because you came here?"

I emphatically shook my head. "No, I *wanted* to be here with you. You'd have done the same for me."

"But you loved that job. You were great at it."

"I never loved it. I liked that I was good at it. And I liked how much it paid. But I never felt comfortable at that firm. And I never loved the work."

"What do you mean, you weren't comfortable there?"

I played with the thick green seam of the rajai folded neatly at the end of the bed. Neel and I had not talked about our race and culture

112

since those early years in Chicago when we were actively trying to assimilate. We knew what the end goal was, but we had never stopped to check in on each other about whether we felt we had reached it. The assumption was that by getting good educations and having successful careers, we'd transcended any suffering it took to get those things. We never discussed the parts of ourselves that might have been lost in the process. It was as if we both knew that if we tugged even a little at the thread, then the world we had built around us would unravel. Neither of us was the type to let that happen.

"It was just hard being the only Indian person around," I said. "Law isn't like medicine; it's still a very white profession. I guess I thought that was a good thing in the beginning. Like if I could make it in a superwhite profession, I could make it anywhere." I'd never shared any of these thoughts with anyone and had barely even admitted them to myself until this moment. "I wonder if maybe it would have been nice to not always be the only *other* in the room."

Neel looked at me sympathetically. "I didn't realize that had bothered you."

I shrugged. "It's not like I have anything to complain about. I have an ocean-view office and a large paycheck. And the financial stability Mom and Dad were searching for after we left India. I work around the best of the best—or at least people who *see* themselves as the best," I said with a wry smile. "But after working so hard to be at that prestigious firm in the first place—*harder* than many of the others who were there—it was annoying that I was still the one partners turned to when they wanted someone to order sandwiches for a meeting, or grab a file from their office, or be the notetaker rather than the speaker. Those things happened every day and were a constant reminder that no matter how far I'd gone, I still had further to go." My words hung heavy between us, and after a few moments I pasted on a forced, bright smile. "But that's all behind me now! At least until my next job, when it starts all over again. For now, my professional life doesn't matter, and we need to focus on you!"

"Maybe there shouldn't be a next job like that, then," Neel said, not letting me off the hook.

"It's a nice thought, but bills have to be paid, right? No trust funds for us!"

Neel let out a laugh. "No, we certainly don't have those. But we also aren't at the same place as when we first arrived. Maybe we are okay enough that the rest of your life doesn't have to be spent chasing something you'll never get."

It was the first time he'd alluded to the fact that the goal we'd set as kids—to blend into white culture at any cost—was one we could never fully attain. But we could never have known that at that age. And I'm not sure either of us would have done anything differently if we had. Even if we could never be fully accepted by our white peers, we still had to strive to get as far down that path as possible. Life was easier that way.

I sighed, beginning to understand that I'd never achieve the goal I'd set as a seven-year-old immigrant, but also not ready to believe there was something this significant in my life that hard work could not overcome. But I knew deep down that Neel was right. Acceptance and belonging were moving targets.

"I'm not sure I know who I am if I stop chasing after that," I said softly. "If I admit defeat now, then what did I spend my life doing?"

Neel's eyes met mine, and I could see him wondering if he'd made the right decision for us all those years ago. "What about devoting your life to something you love? Like photography? Even just watching you take photos here of the days leading up to the wedding. You seemed more comfortable than I've seen you in a long time. It has always been obvious how much you love it, and I never knew why you quit in the first place."

"Mom was right. It wasn't practical," I said, even though I'd asked myself a million times over the past eight years whether I had given up too easily. I'd been a kid back then. A year of trying and failing and living with my mother's "I told you this wouldn't work" face felt like a lifetime. I wondered if it would be different if I tried now. If, even if I didn't have the same financial security that corporate America provided, I would have enough emotional security to outweigh that loss.

"What's the point of being practical if you aren't happy?" Neel asked, his voice thick with his recent pain.

His words caught me off guard because he and I had focused on what was practical since we'd arrived in America. Through the wall, we heard Indira Mami close the heavy wooden closet door in her bedroom, the skeleton keys she kept on a large ring clipped onto her sari clinking against each other as she locked the wardrobe.

Lowering his voice, Neel said, "If you need money or anything, Dipti and I can help you, until you decide what is next."

I held up my hands in protest. "No, no. I'll be fine. I have some savings until I figure out what I want to do. You know when you feel like you've hit a wall? You're not sure how or why you got there, but you just know that you've got to make some changes."

He nodded, closing his eyes as if the feeling was all too familiar right now.

I debated telling him about Alex and New York but held back because the family strain had affected him as much as it had me, and I didn't want to add to his burden now. Besides, my heart knew the right thing was to call Alex and tell him first. If I was choosing him, then I had to commit to that fully. Neel had suggested I devote my life to something I loved, but maybe the right answer was to devote it to *someone* I loved.

"What are you going to tell Mom and Dad?" he asked.

"I'm not sure, but I figured there was no point in telling them until I really have to." Shifting my gaze back to the blanket and feeling emboldened by the conversation we'd just had, I asked, "How do you manage to do it?"

"What?"

"Be so perfect."

"I'm not perfect."

"I know you're not. But how do you get Mom and Dad to think you are?"

"I'm more patient with them." He clasped his hands together, pausing for a moment. "I was older when we moved to Chicago. I remembered more about India and life here. Mom and Dad would put on this act that everything was fine after we moved, but it wasn't. They fought all the time when they thought we couldn't hear them. Money was tight. They weren't good at mixing with Americans."

"It's not like I was *that* much younger than you. I saw all of that stuff too." I tried not to sound defensive, but he often acted like being five years older gave him a lifetime of experience over me.

He shook his head. "You know some of it, but they worked really hard to keep the bad stuff from you when you were a kid. So did I. We wanted you to think moving to America was the great adventure we hoped it would be."

I searched my memories, trying to understand what Neel meant. It had been hard for him and me as we struggled to fit in at the public school, where most of the kids were white or black, but I thought it had been good for our parents when we'd first arrived. One of Dad's friends had helped him get an engineering job at a steel factory. Mom had her social circle with Monali Auntie and her other friends who had also come over from Ahmedabad. It was like they had their perfect Indian enclave in America: modern amenities with old-world culture. They weren't teased and picked on the way we were because they didn't have to go to school and mix with so many non-Indians. No one had ever called them "curry lovers" during lunchtime—a phrase that I did not understand because there were no Indian dishes I knew of called curry. It wasn't until I was in college that I realized *curry* was what white people decided to call Indian food rather than use the names Indians used for our food. My parents never learned to identify themselves as "other" the way Neel and I had to navigate America's color-based caste system. As a child, I'd longed to be something other than "other." After September 11, I got my wish. After that, we all became "brown," and that was far worse than "other." India had no "brown" people, so I'd never referred to myself as such when living there. The first time I had to utter it as an identifier of who I was, it felt so odd. But my parents escaped that. Keeping to their own meant they got to avoid the pressures of blending in and adopting odd labels to make them palatable to the white community around us. For years, when things were so hard for Neel and me, I'd been resentful that they'd made this move thinking only of themselves and not about how it would affect us.

"What were they fighting about?" I asked.

"Dad hated being a factory worker and wanted to come back. I think having an advanced degree but doing lower-caste work really hurt his pride. He thought his education and stature in India would translate here, but those things didn't matter anymore. They ended up making less money than they would have in India and working harder to get it."

"Factory worker? Dad was an engineer." I couldn't picture my father doing manual labor as a profession.

"That's what he told people, but the company wouldn't recognize his Indian degree. He was working on the floor of a steel mill hauling stuff to the loading docks. That's why he has all of those back problems now. It took him years to get an American degree at the local community college that companies would recognize."

My mind was reeling. How could I not have known that?

Neel continued, "Dad thought they'd be better off back in Ahmedabad. They'd have more respect and could afford a better life. Life would have been easier."

"Why didn't they move back?"

"Mom didn't want to."

That wasn't the answer I was expecting. My mother, who was so steadfast in her devotion to Indian culture and who could not get on the plane fast enough whenever we went to Ahmedabad for a visit, hadn't wanted to move back home? This was the same woman who'd forced me to wear panjabis to a public school in Chicago after she'd realized there were no school uniforms like we'd had at our private school in Ahmedabad. I had begged her to buy me a pair of jeans so I could dress like the other kids, but she'd said my tailored Indian clothes were better quality than the cheap, off-the-rack American clothes I wanted to wear. It had taken me over a year to convince her otherwise.

"Why?"

"Not sure."

Neel's version of our family's life was so different from what I remembered. I began scanning my memories, looking for signs I had missed or been too young to notice. When my parents forced us to take leftover Indian food to school for our lunches and made us susceptible to curry-related jokes, was that really because they thought it was more nutritious, or was it because it was all they could afford? Was Mom insistent that I wear panjabis because we already had them, and she couldn't pay for new Western clothes? Did she tell me I couldn't have friends over for dinner because it was just another mouth to feed and every penny counted?

I had so many unanswered questions, but before I could probe Neel for more information, Bharat walked into his bedroom and asked if he could use the computer.

"Sure," Neel said, standing and returning the chair to the desk. "Sorry we took over your room."

I wasn't sure when Neel and I would get another moment of privacy to resume our talk. But we had already come so far in just this single conversation, and I knew he was never going to be able to tell me why our mother had acted a certain way toward me, whether it was because she believed so strongly in our culture or whether she'd rather have me

118

believe that instead of knowing how difficult things were after moving. Only she could give me those answers.

~

That night, I replayed my conversation with Neel and my childhood memories for things I might have missed or that might have been more nuanced than my young mind could have processed at the time. I felt a little betrayed that Neel hadn't let me in on all those secrets earlier. While I'd thought we hadn't kept any secrets from each other, it seemed that loyalty had only flowed one way. And even if the goal had been to protect me as a child, we'd both been adults for a long time now. Loneliness washed over me, and my heart yearned for Alex.

I thought about how introducing Alex back into my life would make it more difficult to learn the things I wanted from my mother. Hearing his name would likely be enough to put the cold war between us back into effect. I asked myself whether he was worth it. I tried to convince myself that he wasn't, but my heart wouldn't listen. And there was no guarantee that even if I didn't go back to Alex, my mother and I could repair the relationship that had begun fraying since those early years in America and had never been mended. I was too Indian to fully cast aside my family, but also too American to not follow my heart. I'd do what I could to make both work, even if that meant being more like Dipti around my mother and biting my tongue to keep the peace.

When the only sounds were the dogs barking and crickets chirping outside, I reached for my phone and unlocked the screen to the favorites page, where Alex's number remained in the number one spot. A smile crept across my face as I realized this time, I was calling him for what he had thought I was calling about from the airport a couple weeks earlier. Below his contact information was Neel's, and then my parents'. My lips tightened upon seeing my mother's number, but I had made my decision, and there was no looking back now.

The phone rang three times, and I did the math to figure out that it was midmorning in New York. Then it dawned on me that he might not answer because it was me. He'd been notorious for screening calls, but never mine. But we weren't together anymore, I reminded myself. To him, I was no different from those people he used to send to voice mail to deal with later.

Then on the fifth ring, I heard his groggy voice, husky and hoarse with sleep, mumble hello. I pictured him lying in bed, the covers pulled over his head and his dark-brown hair tousled from the night. The image took me back to those mornings in our apartment. Except that now he wasn't lying in our bed in Los Angeles. He was in some strange place in New York that I had never seen, in a bed covered by a blanket I didn't know the texture of and couldn't picture.

"It's me," I said, unsure of what else to say but already lighter having heard his voice.

"I know."

"Sorry. It sounds like I woke you." I fiddled with the rajai covering my legs, suddenly nervous about telling him the news that he'd wanted to hear for so long.

"What's going on?" he asked. "Are Neel and Dipti okay?"

"Yes and no," I said. "They are both fine healthwise, but they lost the baby, so it's been a really difficult time for all of us." Not wanting to bring the mood down by rehashing all those gory details and still not able to blurt out why I'd called, I said, "How's the film coming along?"

"Did you really call me about the film, Pree? I thought we said we wouldn't talk anymore . . ."

Pree. He had used my name instead of calling me Monkey. My heart ached for what we'd had. For what we'd been. I'd give anything to feel him hold me right now. The warmth and comfort of being enveloped in his strong arms could make everything else disappear and make me feel safe and secure. I needed to get back to "Monkey." *We* needed that.

"No. I called to apologize, and to tell you that you were right," I said. "I finally did what I should have done a long time ago. I quit my job. What happened with Neel and Dipti showed me how messed up my priorities had been, and well . . . I know you'd been saying that all along." I took a deep breath. "Sheep, I was wrong not to go to New York with you. I see that now, and I want to make it right. Make *us* right."

I smiled as I waited for his reaction. Saying the words out loud felt better than I'd imagined. The past couple weeks had taught me what was important. And that I wanted a relationship like Neel and Dipti's, or at least the way they had been, and the way I hoped they would be again.

He took a deep breath. "You quit your job?" His voice was even.

"Yes. I already called Jared, so I guess there's no turning—"

I heard a soft voice near him ask if everything was okay.

He whispered away from the phone that he would be right back.

Reality set in. My pulse quickened, and the room felt hot. So hot. He was with someone. Another girl had my place in the bed next to him. She now had memories of him when he was asleep, and she could complete the picture because she shared his new home with him. She knew the color of the sheets and the blanket and could trace her way to the bathroom in the dark. My mind began reeling, the room spinning. I hadn't prepared for this. Not even a little.

"Who was that?" I demanded, knowing I had no right to do so.

A few moments passed. I sensed he was shimmying into his boxers and moving from the bedroom to another part of his apartment. The image made me nauseous.

Finally, he said, "Preeti, we both said we had to let go and move on. I wanted to tell you when you called from the airport, but you were so upset that I didn't want to add to that."

It dawned on me that while I had been pining over him for the last few months, restraining myself from calling him, he hadn't been doing the same. He'd moved forward while I had been standing still.

"I thought we'd end up together. I called to tell you I was ready to move to New York. To give you everything you wanted," I said meekly and instantly hated myself for being "that girl."

"I thought that for a while too. You know that. But I couldn't keep holding on to the hope that maybe someday you'd change your mind."

"It's not someday, anymore. It's today. I'm ready."

"I'm sorry, Preeti. It's too late. I had to move on with my life. I hope you will too."

The words stung, but I could also tell from his tone how difficult they were for him to say. Or maybe that's just what I wanted to believe.

"I shouldn't have called," I said, wishing I could turn back time. Unlearn that he was telling me to move on because he already had.

When I hung up the phone, I pulled my knees to my chest. Dogs in the adjacent lot howled at each other as they continued their turf war. Loneliness washed over me, as I thought about the road ahead. I had no job, no Alex, and no idea what I was going to do next.

16

My eyes were red and puffy from crying all night, but I couldn't let my mother see that, so I hid my face under the covers when she came to wake me the next morning. Guilt consumed me. She had no idea that last night I would have done the thing that would have hurt her most if only Alex had let me. I told her I wasn't feeling well, and it was probably exhaustion, so I was left to rest in my room.

After I knew everyone was downstairs having breakfast and the second floor was empty, I called Carrie on video chat. When her face popped up on my phone screen, I could see that she was still at the office even though it was after nine in the evening in Los Angeles. Her red hair was pulled back into a bun with a pen holding it together. It was her standard after-hours work look. I knew that by now she would have also kicked off her shoes and would be roaming around the office barefoot in her tiny defiance for having to work late yet again. Feeling like I always had to be the model minority, I'd never felt like I could do that regardless of the hour.

Upon seeing the face of my closest friend, I could carry on the charade no longer. Carrie would see through my facade in seconds. My face scrunched up, and I felt warm streams on my cheeks.

"You were right," I managed to say through the tears.

"Hey, what's going on?" She leaned in.

"I shouldn't have quit my job," I said softly.

"So fix it," she said. "Call Jared. What's the big deal?"

I took a deep breath. "I quit because I wanted to get Alex back. I wanted to start over with him in New York."

A knowing expression came over her face. "And?"

"And he's with someone else in New York. So I quit my job for nothing." My head drooped away from her gaze.

"It's not too late," Carrie said.

I bit my bottom lip. "For me and Alex?" My tone had the foolish innocence of a child.

She sighed. "I don't know anything about Alex, but it's probably not too late to get your job back."

My face fell, and Carrie chewed on her bottom lip. Her face was strained, and I could see she was debating whether to say what was on her mind.

"Why did you want to be with Alex?" she finally said.

My face scrunched up. "Because I love him."

"But why?" she pressed.

I felt myself shift into a defensive state. I'd never questioned her about why she chose to date certain people. "Because we loved each other. We were able to laugh together, and I could be myself around him."

Carrie arched her eyebrows. Gently, she said, "From the outside looking in, I'm not sure if you were yourself with him. The guy was pretty selfish, and you catered to him a lot. I've seen you stand up to aggressive, football-player-size guys in depositions, but then you'd be this meek, doting person around him. It just looked like you were so desperate to hold on to him, especially because you felt like you had to choose between your parents and him, that you couldn't see him for what he was. You kept holding on to the guy he was during those first few months you were together, but then when he revealed more of himself, and it was clear that his top priority would always be himself, you kept giving him passes."

I felt like I'd been slapped, and wondered how long she had been holding on to those words. She had been my rock during the breakup—the only person in my life other than Neel whom I hadn't alienated during that time. Was she right? She couldn't be. I had been so clear in my feelings for Alex. My jaw stiffened.

"I don't think it was like that. I chose him over my parents because he was worth fighting for."

The skepticism on Carrie's face was evident. "Everyone is worth fighting for . . . until they aren't. All I'm saying is that I think you can find someone who will respect you, your family, and your culture more than Alex. Someone who will meet you halfway and not expect you to abandon everything you knew and adopt his way of life."

I knew she meant well, but her words stung. "If you've thought that this whole time, then why didn't you ever say anything before?"

She looked sheepish. "There's no point in telling someone something they aren't ready to hear. I'm just saying to think about it with the power of hindsight. Maybe you haven't lost the great love that you feel like you have right now."

I mulled over her words and remained quiet.

"I'm sorry to be so blunt," she said. "Maybe it was too soon to say. But going back to the job thing, Jared's had people in for interviews, but he hasn't hired anyone yet. Beg for your job back. What's the worst thing that happens? You don't get it, and you're back to where you are now."

She was appealing to my practical side. I appreciated that. It was hard to be practical when my emotions were clouding my judgment, so I needed Carrie to point me in the right direction. And then I'd never have to tell my parents I'd quit. Biren and Neel would be quiet about the whole thing, so there wasn't really anything else to worry about. I thought about my conversation with Neel and how much we had unearthed about how I felt about my time at the firm, but there was also safety and comfort in a life full of yellow ruled pads, legal research, and every six minutes of my life accounted for. Was my emotional comfort worth more than the financial security that my job provided? If I worked hard, I'd earn a steady paycheck every two weeks until I hit the glass ceiling of partnership, but by then I'd be able to get another high-paying job. I'd avoid the financial instability that had plagued my family after immigrating. It would be nothing like the unpredictability I'd experienced during the year after college when I'd pursued photography and had no idea when my next job or paycheck was coming. Back then, I was too young and too proud to ever have confessed to my parents how much it weighed on me to have chosen a life of financial instability, and part of me was glad they had forced me into law school.

"Just tell him you'll be back in a couple days," she urged. "He hasn't liked any of the candidates yet."

It sounded like the right decision, even though I hated the thought of doing it. It felt like escaping from prison only to go back and turn yourself in. But it was practical.

"You're probably right," I said. "Maybe I can call—"

Before I could finish my thought, I heard raised voices coming from outside my door. I opened it enough to peer out and saw Neel standing and facing Dipti, who was in the doorframe of the bedroom they'd been sharing. My parents and Indira Mami stood in between them, silent but each looking worried about the exchange.

"What is wrong with you?" Dipti hurled at Neel, her voice heavy. "How can you even think about just leaving like that?"

Into the phone, I whispered to Carrie that I'd have to call her back and quickly ended the call. I opened the door fully so I could step outside, but my mother caught my eye, and I knew I should let Neel and Dipti play out whatever this was.

"Because there's nothing left to do here!" he tossed back. It was the first time I'd heard him raise his voice to her since I'd arrived in India.

"Left to do?" She let the words hang in the air between them, before repeating, "Left to *do*? Our daughter died here. Or have you forgotten?"

His eyes widened. "Of course I haven't forgotten! But staying here won't bring her back. We're not going to be able to move on if we stay here in this constant state of purgatory!"

"If it's such torture for you to be here, then why don't you just leave?" Her voice caught on the last word.

Neel looked at her, exasperated. "That's exactly what I'm trying to do! And then you started yelling at me about leaving."

"Go without me if you want to go so bad."

He squeezed his eyes shut and clenched the back of his neck with his hands as if he thought he could release the tension in the air that way. He took a few deep breaths. "I'm not going to leave you here," he said as evenly as it seemed he could muster.

Her eyes welled up. "I can't leave her here."

"She's not really here!"

Dipti's eyes darted around frantically as if she were looking for Uma and expected her to appear from thin air. "She is to me," she finally said. "Her soul is here."

My mother pursed her lips together like she wanted to jump in and say something but knew she couldn't.

Neel was now standing in front of Dipti, trying to reason with her. "Her soul is everywhere. And the river will take her ashes to the ocean. She will be in our hearts no matter where we are, so she is everywhere for us. The best we can hope for is that her soul has already found a new home, and her next life will be a long and healthy one filled with great joy."

Dipti's glistening eyes looked up at him. She looked like a scared child who wanted to believe everything being told to her. Then she put her head down and said, "It just doesn't feel right to go."

Neel exhaled slowly. "For me, it doesn't feel right to stay." He turned and went down the stairs. We heard the front door close behind him and then the driver starting up the Fiat.

It wasn't clear where they left things, but it was clear that they were hitting a breaking point. Dipti noticed us staring at her and retreated to her room like a wounded animal. Mom closed the door to give her some privacy as we all made our way quietly downstairs.

~

A few hours later, my mother, Indira Mami, and I were in the living room and heard a car pull into the driveway. Neel still had not returned, and my father had gone out to look for him. We had all steered clear of the upstairs to give Dipti some space. A moment later, one of our servants brought Dipti's father into the room. A young man trailed behind him, hands clasped in front of him, head and shoulders hanging low, as if he were trying to make himself invisible. Raj Uncle approached my mother first.

"These are hard times for us all." His tone was apologetic and almost deferential.

My mother seemed confused. "Yes, Sahib. The children are in a lot of pain."

Even though Neel had lost his own child, my mother couldn't help but still think of him as her child.

"Can we offer you chai and nasta?" my mother said, out of habit.

He held up his hands and politely shook his head. "That's very kind, but I'm just here to collect Dipti."

I looked up at the second floor, where I could now see Dipti peering into the living room from the railing on the bridge that spanned the middle of the second floor. Her face looked ashen, and I was sure she'd spent the better part of the morning crying.

"Collect her?" my mother asked.

Raj Uncle nodded his head ruefully. "She just needs some time."

"Neel is not even home. Does he know?" my mother said, realizing what was happening.

Raj Uncle looked at Dipti and shrugged his shoulders, clearly not knowing the answer to the question or what had transpired between Dipti and Neel this morning. I now understood why he looked so apologetic. He was doing something that went against custom because once Dipti married into our family, she was supposed to do what was expected as part of that new family. Taking her away from Neel without his permission violated that marriage tenet. But the pleas of his only daughter must have been so strong that he was willing to go against tradition.

Raj Uncle leaned closer to my mother and said in a soft voice that Dipti would not be able to hear, "She is upset now, but she will move past this."

He was trying to save face in front of my family and assure us that eventually Dipti would fall back into her traditional marriage role. After the new sides of her I had seen during my time in India, I wasn't so sure. While she respected tradition, she wasn't going to let it dictate her life. The way she had stood up to the priest about Uma's funeral made that clear. I kept hoping Neel would walk through the door and convince her to stay, but there was no sign of him.

"Please have a seat until Neel comes home, and then we can talk about this," my mother suggested while gesturing to the sofa. "Come. We'll have some chai and nasta." She caught our servant Gautam's eye and signaled for him to bring Raj Uncle some water and make some tea. It was as if she understood Dipti leaving Lakshmi without Neel would have a lasting impact on them and was determined to avoid it.

"Papa, I'm ready to go," Dipti called down from upstairs.

Raj Uncle looked helplessly between her and my mother. His internal struggle between what the culture expected of him and what his only daughter needed from him was etched on his face.

"Varshabhen, it will have to be another time," he said to my mother.

He motioned for the servant who had been standing behind him like a statue to go upstairs and collect Dipti's things. The lanky young man kept his head down as he mounted the stairs in his bare feet and came back with both of the suitcases that Dipti had brought on this trip. Dipti followed him and made her way toward the door.

"Dipti, beta, have we done something to make you feel unwelcome?" my mother said. "This is a lot of effort for one day, no? Your flights are just after midnight tomorrow, so no sense in moving the luggage, hah?"

She looked up and held my mother's gaze. "I'm not going back to Chicago tomorrow," she said simply.

"I thought you and Neel discussed—" my mother said gently.

She shook her head. "I'm not going back. I'm going to stay with Papa at my foi's house."

"If there is a reason to stay, you and Neel should discuss. I'm sure he will be back any minute now. Just have a seat."

Dipti shook her head. "I'm tired." She turned to her father. "Let's go home," she said.

Indira Mami, my mother, and I watched the servant load the luggage atop the car, tying it down with rope, and then Raj Uncle and Dipti sputtered down the road, leaving a small cloud of dirt behind them. My mother and I turned to each other, knowing the implications of what had just happened could be severe.

When Neel and my father returned an hour after Dipti had left, my mother and I were still sitting in the living room. We hadn't said a word to each other but let the sound of the television playing in the background fill the silence. Mom gestured for them to have a seat.

"Dipti went to her foi's house," Mom said to Neel.

Neel shrugged as if this was no big deal. "Fine. It's one less fight we will have before the flight."

Mom shook her head. "Beta, she is not going to fly home tomorrow."

Neel looked at me, exasperated. "What's she going to do? Stay here forever? This seems a bit dramatic."

"I know you're upset," I said, "but she's really hurting."

"No one said she's not! I just don't see how staying here and wallowing will help anything."

"You need to talk to her," I said.

He threw up his hands and exaggeratedly scanned the room. "She's not here. Wasn't that the point of this whole conversation? That she's not here? How am I supposed to talk to her?"

I knew how upset he was even if he wasn't admitting it, so I let his snide tone pass. "Go see her."

He shook his head. "If she wanted to talk, then she would have bothered to have this conversation with me before she left. Seems there's nothing left to say. She's got a key and a credit card, so she can go back to Chicago when she's ready, but I'm not waiting around for that." He rose and headed toward the stairs, taking them two at a time.

Mom's eyes were wide, and she called after him, "You can't leave India without her!"

The only response was the closing of the door to his bedroom upstairs.

17

Everyone in the bungalow, including the servants, had been tiptoeing around even though Neel had not left his room in over two hours. Servants absorbed the dysfunction of their employers like sponges, and they were politely staying out of everyone's way while still finishing their chores. They probably knew more about each of us and our mannerisms than we even knew about ourselves.

I was in my small bedroom gathering up the meager belongings I had brought on the trip. My flight was scheduled to depart at four in the morning, a day ahead of the one Neel, Dipti, and my father were booked on. While I hated that Neel and Dipti were suffering so much, I was looking forward to going back to LA. There had been nothing but disappointment and heartache since I had arrived in India, and I welcomed the escape. That was what LA was to me now. An escape from everything bad that had happened in India.

The cellophane bags of Indian clothes crinkled as I laid them carefully in the suitcase. I had brought only a carry-on with me, but the bulky wedding clothes I'd bought had made it impossible for me to leave with the same luggage with which I'd arrived. Indira Mami had given me an old heavy blue suitcase that my family had left in India when I was a teenager. It was one my parents had acquired in a secondhand shop on Devon Avenue for our first trip back to India, and it was older than I was. My family didn't believe in throwing anything away. A lifetime of seeing poverty all around them made even wealthy Indians frugal.

The suitcase sat on the edge of the bed, and I knelt on the floor arranging clothes in it. My mother came into the room and sat next to the suitcase. She looked inside it and bit her lip. I knew she was fighting the urge to suggest a better way to organize the contents than the way I had done it. She always thought her way was best.

"Preeti, you must talk to Neel."

I sat back on my heels, giving my knees a break from the hard tiles.

"He hasn't come out of his room yet. You know how he is. He needs to be alone."

She glanced at the suitcase.

After a long pause, she said, "I don't think it's good for you to go."

I stared at her, not sure what she was asking.

She continued, "You both are very close. It gives your father and me some peace, to be honest. He will only listen to you in this type of situation."

"What do you want me to tell him?"

"He can't go back to Chicago without Dipti. It's too much strain for them. That type of action cannot be undone."

I didn't disagree with her. I thought about my failure to go with Alex when he first asked me to move to New York and knew that was why he had moved on. But I couldn't tell her any of that. The saving grace in all this was that I hadn't told my parents that I had quit my job and decided to go back to Alex, so they didn't know that for a second time I'd been prioritizing Alex above them. The relief that my mother would never know numbed some of the pain.

"I'm not sure what I can say to change his mind," I said, wishing I did have the answer.

"Maybe you both can stay together," she said, her eyes hopeful. "You can miss a few more days of work, right?"

My stomach sank as she mentioned work. The old me would have lied to her. Carrie had convinced me I should try to get my job back anyway, and I had convinced myself to again repress feeling like an outsider at the firm, so she would never be the wiser if it all worked out. The air-conditioning unit in the window wheezed and sputtered, a sound I had become accustomed to in the past couple weeks, but I still turned my gaze toward it so I could look away from my mother and gather my thoughts.

"I can't miss more work," I said finally.

"Why? You never take any days off. Surely your boss can understand this has been a serious family matter."

I took a deep breath. "That's the thing . . . I need to go so I can get my job back."

"Back?"

I nodded. "I quit my job last week."

"Why did you do that?" Her eyes grew as wide as thalis.

"Because I couldn't be there and here!" I said in a hard tone, instinctively ready to verbally spar with her. "It was either be here with the family or be there at work. Nothing else."

Her face registered a range of emotions. I could see she was surprised I had stayed and sacrificed my job for the family, but I could also see she was terrified of me not having a job. It was the same range of emotions I had felt myself, so we at least had that in common.

Forcing a softer tone, I said, "I should be able to get it back. But I need to return to LA for that."

My mother nodded, knowing that while she needed me to be in two places at once, a hemisphere apart, I could only be in one.

"I don't want you to have the hardship we had in America." Her gaze was steady.

"Believe me, none of this was planned," I said, referring to more than she could ever know.

She sighed. "I don't know what we will do about Neel and Dipti. But we will find a way." Her expression turned resolute. "You cannot throw away your career."

I looked at Neel's closed bedroom door across the hall and feared the worst. In the half day I had left in India, I had to find a way to help him and Dipti. In the past couple weeks, I had realized their marriage was more than the biodata match I had always assumed it to be. They had a foundation and understanding for each other that was balanced in a way that my relationship with Alex probably had never been, and it took all this pain, including Carrie's harsh but necessary words, for me to see that. I couldn't bear the thought of them letting go of something that people, including me, spent their lifetimes searching for and often never found.

~

That evening, Neel still had not emerged from the room and had refused all food offers during the day. My packed suitcase sat in the hallway, yellow rope tied around it to ensure no one at the airport stole anything from it, ready for Gautam to take it downstairs.

I knocked softly on Neel's door, and when he didn't answer, I turned the handle and opened it enough to poke my head inside.

"I'm leaving soon, and I wanted to say bye," I said.

Neel was lying on the bed with an arm slung across his eyes to shield them from the fluorescent light that was mounted above the bed. He rolled himself up to sitting.

"Any chance you can trade your ticket with me so I can leave tonight instead?" he muttered.

"I'm not sure airline regulations work that way." I made my way across the room to sit on the edge of the bed. I turned to him and said, "You can't go and leave Dipti here."

His face hardened. "Not you too."

I held up my hands in surrender. "It's not like that. I'm not sure what Mom said to you, but here's what I have to say." I took a deep breath. "After Hari's wedding, I called Alex."

He gazed at me questioningly, not having expected the conversation to head in that direction.

"I realized a big part of why I had quit my job was because I wanted to be with him. Sure, I also felt uncomfortable at the firm for all the reasons we discussed before, but the reality is that I'm used to feeling uncomfortable and molding myself to what the situation needs. But I wasn't used to the empty feeling of not being with Alex. And that meant being with him on his terms, which meant being in New York. No matter the consequences with Mom and Dad, or anyone else, I was going to move to New York and do what I thought I should have done in the beginning."

"You're going to New York tonight? Does Mom know?"

I shook my head. "I wish I were. By the time I called him to tell him I was ready, he had already moved on to someone else. I never told Mom what I had decided to do, which in hindsight was probably a good thing since it didn't work out."

"That would have killed her," he said.

I lowered my eyes to the marble-tiled floor. "I know. But being without him was killing me, and I had to choose. But the only reason I'm telling you this is because I know how much damage is done when someone leaves."

He rolled his eyes. "Dipti isn't going to run off with someone else. We're married."

"I'm not saying she is. I'm just saying that the hole in a person's heart when someone leaves is hard to fill. It doesn't go away. And it has the same effect as running off with someone else would."

"I've done everything I can. I've been patient; I've been kind; I've been supportive. But I can't live in purgatory. Wallowing in sadness has never fixed a single problem, and it never will."

"You need to give her more time."

"How much time can I give her? I have to get back to work. What good would it be for me to join you in unemployment? If Dipti wants to throw her career away, that's fine, but we don't have the luxury of both of us doing that."

"Trust me; I get it. I'm about to go back with my tail between my legs and ask for my job back, because even a demoralizing job is better than having nothing. But you can give her another few days, few weeks, whatever it is. Just don't let her feel like you abandoned her. That feeling never goes away."

"I hear what you're saying, but there's some self-preservation here too. Pree, I can't sit here in this house and be miserable with no sense of purpose with Dipti at her family's place and Mom and Dad tiptoeing around me." His voice caught. "You won't even be here, and I just can't handle all that on top of everything else. I need to feel productive so I don't feel broken."

I had never heard him speak so vulnerably. I wanted to give him a hug but knew better. It would be the thing that made his tears fall and made him clam up, the same as it would have been with me.

"I've never said this, in part because I never got to know your relationship before now, but what you and Dipti have is special. I now understand what made you fall in love with her and realize that it was love, and not just settling down because it was the right time like Hari and Laila. But love marriages are more fragile than arranged marriages. They can change in an instant. You guys are among the lucky few that have a love marriage that fell within the biodata matches of the arranged system, and you have to protect it." I smiled ruefully. "You have to give me hope that someday, somewhere, I will be able to find that kind of happiness too."

"I appreciate you saying that. Really. But I'm not sure how to salvage what's left. And if I can't save us, then shouldn't I at least save myself?"

It was a difficult question and a difficult decision. I didn't want him to lose himself or his marriage.

"We will find a way to save both," I said, patting his knee before telling him to get some rest.

As I closed the door behind me, I looked at my packed suitcase in the hallway. My ticket away from the family drama. My ticket to getting my hard-earned job back. I wheeled it back into my small bedroom. With a pair of scissors, I cut the taut yellow rope and took the contents out and put them back into the small drawer stand by the window. The only way to get Neel to stay was for me to stay too. I couldn't save my career and help my family, so I had to choose. I put the empty suitcase back in the hallway and lay down on the bed for a moment. The dogs were back at it behind the house, but I had a feeling I'd have many more nights ahead to get used to them.

I went back to Neel and told him I would stay in Ahmedabad with him until he and Dipti were ready to go back together. He reluctantly agreed. As siblings, there was safety in numbers, and he and I had been through enough hard times together that we knew we could weather this storm as well. I knew my parents wouldn't be thrilled about me being unemployed, especially my dad, but I needed to tell him.

Taking a quick breath, I rapped on the door. After hearing a low-murmured "Come in," I pushed it open. My parents were in the bedroom Mom had slept in as a child. She always said it looked the same back then as it did now. Similar to the other bedrooms, there were no personal touches. The room was sparsely furnished, with a bed in the center flanked by two wooden end tables. On the far wall was a wooden vanity. A locked gray metal wardrobe was in the corner opposite the bed. Next to that was a white wooden door leading to a balcony. There were no photos or artwork on the walls other than the framed photo of Bhagwan that hung over the vanity. The only color in the space was the forest-green paisley-patterned rajai that covered the bed. It was such a contrast with their cluttered bedroom in Chicago, where there were so many pictures on the walls and so many baubles on the flat surfaces that my gaze never knew where to rest.

Mom was folding some laundry with the same careful precision I would have, while Dad was lying on the bed, eyes closed. He wasn't snoring, so I knew he was awake.

"Can I talk to you?"

Dad opened his eyes and blinked a few times, readjusting to the light. Mom looked up from the neat piles of petticoats and underwear. The chair in front of the vanity was piled with clothes to be folded, so I sat on the edge of their bed with one leg crossed under me and the other dangling over the side. My parents looked at me expectantly.

"Given everything that's been going on, I'm going to stay in India with Neel. He's going to stay until Dipti is ready."

Mom stopped folding. The creases on Dad's forehead became more pronounced. He sat up.

Dad raised his eyebrows. "You can never even get one day off," he said, referring to the number of times I'd used work as an excuse to avoid family events. "How are you going to get so many days off like this?"

"Actually," I said slowly, "I quit my job."

Mom remained still while Dad sat up. "Why would you do that?" He turned to my mother. "Why would she do that?"

She scrunched up the shirt she had been about to fold and remained silent.

He raised his eyebrows at her. "You knew about this, then? Hah?"

"Just listen to her, yaar," my mother said, even though I could see the conflict dancing across her face.

My dad said, "You can't just take a leave or something?"

I could see my parents thinking that their very successful and financially stable daughter was about to throw away *their* sacrifices. Because in the end, it was their sacrifices that allowed me to have the life I had. They had given up their posh upper-caste lives to become lower working class in America, trying to build their way back to the comfortable lives they'd already had in India. It was an immigrant story that was hard to comprehend but was common for many of the Indian families that had immigrated there, certainly for the ones in their circle. They had never shared that story with me, nor had I ever asked such a personal thing of them, even though I longed to understand.

The air-conditioning unit sputtered, and the cold air that had been gusting out grew warmer. Mom got up and rotated the dial to turn off the machine to keep it from overheating. The unit was probably as old as I was, still having that faux-wood paneling I hadn't seen in America since I was a little girl. Mom propped the window open. With the unit off, we could hear people shouting in the distance and horns honking. A smoky smell wafted in: fresh roasted peanuts from a street vendor across from our subdivision.

My thoughts swirled. I couldn't tell them that, as the only Indian associate at the firm, I didn't have the liberty of speaking up. They wanted to believe that America had accepted their children, and if we didn't let them have that lie, then they'd be left wondering if their sacrifices had been worth it. They'd be left wondering if they had made the wrong decision. It was a question that was cruel to ask because it could never be answered. I had given up nearly all my culture to blend into that firm and the life that came with it: eating the foods they liked and lying to my parents about the fact that I had stopped being vegetarian, celebrating their holidays and ignoring the ones I'd celebrated with my family in our home, dressing in cardigan twinsets and pearls, and speaking in a way that was comfortable to those in power. I had given up a lot of myself no doubt, but how much was another question too cruel to ask because I'd never know the answer. I could only acknowledge these transformations in hindsight, now realizing how brief life could be and looking into the past through a shorter lens.

"That job wasn't a good fit for me," I finally said. "I want to do something that has more meaning."

"Meaning is something reserved for the rich," Dad said. "We don't have that luxury. You know how hard life is without money. We didn't go to America and struggle so you could throw it all away like this! If you were going to do that, we should have just stayed here in the first place! If we'd stayed here, none of us would have struggled."

I could hear the desperation in his voice, and I hated him thinking that his struggles—*our* struggles—had been for nothing. But I still knew that I had to put Neel ahead of that.

"Dad, this is about more than a job. Neel needs me. I have to make sure he and Dipti are okay."

I could see my parents envisioning a future in which both of their highly educated, once-successful children were unemployed, and weighing that against Neel ending up divorced. Both were bad outcomes in the Indian gossip circles.

Worry spread across my dad's face. "You kids have never been in India without us."

Before I could respond, Mom said, "I'll stay with them."

"You don't have to," I said quickly. "Neel and I can stay on our own. Really." He and I would both have clearer minds and more peace if Mom wasn't helicoptering over our every move. "You should go back with Dad tomorrow like you planned."

Dad shook his head. "Varsha, I don't understand how you can be so calm. She's throwing her life away."

"Maybe, but yelling at her won't fix anything," Mom said.

Dad's hand went to his forehead as if he had a headache. "Maybe they are both throwing their lives away," he said, defeated. "Maybe we all threw everything away when we left here," he muttered, more to himself than to us.

"Trust that you raised us better than that," I said to him. "And I'm sorry if you don't like my decision, but I'm staying."

"See! That is exactly the type of attitude that will not last long here," Mom said. "This is why I need to stay. You kids are too Western for this culture."

"This isn't a time for an Eastern or Western culture debate, Mom. We need to pull together as a family and help Neel. No matter the cost."

18

The next day I woke up to the dogs barking outside the window. I adjusted my head and felt a crick in my neck from fitful sleep on the dense, brick-like pillow, and looked around the bare room and realized I was single, unemployed, and staying in a country I had spent most of my life running from. I groaned when I realized what I had done and had a pang of regret that I was waking up here again rather than on a flight halfway back to LA like I had planned. I would do everything in my power to bring Dipti around so we could all go back home as soon as possible.

When I went downstairs to breakfast, Neel shot me a look of gratitude and annoyance: annoyance that I had agreed to stay behind with him so he knew he couldn't go back home either, and gratitude for the sacrifice I'd made for him. Doing the right thing was rarely the easy thing, but we were both trying.

That afternoon, the sounds of scooters and rickshas honking flowed in through the window even louder than usual, but the breeze tempered the stuffiness in my room, so I left it open. It was Saturday, and more people were out and about than during the week. The house still had a heavy sadness that rested upon it. I had to try to do something to break the spell.

I went out to the driveway, where the driver had reclined his seat in the Fiat and was napping. He must have heard the gravel crunching under my feet as I approached, because he bolted upright as soon as my hand touched the door handle. I climbed into the back seat and in Gujarati told him to drive me to Dipti's foi's house. Maybe there was a way to get Neel and Dipti on their flights tonight, and we could all go back home. The engine roared when we pulled out of the driveway.

Her family house was only a couple miles from Lakshmi, but with the Ahmedabad traffic, it took us nearly thirty minutes to get there. We had to push our way through various animals ambling through the streets. The cacophony still took some getting used to.

She and her father had been staying with his sister in a large bungalow similar to Lakshmi in a similarly affluent gated community. Her family came from similar wealth and stature as ours by virtue of being part of the same major and minor caste. I recalled how sold out I had felt when Neel met her on his own in medical school. For years before her, he'd dated plenty of non-Indian girls, albeit behind our parents' backs so they had never known about them, but I thought he was going to be the one who blazed the trail such that I could also bring home whoever was the right match for me, regardless of biodata. I was surprised and disappointed that the first and only girl he'd brought home was Dipti. So much for solidarity in rebellion.

When Dipti's father led me to her closed bedroom door, I gingerly knocked on it.

"I said I don't want any food." Her voice came through the door.

"You have a guest," her father replied.

"Neel, go home," she said from inside. "I'm not going back tonight."

I pushed it open slightly and stuck my head inside. "It's not Neel."

She stared at me and blinked twice and then gestured for me to enter.

"I hope it's okay that I came," I said.

Showing up unannounced was part of the culture in Ahmedabad, so while she was surprised to see me, she wasn't surprised that someone had arrived unexpectedly. I'd been worried that if I'd called ahead, she would have said not to come.

"Weren't you supposed to fly home last night?" she asked.

I nodded. "I didn't want to leave while things were like this with you and Neel."

"Since when do you care about us?" she said.

The air-conditioning unit spewed cold air into the room. She sat on the bed, a rajai tucked tightly around her outstretched legs and a notebook resting on top.

"That's fair," I said. "I haven't been the best advocate in the past. But during my time here, I've seen the way you balance each other, and until now, I hadn't."

"I'm not going back tonight," she said, staring at the notebook.

"I'm not asking you to. Is it okay if I sit?" I asked, slowly approaching her the way Nana had taught me to approach the peacocks that came to the garden at Lakshmi when I was a little girl.

She nodded, and I sat in a chair near her side of the bed. I imagined her father had been keeping vigil over her from that chair.

Once seated, I said softly, "I just think you and Neel should talk. You left without doing that, and he's really hurt."

She glared at me. "He didn't have a child ripped out from his insides."

"I know. But he did lose a child. You both need each other now more than ever."

"He apparently just needs to work, and then everything will be fine."

"He's not going back tonight."

She looked at me skeptically.

"He's not," I repeated. "He's going to stay until you are ready. We both are."

I could tell she wasn't sure how to process this new information.

Eventually, she said, "I can't imagine either of you will last long here." Then she turned back to the notebook on her lap.

"What are you working on?" I asked, motioning toward it.

She looked down at it before answering. "A letter."

I nodded, knowing from her hollow eyes that it was a letter to Uma.

"How are you holding up?" I asked.

"Fine. I'm almost done with the antibiotics," she said, her expression cold and unwavering, like a stone statue.

"That's not what I meant."

"Oh."

"You can talk to me if you want. I can only imagine how difficult this must be for you."

The breeze from the air-conditioning unit caused goose bumps to pop out on my arms as I adjusted to the cold room.

"I'm fine," Dipti said, crossing her arms.

She had a slight edge to her words that I recognized well—it was the same tone I used when I wanted people to leave me alone.

I leaned toward her and put my hand on her forearm. "I know things are hard right now, but please don't blame Neel. He loves you, and he loved the baby. He had to make an impossible decision."

She jerked away from my touch as though I had burned her skin. Pain flickered across her face.

"I'm fine," she repeated and looked at the door, making clear she wanted to be alone.

I slowly rose and made my way to the door. Before leaving, I turned around and said, "Please don't shut him out."

When I returned from seeing Dipti that afternoon, for the first time since arriving in India over two weeks ago, I found myself alone in the bungalow. With so many people staying there and a constant rotation of servants who'd been hired to help with the wedding, it was the first time that the only sounds in the house were of my feet shuffling across

146

the marble floor in my champals. Neel had gone out with my parents to buy some last-minute things like spices and nasta for Dad to take home with him. He was now the only member of our family who was flying home that night. Hari and Laila were on their honeymoon in Udaipur. Virag Mama and Bharat were at the office. Indira Mami must have been out running errands. Even the servants seemed to have made themselves scarce for the moment.

I gathered the bangles I had borrowed from Indira Mami for the wedding and took them to her closet, which was a room off her bedroom with wardrobes along three sides. I used to play dress-up with her jewelry as a young girl and knew she didn't mind me opening the wardrobes. A quick tug on the closet door reminded me that the cabinets in the house were always locked for fear that the servants would steal or looters would break in. It took some getting used to for me to keep everything under lock and key and never leave clothing or my laptop or earbuds lying around. Virag Mama and Indira Mami didn't want to leave any temptations in plain sight.

There were horror stories of servants who had been with families for years learning their secrets and then robbing them and taking the money back to their families in the villages they grew up in. It saddened me to think that the caste system forced some to steal from the people who employed them to help feed their families. Equality was not even a topic of discussion in India, let alone something people strove for. Unlike in America, in India, the presumption was that the caste you were born into reflected your karma from past lives, and a life better lived meant that you'd elevate in the next life. Of course, the opposite held true as well. The fear of the unknown was enough to keep an undecided like me on the karmic straight and narrow as much as I could manage.

Indira Mami kept a large ring of dozens of skeleton keys on a clasp that tucked into her sari, and they jingled with each step she took. When we were kids causing mischief around the house, we knew to disperse and pretend we were behaving as soon as we heard that sound. Those keys were always on her. She had given me a small key to open the key box that hung on the wall in the foyer. I rummaged around the ones dangling on the hooks, until I found the spare set for her wardrobes.

After trying several keys in her closet, I heard the latch release, and the large cabinet door swung open. Indira Mami's colorful bangles were organized on red velour rods on a higher shelf. I pulled a stepping block over to the cabinet and removed a rod that had space on it. When I slid the bangles back in their place, I noticed the thick cardboard boxes I had seen as a child—the ones that held old family photos.

It had been decades since I had looked through those. I removed a couple and sat on the floor. The photos were yellowed with age, some in sepia tones rather than the vibrant colors of modern-day prints. There were photos of Hari and Bharat when they were young. Neel and I were in some of them: playing in the yard, climbing on the hichko, sitting at the dining table. In some, my family was dressed in traditional Indian attire for weddings or dinner parties. In others, Neel and I wore our Western shorts and shirts, grinning at the camera like happy fools.

When I met people in Ahmedabad, they always knew I was American. Without me saying a word. Something in my clothing, hairstyle, or general presence projected that I was not a local. Comparing the photos from when I was a little girl in Ahmedabad to the ones from our visits after moving to America, I realized it had become obvious I was now NRI. In the later pictures my smile was bolder and more direct compared to the demure, deferential looks on my relatives' faces. I stood with my hands on my hips, rather than clasped neatly in front of me like the other girls in the photos. My subconscious self in India hadn't been as focused on blending in or hiding, which seemed ironic because my conscious self in America had thought of nothing else since the day we moved there.

In the second box were photos of a little girl who had my familiar smile and large eyes. For my entire life, relatives had commented that

I was a "copy" of my mother. I held the photo of her next to one of myself, finally seeing what everyone else had. How could two people who looked so similar on the outside be so different on the inside?

I continued sifting through the box. There were photos of my mother from her Kathak dance performances when she was a teenager. Her smile was soft and demure, but she beamed into the camera, her eyes shining brighter than the diamonds around her neck. I couldn't remember the last time I had seen her with such a genuine smile on her face, but I also couldn't recall the last time I had seen her dance. There were also photos of my parents as a young newly married couple. Their smiles were shy and awkward. I had seen those paired smiles countless times. I thought about what it must have been like for Mom to have met Dad only once before her wedding day. I had always been sure that if they had ever dated, they never would have married, because they didn't seem to have any common interests from which to build a foundation. But that wasn't the criteria for a marriage in India, and theirs, by Indian and maybe even Western standards, was considered a successful one. They had been married over thirty-five years and had two professionally prosperous kids to continue their legacy.

My thoughts were interrupted by a clinking sound coming toward me. Keys. I looked around at the mess I'd created, wishing I could have put everything back before Indira Mami had come home.

"Here you are," Indira Mami said, stepping into her closet room. "How—" She stopped when she saw the photos spread around me. "What is all this?"

She hoisted up the pleats of her soft pink sari and sat with me on the cold tiles. "I haven't seen these in many years." She picked up a photo of Hari when he was ten years old. "Now he is married," she said, a nostalgic look creeping onto her face. She had remained calm and collected during his entire wedding, but it was interesting to see how a picture from the past could now pierce her stoic facade.

My eyes fell on a stiff wedding photo of my parents. It reminded me of some of the pictures I had taken of Hari and Laila in the days leading up to their wedding, two virtual strangers thrown together and hoping for the best. My family thought that even a less-than-perfect marriage was better than the public shame of ending up alone. It explained why my parents were so desperate to see me settle down. It would have given them some relief that if something happened to them, then I'd be taken care of. I appreciated the sentiment but had a hard time getting them to understand that being single didn't mean I could not take care of myself. And I'd rather take care of myself than be tied forever to someone I hardly knew, or worse, be stuck taking care of someone else for whom I had no feelings because his parents had not taught him the necessary life skills to take care of himself. I could not deny that despite the many problems my parents and I had when dealing with each other, they had taught me how to survive, no matter how difficult things became.

I picked up another photo of my mother, one in which she was dressed in a traditional sari like the elaborate one she wore in the wedding photos with my dad. But I didn't know the man in the photo standing next to her. He was shorter than my father and had broader shoulders. My mother's smile in that photo was more natural. It was a look of which I had only caught glimpses because Mom was typically so reserved. I couldn't recall when I'd last seen it.

"Who is this?" I asked.

When Indira Mami took the photo, her expression darkened. "I don't know him."

It was clear she was lying. "You must. Who is it?" I persisted.

She shoved the photo back into the box and dumped a stack of photos on top of it before she rose awkwardly to her feet. "That's enough for now. I should start the chai before everyone returns."

I bit back my instinct to chase after her and make her answer my questions. That sort of behavior would never get me any results in this country. I gathered the remaining photos and placed them back in the cabinet. I heard the click as the bolt slid into place. I thought back to the conversation I'd overheard at the wedding and still wasn't sure what *nasib* meant, but I was certain this man was part of it.

~

Later that day, I was at the snack shop in the small shopping center across from our subdivision picking up the preordered sev for my dad to take back with him when I heard Biren call my name.

"Mingling with the locals, are you?" he asked with a smile. He was wearing blue jeans and a plaid button-down shirt with the sleeves rolled up.

"Running errands." I held up my purchase.

"You'll give yourself a heart attack if you eat all of that!" He laughed and pointed at the large two-kilo bag of sev.

I laughed. "It's not for me, but you can let my father know that! So what are you doing around here?"

"On my way back from the gym." He ran his fingers through his hair, still damp, with the ends curling slightly. It was a good look for him.

He took the bag from my arms and walked back to Lakshmi with me to deposit the sev. "How are you adjusting?"

"Okay, I guess. My mom decided to stay with me. Us, I guess. Neel and Dipti aren't leaving yet either. Only my dad is flying back tonight."

He laughed. "I suppose that'll make for an interesting stay."

"Tell me about it."

"She's not so bad. Maybe you'll enjoy having her here."

Once we arrived at the house, Biren placed the sev on the dining table. Indira Mami insisted on making him some chai for his trouble, so Biren and I sat on the hichko in the garden while she prepared it. Sitting next to a guy wearing jeans and having a conversation in English felt so normal. A feeling I hadn't had since I'd arrived, because I'd been so steeped in the pain of losing Uma and then Alex. If it weren't for the monkeys in the green mango tree opposite us at the end of our yard, and the fact that Biren was Indian, I'd have thought I was back in LA.

The garden wrapped around to the back of the house, and from an upstairs window, I saw my mother peeking out and watching us. I kept a respectable distance from Biren. A few minutes later I saw the curtain in the living room pull back. Indira Mami. Clearly if I so much as talked to a member of the opposite sex, it would be considered a family activity.

Apologetically, I said, "It seems like everyone in the house has busied themselves with studying us."

Biren shrugged and resisted looking over his shoulder to see what I was talking about. I respected that.

"Not a lot of guy-girl friendships in India," he said.

"My mom can't help herself. You're the first biodata-appropriate person she's ever seen me talk to!" I said to him while motioning for the gawkers inside the house to leave us alone.

Biren laughed. "I'm sure our parents dreamed of arranging our marriage when we were little kids. They probably think this is exactly where our Janmakshars are meant to intersect. Actually, I bet they think we're both quite late on the Janmakshar plan!"

I nodded, wondering how far I'd deviated from my birth horoscope. "How have you dodged the bullet?"

He shrugged noncommittally. "Hasn't been a priority."

"Your parents aren't breathing down your neck to introduce you to a nice girl?"

"They've tried, but I ignore it. There are a couple perks to having spent several years in the West, right? We can stand up to our parents, whether they like it or not!"

"Couldn't agree more," I said with a relieved smile.

Playing the part of the dutiful Indian daughter for the past couple weeks had been exhausting and unnatural for me. I missed Carrie and our ability to speak our minds without worrying about offending the other person. Maybe Biren could help fill that void.

"So, now that you're staying, we should spend some more time together. Maybe we can spend Christmas Eve or Christmas together in a few days. The local Indians don't have much cause to celebrate it, but I've always enjoyed it."

Christmas was only three days away, and I had completely lost track of it. It was hard not to think about Alex when I heard the word *Christmas*, and it might be nice to share those Western holidays with Biren and take a small break from everything going on with the family.

"I'd love that, assuming everything is okay—or at least not *worse* than things are now—with Neel and Dipti."

"Of course."

I smiled at him and realized how much better India would be with someone to talk to outside my family.

19

I had barely opened the front door to the house after Biren left before Indira Mami charged at me.

"So, Biren is a nice boy." Her tone was anything but subtle. "Good family."

I heard the clapping of Mom's champals against the marble stairs. She'd been moving so quickly she was out of breath by the time she reached the main floor. She didn't say anything, but it was clear she wanted to hear every word Indira Mami and I exchanged about this subject.

"Yeah, he's nice." I was careful. Giving them even an inkling that I had noticed he was attractive would probably be enough for them to confirm our marriage for the very next auspicious date.

Indira Mami began to reason through the scenario out loud. "Right age. Good height-body. Education. Job. Proper family."

In her mind, all the appropriate biodata boxes had already been ticked and the only thing left was to approach his parents to strike an arrangement.

I held up my hands to stop her. "Make sure you get at least four goats in exchange for me," I said lightly.

Indira Mami said seriously, "Oh, no, we don't have to worry about your dowry these days. Times are more modern."

Mom stifled a laugh.

I threw up my hands in defeat. "I'm kidding!"

"You know, when you were little kids, you and Biren used to play together all the time. We even dressed him up in a chaniya choli just like yours one day. It was so cute, both of you in matching clothes like that. I should find that photo so you can show him."

"I doubt he wants to see that," I said, remembering a similar photograph of Neel dressed in a chaniya choli when we were little. Before she could keep going, I excused myself to take the sev upstairs so we could finish packing Dad's suitcase.

While my mother and Neel were busy weighing my father's suitcases before tying them with yellow rope to take them to the airport, my father stopped by my bedroom. It was now two in the morning, and the bags underneath his eyes hung heavy.

"You know this is not the life I want for you," he said.

"I know," I said evenly, not wanting to start a fight before he left for America.

"You get this stubbornness from your mother, you know?"

"Maybe." All of us were stubborn, my father included, so the truth was that I could have gotten it from anywhere.

He lowered to the bed. "It's not because I don't want you to be happy. I don't want you to have to struggle for money the way your mother and I have. A good job like yours takes away that stress."

"I know, but money comes at a price. And I won't be reckless. What you don't understand is that we grew up differently from you. Neel and I learned to grow up without a safety net. We didn't have the prestige of the family name like you and Mom had when you grew up in India. You never thought about money and finances when you were a kid because you were here. You never had to worry about it until you went to America. But Neel and I thought about it all the time. We had to fight for everything, and we know if we screw up, there's no money coming from anywhere else, except maybe each other."

My dad looked surprised to hear me say that. I could see him mulling over the comparisons between our childhoods.

"That fire in you comes from her too," he said.

I'd never heard either of my parents compliment my passionate streak. I had always assumed that to them, it was the reason I couldn't be the obedient Indian girl they had wished for. It was why they said I walked like an elephant.

"Then you should know I'll be okay. I'll fight to make sure I never go back to the life we had when we got to America."

He smiled at me, pride in his eyes, and I basked in it.

"You are strong like her," he said.

"I wish she knew we'll be okay if we stay here alone. We don't need her to babysit."

Dad sighed. "Did you ever think she needs this for her?"

I opened my mouth to speak but then paused. I hadn't considered that.

"I moved her from India too soon. I know that now. In our culture, first you marry, then you date, then you fall in love. I thought a fresh start was what the family needed to grow together. To bond us together in our family love without the distractions and obligations that come from society in Ahmedabad. I didn't know how hard life in America would be for us. Especially for her."

I wanted to ask him more about the difficulties of our life in America during those early years, but we had mere minutes before he had to leave for the airport, rather than the hours it would take to unlock those stories. I knew that conversation would be one for another time when I was back in our home near Devon Avenue.

His knees creaked when he stood up. "Take care of her." He patted my leg.

"Who's going to take care of you?"

I couldn't imagine him doing all the cooking and cleaning. Even on days when my mother was away, she made sure there was food in the freezer, portioned out and vacuum sealed, that my dad could reheat.

"Don't worry about me." He smiled as if he had a secret. "Varsha likes to feel needed, but I can handle myself."

I'd never heard my father speak about my mother with this level of affection. He was a man of few words, so the ones I'd heard most were when my parents were shouting at each other about some foolish thing like buying the wrong kind of milk or shoveling snow off the driveway.

His demeanor reminded me of when he'd quietly handed me the money for my eighth-grade field trip. That time he hadn't said anything, but his actions spoke volumes. I felt the same way today. It seemed I was never too old to have my parents surprise me.

20

The next day, we were all exhausted from saying goodbye to my father at the airport in the middle of the night. Neel and my mother were sleeping in, and when Indira Mami was busy in the kitchen making lunch, I crept back to her closet and flipped through the photographs we'd placed back in the wardrobe until I found the one I needed. Then I walked to Monali Auntie's flat, which was just five minutes away. She and Kamal Uncle had done well for themselves after immigrating to America, much better than my parents had fared. Kamal Uncle's investment business sailed, and they were among the class of NRIs who could afford to keep an apartment in India for their yearly visits.

Her place smelled of mustard seeds, cumin, and lentils—homemade dal. It was familiar and comforting. My mother had taught her how to cook. The two had been as close as sisters while growing up in Ahmedabad, but my mother managed to do everything a step ahead of her, including marriage. Before Monali Auntie's wedding, she came to our house in Illinois and learned to cook and do laundry, chores that servants in India had done for her until that point. I imagined it was challenging for my mother to watch her best friend's family rise financially, while it seemed no matter how hard my parents tried, they could not get ahead.

Monali Auntie handed me two shallow Corelle bowls to set on the dining table. The scent of the fresh lemon she had squeezed onto the dal permeated the air as she carried over a trivet and pot, both items she had brought over from America.

"You know I am always happy to have you," she said, "but I suspect you are here for a reason, no?"

She passed me a steaming bowl of dal dhokli. I blew on a spoonful. When the steam dissipated, I took a bite. The tender pieces of dough melted in my mouth, complemented by the fiery broth.

I sank onto the dining chair, glad Uncle was at a carom game with his friends so Auntie and I had this time alone.

"I found this photo, and Indira Mami wouldn't tell me who this was. Do you know?" I asked, handing the photo to her.

She held it up closer to her face. "Where did you get this?"

"I found it at Lakshmi."

She remained quiet, an unusual occurrence for her. Finally, she said more to herself than to me, "I'm surprised they kept any of these."

"Why? Who is he?" I asked, even though I already knew the answer.

"You should ask your mother," she said, resigned.

"It seems pretty clear that this is an engagement photo and the guy in it isn't Dad. It is, isn't it?"

Since I'd first seen the photo, I'd suspected that was the case, but seeing the confirmation on her face felt like whiplash. It was not every day I learned my mother had some secret life before my father. Such things were far from common in this arranged marriage society. I recalled Hari saying how Laila's reputation would have been ruined if they had spent any time alone together outside the presence of their parents. Surely something like a broken engagement was far worse than a young couple trying to date, and on top of it, this would have been over thirty-five years ago. I had never heard my parents speak of anyone from their generation dating someone, let alone being engaged to someone other than their spouse.

"Beta, some things are between you and her," Monali Auntie said, sinking into a chair across from me.

She'd always been so candid with me, and I couldn't believe she had picked now to be discreet.

"She doesn't talk to me like that," I said.

"I know the past few months have been difficult for you, but she has a lot of pressure too. Do you know how hard it is for an Indian mother to not speak to her daughter for four months? I call my boys every one to two days, and she was doing the same with you and Neel. On top of that, with everything now, she is the only mother Dipti has. Meanwhile, there is no one left to comfort Varsha."

I twirled my spoon in the soup, letting steam escape. "But when I tried to talk to her this week, she shut me down. What am I supposed to do now?"

"Oh, beta!" She threw up her hands. "I had this same conversation with your mother after her trip to LA, and I'm going to tell you the same thing I told her then. Bandar kya jaane adrak ka swaad."

She crossed her arms, satisfied. The words were familiar enough that I knew she was speaking Hindi, but I could no longer understand them. "What does that mean?"

"Let me think of how to say it in English." She cocked her head for several seconds. "A monkey does not know the taste of ginger." She grinned, proud of her translation.

"Meaning what?"

She thought about it more. "You cannot appreciate that which you do not know."

"So give the monkey some ginger," I said. "Problem solved."

She raised her hand, as if she were going to reach across the table and playfully slap me. "Such an American answer."

"I know, I know. Sorry, it was too easy."

"It would be good if you both stopped being such stubborn monkeys. One thing is certain: you don't understand her life, and she doesn't understand yours. Until you both start trying the ginger, you never will."

I pondered her words. She had a point, but how could I build a bridge between two different worlds that was strong enough to support us both, and was it too late to try?

She took a deep breath. "I should not be telling you this, but part of why losing Uma is so hard for her is because she felt it could be her second chance. She knows she made some mistakes with you, but she is too proud to ever admit them."

Her words shocked me. My mother wasn't the type to own mistakes, certainly not when it came to me. I wondered what she would have done differently. How would I have reacted in response? Maybe we could have ended up confiding in each other like friends rather than always filtering the substance from our conversations and only speaking about what we had to eat for dinner or how work was going.

She reached for my nearly empty bowl and refilled it. "You must understand your mother and I didn't grow up expecting love. It wasn't something we looked for when choosing a husband. I was lucky. I didn't know anything about Kamal when I married him, but our relationship grew into one of love over the years." She gestured toward the family photo on the window ledge. "But we didn't face the same challenges your parents did. In an arranged marriage, when the money stops flowing, then so does the love."

"Maybe that's the problem. I didn't grow up dreaming about marriage contracts and dowries."

"For us, marriage is a business arrangement between two families. What do you lawyers call it?" She snapped her fingers as she found the word. "A merger! The woman fulfills her duty, the man fulfills his, and there's nothing left to discuss. With you chasing this Western love, it's hard for your mother to understand that. All she saw was that you had hurt your reputation in the community. With something like that, she feared you would end up unhappy and alone."

"She was right about that, even if not for the right reasons." My eyes met Monali Auntie's.

"Beta, I'm sorry." She reached across the table and placed her hand on mine. "When it comes to love, the gods control it, not us." She then smiled. "You know, maybe you are more like your mother than you realize."

"Except that she doesn't think love factors into major life decisions. Why can't she see that there's more to life than money and biodatas? You were raised the same way, and you get it."

"Because, beta, I don't have daughters. I love my children, but the bond between a mother and daughter is different. Boys are supposed to grow up and do whatever they wish. But the girls"—she sighed—"the girls are the ones who carry on the family traditions."

I'd been so focused on my career that I hadn't really thought about children. In fact, during this past week of watching what Neel and Dipti were going through, it made me wonder if I'd ever want to put myself in a position in which I could be hurt so badly. But I suppose Auntie had a point that mothers and daughters were different. Mine had been so much stricter with me than she had ever been with Neel, and maybe that was because she expected more from me than she ever had from him.

She reached across the table and touched my forearm. While gesturing to the photo, she said, "This is something between you and her. Not me."

I had so many questions for my mother but didn't know how to bring up something so personal after we'd been keeping each other at arm's length for so long. I still hadn't told her what really happened with Alex and why we ended things. She didn't know I had tried to go back to him even if it meant losing her. If I was still keeping secrets from her, it was hard to convince myself that I had a right to know hers.

She'd ended up with my father, and maybe she wanted to leave the rest in the past, like I now did when it came to Alex. But Monali

Auntie seemed to think the information might help me understand her in a way I never had, possibly even bridge the gap between us, so it was hard to think that we could continue to ignore it. I thought back to her message in my birthday card and the calls that I had ignored following the breakup. Maybe this was what she'd wanted to talk to me about.

I squeezed Monali Auntie's arm and said, "I'm glad you're here, Auntie. If it had been any of Mom's other friends here, I don't think I could have handled it."

She laughed. "Of course not! If it were just that pesky Gita Auntie here, you would never get a moment of peace. That woman is more trouble than a goat in the vegetable garden!"

21

Night jasmine perfumed the air, and crickets chirped as I swayed back and forth on the hichko in the garden. The sun had long since retreated to the other side of the world—the side that had been my home. It had been another hot day, and the cooler night air against my skin was a relief. The rusty hinges holding up the swing creaked with each movement. The front door opened, and footsteps shuffled toward me.

Mom sat next to me. Her weight disrupted the smooth motion, and the hichko wobbled as it rocked back and forth, eventually settling back into a rhythm.

"I'm worried about Neel and Dipti," she eventually said, a big emotional concession for her.

"So am I," I said.

Mom took in a deep breath. "This was my favorite smell when I was little."

"Mine too," I said, realizing how much this floral smell reminded me of those early years in Ahmedabad before we had left for Chicago.

"When I talk to Neel, it doesn't feel like he is there anymore."

"It felt the same way when I talked to Dipti."

She nodded. "You never expect something like this. You never expect to watch your child bury his child. I'm supposed to be well into another life before even thinking about burying my child, let alone a grandchild."

We continued to rock slowly back and forth on the swing. "I guess no one can be prepared for something like this," I said.

"And to not lean on each other . . ." She shook her head. "That's what love marriages are for, right? You have a partner?"

She was admitting she did not understand such a central part of Neel's life. Of mine. She could not understand marrying for love because it was such a foreign concept to her. I thought about how much romantic love wove its way through my being and wondered how a parent and child could be close when they lacked the ability to understand the other's worldview on love at such a basic level.

I found myself wondering about her life before marriage. About more than the man in the photo. I knew she had a degree in pharmacy from a prestigious Indian university, but I had never heard her speak of a career or any professional aspirations. I had never heard of any of the women in our family seeking such goals. It had never occurred to me that my mother might have wanted something different. Something more like the life I had back in LA: career, choices, freedom. I wanted to ask her but didn't feel like I could be that direct. My family didn't talk about the past or hopes and dreams like that.

I started with a soft approach. "Why did we leave India?" I thought back to what Neel had said about those early years in Chicago. It would have been so easy for them to see how hard it was going to be and just turn around and go back. Return to a caste system and life in which they were in a dominant, rather than subservient, position.

Mom stared ahead at a spot on the lawn, seemingly concentrating on what she would say next. I continued to push my feet against the dirt, rocking the hichko back and forth.

She said, "We moved from this country so you and Neel could have more options than you would have had here. We were thinking: Our kids are smart, and we want them to have all the opportunities."

Her voice was heavy. I wondered if she doubted whether she and my father had made the right decision all those years ago.

"But why did you think we couldn't have done that here? Wouldn't it have been easier with all of the privileges that come with our family name?"

She stared at the large bungalow she grew up in. "Maybe for Neel. But not for you." She sighed. "Maybe not even for him. There's no reason to work hard when everything is handed to you. Who knows if Neel would have pursued medicine. You would not be a lawyer. Seeing how well you both can take care of yourself now . . . it's hard to say the decision was wrong."

"But why did you keep saying how misbehaved we were after moving to America and we should have stayed here?"

"We wanted you to have a good education and job, but not give up all of your culture. We wanted you to have both. Perhaps it was silly to think that, but because Neel could keep both, we thought you could too."

I pushed my feet into the ground to stop the hichko. It creaked as it fell out of sync and shifted from side to side. "I'm not like Neel."

Her expression grew weary. "I know," she said.

We sat in silence for a few moments, each of us escaping to our own thoughts.

I thought about her words. Had I lost my culture? I felt like I was constantly reminded that I was Indian—at work, at a store, when talking to white friends—some part of me was always aware that I wasn't like the other people around me. It crept into every facet of my life, whether it was someone mispronouncing my name and me grinning and acting like it didn't bother me, or people assuming I knew every other person with the last name Desai and not understanding it was as common as Smith and in a country far more populated than America. It followed me as I moved about my day, mentally tallying whether I was positive or negative on the karma scale, because while I wasn't sure what the afterlife entailed, in the event reincarnation was our fate, I wanted to make sure I was on the right end of it. I still understood our native language, wore the clothes when needed, and ate the food mostly without complaint. I certainly never felt like I had "lost" it, but I wondered what made my mother think I had.

"With everything that happened this year in LA and then here in India, I've had to ask myself what is truly important to me. The truth is I'm not sure if I've been fighting for the right things. I fought so hard to be accepted since the first day we arrived in America, and I've never stopped trying. I always thought being different from white people was the problem, but then I realized how exhausting it is to try to be the same as everyone else."

She gazed into the distance, contemplative.

"We thought you kids would be okay. You learned the language quickly and could speak with no accent. You learned the customs. With those things, you could mix with the Americans. Your father and I had spent too much time in India to do those things the same way."

I realized that my parents didn't know how hard it had been for Neel and me. They'd been busy protecting us from financial hardship, and we'd been busy protecting them from our social hardship. We'd all fallen into this pattern, and it had become second nature to each of us. What would have been different if we'd shared those struggles with each other rather than growing apart because we didn't trust the other to handle the truth?

"You know what Nani used to say?" Her voice quivered in that same way it always did when she remembered her mother. "It is better to fail at the right thing than to succeed at the wrong one."

Was my mother saying that she thought she had failed by moving us, but that it was still the right thing? I looked at my life through that lens and wondered how much of it I had spent trying to succeed at the wrong thing. I had been on such a lifelong quest to fit in—with my family, with my job, with Alex, with everything—that I never stopped to ask myself whether it was the right fit. Had I picked law because it was one of the whitest professions in the country and if I could succeed there, then it meant I would be accepted as an American? Had I picked Alex because I thought he would make it easier to blend into the world around me because he fit in so naturally that surely I would, too, simply by association? As I studied the wistful expression on Mom's face, I wanted to know how she felt about Nani's words. Had she pursued the right path?

"Do you ever wish you had stayed in India?" I asked. It was the first time I had touched upon whether she was happy with the life she had chosen.

"It is not sensible to think that way. We can only know the path we chose." Her expression grew somber. "I wish I could have spent more time with Nani and Nana before they passed. It was hard being so far during that time." Her eyes welled up as she remembered her own parents.

"I'm sorry you couldn't," I said, guilt rising within me.

Money had been so tight when Nani passed away that my mother could not even fly back for her funeral because it was too expensive. She'd been practical and said that it wasn't worth spending that kind of money when Nani was already gone. That year Neel was going to be starting college, and they needed to put as much as they could aside for his education.

Mom had married my father based on the families' suggestion when she was twenty-four years old. Thirteen years later, she was whisked off to America—a country she had never set foot in. She was half a world away from her parents and brother and surrounded by strangers who didn't understand her language or customs. I couldn't imagine a lonelier or more terrifying situation.

Tears were now brimming in both our eyes. I couldn't envision a time when I had felt this close to her.

Finally, Mom said, "But we cannot dwell on the past. Now, we must focus on Neel." She looked me straight in the eyes, something she rarely did. "Together."

I looked at her, knowing we were on the precipice of a great shift. She and I had never acted as a team in anything that truly mattered. We had worked together on homework when I was a kid, but since then we'd both been on our own paths and existed as part of the same family, but I'd never felt we were emotionally together. After I moved away from Chicago, the physical distance let us mask the emotional one that had formed between us. In many ways, it had seemed like we were both more comfortable with that game of pretend. Now, we needed to join forces for the first time in my adulthood, and I hoped we could do it.

22

Ahmedabad hadn't been home for such a long time, and time passed slowly without day-to-day distractions like work and errands. It seemed all we did was spend each day milling about the bungalow consumed by the grief. So, when Virag Mama suggested I create an album with the photos I had taken from the wedding, I was ecstatic to have a project away from the sadness and some sense of purpose to my days. As was the Indian way, Virag Mama knew someone who was willing to let me share the darkroom space he had for his photography business. December 24 was just another workday in India, and I was happy to be distracted from the memories I had with Alex last year at this time. Virag Mama and I went to the workspace together so he could make the introductions and leave me there to work as he headed to the office to meet Bharat.

As we made our way through the Ahmedabad traffic, I tried to remember what it had been like in India before we moved. My conversations with Neel and my mother had brought back a flood of memories, but they were now filtered through an American lens. I'd been happy in Ahmedabad but now wasn't sure if that was because I hadn't known any different. I hadn't yet seen the Western world outside of television and had never experienced what a life of so many choices had to offer. But maybe that didn't matter, and happiness was happiness, no matter how it came to be. Ignorant bliss, as they say.

What I recalled most was that life in India had felt simple. Neel and I went to school six days a week, had tutors seven days a week, and played with other neighborhood kids when we weren't studying. There were no chores because those tasks were handled by the servants. I recalled enjoying certain things like helping my mother or Indira Mami shell peas or trim green beans because they were novel rather than required. Those were fun times in which I'd heard them gossip about other families, and I'd been excited to be sitting with the adults and be a part of their club for a short while. After we'd moved to America, chores became a part of everyday life, and prepping vegetables was work that was needed, so there was no joy in it. My mother and I often did the tasks in silence, and I could always see the strained look on her face, as if her mind were racing a thousand miles an hour, so I never wanted to disturb her.

As Virag Mama drove, we passed some kids playing a heated game of cricket in a field. I had enjoyed playing cricket as a child, but I was so far removed from those days. I longed for how carefree they had been. It took returning to India for me to realize how quickly I had grown up after moving to America. While I hadn't realized it at the time, stress had become a constant part of life because money had been scarce and the feeling of being an outsider was pervasive. It was something that clung to me like skin and was part of everything I did. I'd never felt that during my early years in India.

There was certainly stress in India, and surely the adults must have felt it during my childhood, but I thought about Hari and Bharat and saw how much children in India were sheltered from it. I thought back to my conversation with Neel about our dad having worked a manual-labor factory job when we first moved to Chicago but telling me it was his same engineering job. In India, adult matters were handled by adults, and children were not meant to be burdened with them. While it made me less angry and hurt about the lies I'd been told, it made me even more curious about how many there were and what the truth really was. It seemed Neel knew more of it than I did, but it would surprise me if even he knew it all. Other than my parents, who had lived it, I doubted anyone could know the full truth. With my dad having returned to Chicago, that left my mother as the person who could answer these questions, and I wasn't sure how to even begin to raise them with her. She and I didn't speak of such things, and I'm sure she'd never spoken of such things with her own mother. That was the Indian way. But I also knew that my American side would have to try to find the answers, because they would help me complete the picture of my identity. And there was nothing more American than the search for one's identity. But I also knew my curiosity and questions would have to wait because right now we had to focus on Neel. His visit to see Dipti had not gone as well as he'd hoped. They had only spoken for a minute before she stormed back to her room. Dipti's dad then stepped in to tell Neel that she just needed more time. He sympathized with Neel, knowing how good Neel was for his daughter, but in the end, his loyalty had to remain with her. They were blood. Seeing the hurt on Neel's face when he returned was too much for me. I was happy for a day away from the bungalow.

After forty-five minutes, Virag Mama and I pulled into the dirt parking lot of a three-story shopping complex that looked like so many others. The businesses with colorful signs in a mix of English, Gujarati, and Hindi script all faced the street. One storefront on the second floor boasted a far-too-cheesy blue sign with the words HAPPY SNAPS on it. The window was decorated with cheap-looking red-and-green tinsel and a cardboard cutout of a tree. Christmas was acknowledged only for the NRIs.

When we walked in, I instantly recognized the man behind the counter.

"I didn't realize it was you," I said to the overzealous photographer from Hari's wedding.

"Yes, please, madam. It is my pleasure to see you again. Namaste," Tushar said, hands in prayer position and bowing at the waist to greet me.

Tushar, a mild-mannered man around my age, ran Happy Snaps. Tushar was only a few inches taller than me, maybe five feet seven, and was skinny in a way that American models aspired to be. His hair was short but kept in place with castor oil—a cheaper option than the almond oil my relatives used. Its potent smell lingered after him as he moved around the store.

As he guided Virag Mama and me toward the back, he said, "You see, the room has become mostly used for storage, madam. When we changed—"

"Hold on." I stopped to make sure I had his attention. "This 'madam' business needs to stop. I'm not your ba!" I said.

Virag Mama was standing next to me and put a hand on my shoulder. "If Tushar wishes to treat you with respect, then it shows he was raised by a good family."

Something about the careful way my uncle spoke made me uncomfortable. When I turned back toward Tushar, I realized what it was. Even in the dim light at the back of the shop, it was evident that Tushar's skin was darker than mine. He was from a lower caste. So even though we were around the same age, he was treating me with the same respect and deference he would have paid to one of his elders.

These caste formalities seemed so unnecessary to me, especially when dealing with peers. "Ignore him. Seriously, call me Preeti."

Virag Mama forced a cough to show his displeasure at my comment. Before I could respond, Tushar's cell phone began belting out a tune from a recent Bollywood movie.

Tushar bobbled his head in that familiar side-to-side way and said, "Yes, Ba," in a voice low enough that Virag Mama couldn't hear him. He then moved to the front of the shop to take the call.

When he called me Ba, I knew there was more to Tushar than I had initially thought.

He returned a moment later, apologizing for the interruption, and swung open the door to a small darkroom. I couldn't help but notice his calloused palms and the lean muscles on his thin arms. He was no stranger to manual labor. I liked the contrast with the preppy lawyers at my firm in California with their manicured fingers.

Inside, boxes and crates were piled in a corner. Stained developing trays were stacked near a sink. A single light bulb emitting a yellow glow dangled in the center with a red bulb next to it. The familiar metallic smell of solvent hung in the air. I felt the tension that had permeated through me ever since I'd gotten the call from Neel that Dipti was in the hospital start to dissipate, and a hint of calm took its place.

"You see, it may not be what you are used to," Tushar said, wringing his hands together.

Even though the space was much smaller than what I had used in college, I grinned when I realized I'd be spending time here. The room was a far cry from the splendor of my old law firm, but that was the best part.

"It's perfect," I said, already knowing this place would be my Ahmedabad oasis.

~

We sat down to dinner that night as a family: Neel, Mom, Virag Mama, Indira Mami, Bharat, and me. Usually Bharat or Virag Mama was stuck late at the office, so it was a nice change to have everyone together.

After spending a day in the darkroom, I felt more animated than I had in years. And for the first time in the months since Alex and I had broken up, I felt alive again. It felt good. Even though I felt guilty finding some pockets of joy while there was still so much pain around me, I allowed myself that tiny indulgence. An easing of the heaviness even if only for a day.

Before each of us, Gautam had placed a steel thali of dal, bhat, rotli, and shaak. It was our standard weeknight meal, and tonight's shaak was eggplant and potato. I hated eggplant but ate it without making any fuss. Today, it tasted delicious.

Mom asked, "How was the photo shop?"

Clapping my hands together, I said, "It was great! Tushar is going to teach me what he knows about photography. He uses digital cameras now, but he started on film, and he can show me the basics, so I have a refresher course. Hopefully I'll remember the tricks from college too." I smiled in Indira Mami's direction. "I'm going to try and finish the album before Hari and Laila return from their honeymoon, but it just depends on how many good shots I have."

Mom nodded. "That sounds good."

Virag Mama stopped slurping his dal and cleared his throat. "Have you spoken to her?" he asked my mother.

Mom shifted in her chair. "Hamna nai." *Not now.*

The way she said the words to her younger brother was the way Neel addressed me when we were in public and I was broaching a private subject he didn't want to share. I was anxious to know what they were talking about, but Gautam had returned to the room with fresh rotlis hot from the stove. They'd never discuss a personal topic in front of him.

Mom waited until Gautam went back into the kitchen before saying, "You must be careful about how you interact with Tushar."

Virag Mama leaned forward and said, "It is not proper for an unmarried girl to be seen with a boy. Especially not with someone from a lower caste."

I resisted the urge to roll my eyes and glanced at Neel for help, but even though his body was at the table, it was clear his mind was elsewhere, and he wasn't listening to the exchange.

Indira Mami said, "You know how people talk here, beta. So be careful."

This was absurd. I had spent a few hours with the guy in his shop, but they were acting as if he and I had been caught making out in a temple. I searched Bharat's face to see if he was as offended by this assumption as I was, but he sipped from his water as if this conversation was no different from one about how his day at work had been.

Mom, with what appeared to be some degree of reluctance, said, "They are right. You are already NRI, so people here are watching you more closely. No reason to give them anything to gossip about."

It was clear the resignation in her voice had something to do with her past experiences in India and not just the discussion at hand. I thought back to the picture I had found of her and that other man, desperate to know the story behind it, but I still had not found the courage to ask.

Gautam came back into the room, so we began talking about the upcoming kite holiday—Uttarayan—that would be just after the Western Christmas and New Year's holidays. I was excited because I had fond memories of the holiday from when I was a kid, and part of me hoped I'd still be in India then and could photograph the sea of kites swaying in the sky. Virag Mama and Bharat began regaling us with tales of some of their greatest kite victories. I was only half listening because I had noticed something about Gautam.

He had darker skin than all of us who sat around the table. It was also darker than Tushar's. That suggested that Gautam was a step below Tushar on the caste ladder. I now realized that even in India, it was possible to tell a person's caste by that single factor. Shades of brown had not mattered among the Indians in America because mostly it was the wealthy upper-caste families who could afford to be there in the first place. In America, I had constantly thought about how I stood out because I looked different and did everything I could to compensate for that. But I had never thought about the color of my skin in India. Realizing that, I wondered if it was because there was no question that I belonged to the dominant caste. Was that what it felt like to be white in America? Was that how Carrie and Jared and the countless others at my firm walked through their lives? I was a hemisphere away from all that and realized I had just traded one caste system for another but had landed at the top. It would be impossible for Tushar and me to spend any time together without local people noticing that something was amiss.

~

On Christmas Day, I woke up to the dogs in the empty lot, but even they could not spoil my mood. I was getting ready for another day at Happy Snaps and would be meeting Biren afterward to celebrate the holiday. While I was in the pantry searching for the container of khari biscuits, the doorbell rang, reverberating throughout the bungalow like a gong. I could hear Gautam mopping the floors in the bathroom, so I went to answer it. Standing outside was a scrawny young man who could not have been more than eighteen years old. He wore thread-bare brown linen pants and a peach button-down shirt with the sleeves cuffed to his elbows.

"Good morning, madam. I am Sangiv, the driver for today," he said through red-stained teeth as he bent at the waist.

The drivers all had similar-colored teeth, tinged by the saffron found in paan. I'd tried one at the wedding, and it was a taste I found as acrid as the cigarette I'd tried in high school.

"Okay, I'll get Neel," I said.

I contemplated inviting him in for tea but stopped myself. On a few occasions, I'd done that with other drivers, and they felt obliged to accept and would sit silently on the edge of the sofa with the ceramic tea mug clinking against the saucer because their hands shook from nerves. It felt rude to let them wait outside, but seeing them joking around and laughing with the other drivers made clear that was the environment they preferred to the stuffy upper-caste home. Rather than forcing them to spend time with me, I'd started bringing them chai and nasta while they waited outside. That seemed far more socially acceptable, and while I was here, I'd better learn which behaviors were appropriate.

I asked Gautam to deliver the chai before bounding up the stairs to find Neel.

Neel stood next to the bed, rummaging through his suitcase. Ever since Dipti had gone to stay with her relatives, Neel had been distraught. He was going to see her again and hopefully get her to talk to him.

"Your driver's here," I said, plopping onto the bed.

Startled, he looked up at me. His eyes were blank. "Sorry, didn't hear the door."

"Do you want me to come with you?"

He shook his head. "She's so delicate these days. I don't want her to feel ganged up on. I'm hoping to use Christmas as an excuse. Would be pretty Grinchy to kick me out on Christmas Day," he said with a rueful smile.

I nodded. "She's going to come around. She just needs some time. I can't imagine how hard this is for her."

"That's the thing," he said. "I can. We should be going through it together."

"People heal in different ways. But the important thing is that they do heal. You guys will too. I'm going to be hoping for a Christmas miracle!"

23

After Neel left, I called Carrie to wish her an early Merry Christmas, given that it was still Christmas Eve in LA.

"I was getting worried about you," she said. "It's been a few days since I've gotten a text or anything."

"Sorry," I said. "With me being at the photography studio during the day, and then the time difference, it was hard to find a good time. It's been nice to distract myself with something that feels productive, so I've let myself enjoy that a little."

"How long are you staying?" she asked.

"I'm not sure yet. It depends on Neel and Dipti. Honestly, it hasn't been as bad being here as I thought it would be. I'd forgotten so much about Ahmedabad and India, and it's nice to reconnect with my old life a bit."

"One of my cases is on the verge of settling," she said. "If that happens, then maybe I will come see you. If you don't mind the company, that is."

I nearly dropped the phone. Carrie's idea of roughing it was going to Kauai instead of Maui, so I suspected she was really coming to see if I had lost my mind since I still couldn't tell her when I was returning. Either way, I was excited at the thought of seeing my best friend in a part of the world that I could never have pictured her in.

"I'd love that!" I squealed.

She laughed at my reaction. "Let's cross our fingers that the settlement doesn't blow up on us, but we are trying to get it resolved before the end of the year."

~

After hanging up with her, I jumped into the back of a ricksha and recited the directions to Happy Snaps in Gujarati, a task far more complicated than it might seem. Ahmedabad had the same population as Los Angeles but had all those people crammed into a much smaller area. There was no use for GPS because without street names or numbers, the device would be nonsensical. The translation of the "address" for Happy Snaps was "the Jodhpur intersection, across the street from the fruit vendor."

Everyone traveled through the city with these types of directions, and I was amazed that the ricksha driver knew exactly where to go based on my description. The three-wheeled buggy sputtered down the road and into the traffic. The streets were filled with a cacophony of animals calling, horns honking, and people yelling. I covered my nose and mouth to minimize breathing in the harsh pollution from the exhaust.

Pulling up in front of Happy Snaps gave me a sense of accomplishment. It was my first time taking a ricksha across the city by myself. I felt like a local.

That is, until I walked up to Happy Snaps and found the metal grille covering the door and windows. Closed. The other shops all looked the same way. Then I remembered the Indian workday started after ten. Sometimes closer to eleven when you factored in "Indian Standard Time." It was 9:10. I was acting the same way I had when it came to my lawyer job—get into the office as early as possible. A local would have known better.

There was no point in fighting traffic back and forth, and I was too laden down with my heavy camera and assortment of lenses to walk around, so I sat on the stoop outside Happy Snaps and waited for Tushar to come and open the store.

People who passed by made a point of staring at me. I realized that in my jeans and T-shirt I stood out among the other women, who were dressed in saris and panjabis. My time in India reinforced that no matter where in the world I went, I'd be considered a foreigner.

Monkeys leaped across the rooftops of the buildings. Some crawled down and sat atop the cars parked along the side of the street. The American notion of parking lots did not exist here. Bicycles, motorcycles, scooters, rickshas, and cars parked on the dirt alongside the road without any semblance of order. When a scooter had blocked in a woman's Maruti hatchback, she sat in her car honking her horn until the owner of the offending scooter came out. Though they yelled at each other, their exchange seemed routine, and neither party seemed fazed as they drove off in separate directions muttering to themselves.

I'd been watching the scene when I heard someone say, "Why are you sitting on the ground like a commoner?"

Tushar had arrived and was searching for the right key to open the large padlock on the front of the shop. I leaped up and swatted off the dirt from the back of my jeans. Another thing to learn about the caste system. Apparently where I sat mattered as well. When I was a child, these things had been ingrained in me, and I'd known them implicitly, but my years in America meant I had to relearn everything.

"I was waiting for you."

The metal grille rattled as it rolled upward. A bell dinged when he opened the front door.

"After you, madam," he said.

Back to the "madam" thing. We'd have to work on that.

∼

As the day progressed, Tushar reintroduced me to the basics of developing film. I had not developed my own photos since my internship before law school, but as we began to work through the process, I realized not much had changed.

We spent much of our time in the darkroom, except that he would run out to the front whenever he heard the chimes signaling that a customer had walked in.

Tushar pointed to a large poster in the corner, which was fortunately written in English: *Massive Development Chart.* "If you choose to use black-and-white film, you must remember to check this paper. It will tell you how long the film is to be kept in the developing chemicals."

I had seen that chart in college, but in America the poster had become obsolete. Everything was digital, and apps reigned supreme. I appreciated that some things in modern-day India were closer to where I had left off with photography in the past.

"Thanks. You know, your English is pretty good," I said, cringing after I said it, remembering the times when people in America had said that to me even after I'd been living in the country for years and had no accent. He didn't look offended, but I tried to recover and said, "I meant, where did you learn it?"

I admired his mastery of another language and had no doubt his English skills were better than my Gujarati skills.

"Thank you, madam."

I stopped loading my film onto the spool. "Seriously, you can call me Preeti. I would *prefer* that you do."

Despite the lack of lighting in the darkroom, I could see him shift his weight as if searching for the words to convey his thoughts.

"It is as your uncle explained. Your family must be treated with respect. Your uncle has been very kind to us—provided my family with much work."

The hue from the dim red light hanging over us seemed to erase our different skin tones. In this room, we were just two photographers.

I moved closer to him. "I'm American. I don't believe the same thing he does."

Tushar stepped back. "But I am not American, and we are in India. What matters is how the Indian culture believes."

"Fine. But at least in here, in the darkroom where no one is around, you don't have to treat me so formally."

He bobbled his head from side to side. "Very well then. What shall I call you here?"

"Anything other than madam!"

He paused for a moment, his lips curled into a slight, shy smile. "You are the only girl I know from California. I will call you California Girl."

I laughed. "Suit yourself."

He looked at me quizzically.

"Never mind. It's an American expression."

I slid the spool of film into the developing chemicals while he stood over me, checking to see if I was doing it the way he had shown me earlier.

"Did you go to an English-medium school?" I said, assuming he had learned English the same way my cousins had.

It was Tushar's turn to laugh. "No, of course not. English-medium schools are all private. I went to the public Gujarati school."

He had no malice in his voice and spoke matter-of-factly, but my cheeks warmed as I realized how insensitive my comment must have sounded. During my Indian childhood and infrequent trips back, I never had occasion to be around anyone from another caste outside of servants and vendors, and I wasn't familiar with the differences in lifestyle between them. It hadn't even occurred to me that there were public schools here because I'd only ever known people who went to private ones. What I knew of India applied only to the upper caste, and I realized I knew nothing of how most of the country lived. I vowed to be more careful about what I said around him and to be more observant of the rest of the country.

"Sorry. I shouldn't have assumed."

He poured enough chemicals into the tray to submerge the film and then covered it with a push cap. While showing me how to agitate the film, he said, "My father knew some English from running this store and speaking with the NRIs. I learned what I could from him. After that, I watched all the Hollywood movies I could find. Hearing it helped me learn more than what I would need simply for the shop. Now, I can read it—slowly, but it is better than nothing."

I thought about how even though I could speak Gujarati with relative ease considering I was now classified as a foreigner, I could no longer read a word of it. The symbols might as well have been hieroglyphics considering I had not used them since I was seven years old. That he had taught himself to read something with a different alphabet was beyond impressive. The more time I spent with him, the more interested I was in learning more. In just one day, he had made me question so much of what I thought I knew about India. I knew that for the rest of my time in Ahmedabad, I wanted to keep learning more.

He removed the push cap and gently lifted the film from the tray. With a steady hand, he used a watering can to stream water over it to clean it. In college, I recalled using a faucet to do that step, but running water was much more of a scarcity here, and clean running water scarcer still.

As he worked, I could not help but notice how his bicep flexed from the weight of the can or the way his calloused fingers handled the film with such delicate ease. *Stop it!* I scolded myself. I needed to focus on what he was doing rather than the way he looked while doing it!

"How did you learn so much about photography?" I asked when he handed me the film to hang on the line to dry.

"How you learn anything—I practiced. I took photos. This shop belonged to my dada and then my father. It has been a part of our family for many years. I believe I may have taken my first photo before I took my first step!"

I pictured an infant Tushar with a giant camera dangling from his neck. "Why not travel beyond Ahmedabad and take photos? Turn it into a larger-scale business?"

"My family is here. It doesn't make sense to be anywhere else."

"I wish it were that easy for me."

He shrugged. "This is home."

Tushar was thirty-two years old and had never gotten a passport because he had nowhere to go, and probably couldn't afford to travel even if he did have the desire. Maybe for someone like Tushar who lived in a place where he truly felt he belonged, there was no need to explore the rest of the world. Maybe the rest of us were so restless because we were searching for that feeling of belonging that Tushar already had.

~

Biren had suggested we meet at a new dessert shop near me to celebrate Christmas as best we could. Swiss Cottage was Ahmedabad's answer to a nightclub—without the alcohol, mingling with strangers, or physical touching. It was full of groups of twentysomethings dressed for a special night out. We shared a belgian chocolate torte that tasted nothing like the Western version would have. The absence of eggs changed the flavor and texture dramatically, but it didn't matter because I was there for the company and not the food. Biren had become the only friend I had outside of my family and had been a welcome respite from drama over the past few weeks.

As we picked at our dessert, Biren shared his stories of going to school in Australia. I shared the few stories I had from when Alex and I had visited there, leaving out my travel companion and focusing on the gorgeous landscapes and laid-back people. He spoke of how he'd learned to surf and become decent at it before moving back to India and retiring his board.

His laugh was natural and frequent, the lines around his eyes evidence of his happy demeanor. We shared stories like old friends, and I realized that in many ways, that was what we were. There was the safety and comfort of knowing he'd been part of my childhood, even if the memories were difficult to conjure. I trusted him, and with Carrie so far away, it was nice to have that feeling with someone nearby.

I leaned closer to him. "Can I ask you something?"

"Sure," he said, pushing some crumbs around the plate.

"Doesn't all of this caste stuff bother you? Especially after spending time in Australia, where you don't see this?"

He shrugged. "Every culture has a caste system, even if they don't call it that." He chuckled and said, "Including your precious America. And definitely Australia."

There was truth to what he was saying. There were degrees of segregation everywhere, and America's was color based, while India's was caste based, given that on the surface everyone looked the same. Even my law firm had a hierarchy, and when I had quit, my limitations within that hierarchy became clearer.

"I know that's true, but isn't it harder for you to ignore after spending time outside of the country?"

"There are a lot of things I would change about this country. There are a lot of things I'd change about Australia too. But there are also a lot of things I wouldn't change in either place. Countries are like people—you have to accept all sides of them. The good comes with the bad. India has a sense of community that has always resonated with me more than anywhere else. Guess I was built for a collectivist culture over an individualistic one."

I envied his clarity and pondered his words. It wasn't that easy for me. I wasn't as clear on who I was or even wanted to be. Until this trip, I would have chosen America and its values—the good and the bad—over India's without hesitation. I wondered if that was because I had put on blinders. When the goal was assimilation, there was no blending and balancing of cultures. Assimilation required total devotion. And I had devoted myself to America's dominant caste, doing everything I could think of to be accepted. Not realizing privilege was something you were born into and could not earn.

"Do you have friends from other castes here?" I asked him.

"Not really. To be honest, it doesn't come up much. The reality is that the people who have a similar background are likely to be from the same caste anyway, and that's who I interact with. The only people I meet otherwise are when I help my papa out with his foundation work. But those are all such tragic stories, and people are in so much pain, so it's not a breeding ground for friendships."

"Monali Auntie mentioned that. What exactly does he do?"

"The work of the gods, if you ask my mother!" Biren laughed before turning serious. "It's great work, really. He helps abused women and children find safe new homes—often overseas because we made so many contacts while living outside of India. Mostly women and children, and he helps them start over. Works with them to get them set up with immigration papers and jobs and money to start off with. For so many, it's a step up because while the West has its own caste system, too, Western poverty is rarely like Indian poverty!"

I thought back to the single immigration case I had worked on with Jared. He had taken on a pro bono case to help his image within the firm, which meant that he had me do all the work while he took the credit. But I hadn't minded because it had been interesting to hear the story of the family who had arrived from Nicaragua to seek asylum, and it was impossible not to think of my family's journey to America and want to help.

"I'd love to learn more about the foundation."

Biren's eyes lit up. "Papa would love to talk your ear off about it! And he'll probably try to get some legal advice out of you if you know anything about American immigration laws. They've become so strict, so he's been placing more people in Canada and Australia, but I'm sure he would take any advice you could give."

"I've done a little bit of immigration work, and if there's anything I can do to help him, I'd love to do it."

"Don't seem too eager," Biren said with a wink, "or you just might end up with another lawyer job! Papa has been trying to hire an American lawyer to help him all year."

I smiled, thinking maybe that wouldn't be the worst job in the world.

24

When I returned home that evening, I found Neel slumped in his bed staring at his laptop screen. As he had as a child, he was burying himself in video games to avoid the world around him. Some things never changed no matter how much we aged.

"How was work?" He said the last word somewhat sarcastically.

I tried not to bristle at the edge to his voice. "If only photography could be work," I said, sitting on the edge of the bed. "Was happy to even do it on Christmas. How was she today?"

He shut his eyes as if exhaustion had just overtaken him.

"Were you able to talk to her more?" I pressed.

He closed the lid of his computer, his head resting against the wall. "She's in a bad place."

"What did she say?"

He now opened his eyes, and I saw the hard look in them. "She is even more determined to stay here. She just mopes around in bed all day writing letters to Uma. That's just not healthy."

"If that's what she needs to heal, then you have to support her in it."

"I know you're trying to help, but how can you possibly know how to deal with this?" he spit out.

I was taken aback by his tone. "I'm not saying I do. I'm just saying that people heal differently. Our family has never been one for emotional discourse, so if that's what she needs, then maybe that's why she's with her family."

He threw up his hands. "No Indian family is big on emotional shit! That's the defining characteristic of being in an Indian family. We all grew up that way, and we're all fine, right? Doctors, lawyers, we all turned out fine."

He was right. The Indian measure of "fine" was your profession. By that standard, we were fine. But looking at the disarray my family had been in over the past few weeks, in terms of emotional well-being, it seemed we were all a long way from "fine."

"Nothing seems particularly fine right now," I said quietly, not sure if I was saying it to him or myself.

"No shit. That's why I tried to go home! Then *you* convinced me I had to stay, or I'd lose my wife!"

I couldn't recall a single time he'd lashed out at me like that. Maybe when we were kids and were fighting over the remote or something stupid like that, but never about something serious, and never as adults. I was too stunned to respond, but that was just as well because he hadn't finished yet.

"All we do is mope around here, falling deeper and deeper into whatever depression cycle this is. I knew I should have gone home. What good is keeping my wife if I've lost my mind? Worse still, what good is losing my wife *and* my mind?"

His eyes were hard, but they couldn't mask the pain.

"I was only trying to help."

"You're always trying to help, but the person you really need to help is yourself. How can you possibly give life advice when your own is such a mess? I was stupid for taking it. I should have known better. It's probably no accident that I'm the one who bails you out of stuff, not the other way around. Do you ever think about how easy you had it growing up with all of us sheltering you from everything bad and making excuses for you?"

Tears pricked my eyes. I knew he didn't mean the things he was saying, but they hurt just the same. When the person you loved and trusted most in this world said such harsh things, you couldn't help but wonder if they were true. And for how long he'd thought them. There was a resentment in his tone that felt rooted rather than sudden. The words came out so easily. As if he'd uttered them before. Maybe to Dipti. Maybe to friends. But they weren't new thoughts. Those took time to form, and these had taken no time at all.

There was no response I could give in that moment that would help him or me, so I stood up and went to my room and closed the door behind me before I slid against it and let silent tears fall down my cheeks. I had thought loneliness was losing Alex. I'd been wrong. True loneliness was losing Neel.

~

In the days that followed, I wanted to avoid Neel and process my thoughts, so I spent as much time as I could at Happy Snaps with Tushar. During that time, I learned that Tushar was someone who laughed out loud when he read something funny and savored every drop of the chai he drank three times a day. Just like Hari and Bharat, Tushar was overly formal and polite in the way that many locals seemed to be when dealing with people outside of their family. He never talked back to his parents, who called or stopped in the store several times a day, and he often raised an eyebrow when he overheard my casual way of speaking with my mother on the phone. Despite our differences, we settled into a comfortable pattern, and I looked forward to my time at Happy Snaps in a way I never had when I went to work at my old law firm. Being in the studio brought a sense of peace and calm to this otherwise frenetic and painful trip to India.

"I see you have given up your Western ways," Tushar joked when I emerged from the darkroom on my fourth day at Happy Snaps with telltale streaks of finishing chemicals on my parrot-green panjabi.

After wearing jeans my first two days in the shop and having customers stare pointedly at me, I had decided to wear Indian clothing to hopefully not be pegged immediately as NRI. Spilling toner on my favorite pair of jeans a couple days earlier had also helped me arrive at that decision, and I had asked Mom to take me to get some daily wear that would allow me to blend in more with the locals. We didn't talk about it, but I could see from Mom's expression that she approved of this transition.

"Not quite." I smiled. "I still prefer jeans, but when in Rome . . ."

"It suits you, California Girl," he said before burying his nose back in the book he was holding.

I was surprised by how comfortable it felt to have him call me that. It occurred to me that maybe I could share with him the question I hadn't wanted to press with anyone in my family. I placed my hand on his forearm to get his attention.

"What does *nasib* mean?" I asked.

He froze, staring at my fingers wrapped around his forearm, fixated. Until that moment, we hadn't broken the touch barrier. I hadn't thought twice about reaching for him until I saw the shock on his face. I let go and repeated my question.

He took a step backward. "I don't know how to say in English. Something like what you might call fate? Maybe fortune? Maybe destiny?"

His cheeks burned red, so while I knew I had to learn how the man in the photo had changed my mother's fate, I also needed to make Tushar feel less uncomfortable.

"What are you reading?"

He held it up so that I could see the cover: *The Eyewitness Travel Guide for Australia.*

"Planning a trip?" I raised an eyebrow, excitement creeping into my voice, especially at the thought of someone traveling to the part of the world I had enjoyed so much. "You would love it there. There's so much great scenery to capture."

"No, just learning. Appreciating the natural beauty captured in the photos." Tushar held up the book and showed me a picture of Uluru, the vermilion-red sandstone structure standing out against the barren backdrop.

I smiled. "Do you ever wish you could see these places with your own eyes?"

He shrugged. "Not really. There is no point in thinking about such things."

His answer was so simple and yet so complex. During my childhood years in America, I had constantly heard that there was nothing in this world I could not accomplish. I was told that if I worked hard, then jobs and places and people would not be cut off to me. It wasn't until adulthood that I realized this wasn't true. My life would have been so different had my family stayed in India. I would have learned the same rules as Tushar, and my life would have been predetermined for me the same way Tushar's had been for him. The caste system would have put me in a different lane from Tushar, and my life would have been planned alongside Hari's and Bharat's. And the interesting thing was that I probably wouldn't have longed for the passions I now had, like photography, because I'd never have known it could have been a profession for me. I wouldn't have longed for the Western notion of romantic love because people here didn't seek or desire it in the same way.

"What do you dream about in life?" I asked, a question posed to nearly every child in America, but a rather foreign concept in India.

He stopped flipping through the book as he thought about the question. "Maybe buying a bigger house for my family if this shop can make more money," he said.

Had I been asked that question, I could have rattled off a list of a dozen things ranging from tangible to intangible. My dreams were limitless. I appreciated the selflessness and simplicity in his answer. While I saw an upside to the Indian way of life in which people didn't spend most of it wishing for things they did not have, my problem was that I had grown up around American values, had desperately tried to emulate them without question, and now I didn't know how to unring that bell. I had become a dreamer, and the Indian way of life was acceptance over passion and pursuit. While I appreciated that type of existence, I wasn't quite sure if I could live it.

Maybe my mother felt that same way too. Maybe that's why she wanted to be in America. But if that was the case, I'd never seen her pursue anything in America that she could not have sought in India. The more time I spent in India, the more I wondered what had led my parents to leave in the first place.

25

Later that afternoon, I emerged from the darkroom to find Tushar slumped over the counter, his nose in yet another book.

I dried my hands on an ink-stained towel. "What are you reading now?"

He held up a book with a vivid picture of penguins in Antarctica on the cover.

"I'd love to see those in real life," I said.

"Finally, we have found a place where you have not been," he joked, still not fully understanding my desire to travel to countries in which I had no family or connection.

I moved toward him to get a better look. My arm rested next to his on the counter. I could feel his arm hairs brushing against my skin. "There are lots of places I haven't—"

The bell chimed above the doorway. We bolted upright and apart as though we had been caught breaking some rule.

But it was too late. From the look on her face, I could tell she had seen enough to have her answer.

"Hi, Mom," I said, feigning nonchalance.

She bit her lip in that characteristic way that made clear she was holding something back. Tushar scurried around the counter to greet her.

"Welcome, madam. Namaste." He bent at the waist to greet her. "Some chai?"

Mom held up a hand and shook her head. "I only wanted to see how Preeti's photo project from the wedding is coming along. She has spent so much time here this week that I thought I better see what she is doing."

Tushar had clasped his hands behind his back and was swaying back and forth as if he didn't know what else to do with himself. Eager to keep things from getting more awkward, I motioned for my mother to join me on the other side of the counter.

From underneath it, I pulled out the box in which I had been storing my prints. It was cardboard covered in thin red cloth and had once held kaaju katli. It still released the smell of sweetened cashews when I lifted the lid, but now it housed the photos I was considering for the final album. I'd consulted with Tushar on each of them before they earned a place of honor in the box.

"I've got some prints from the baithak I'd like to show you. There are some others I developed this morning, but those are still drying in the back room," I said.

"This is nice." Mom nodded, looking at a photo of the maharaj applying vermilion to Hari's forehead. Hari's eyes were closed, while the priest's were focused on the tip of his right ring finger, covered in bright-red powder.

My lips curled into a huge smile. It didn't sound like much, but "this is nice" was one of the highest compliments that Varsha Desai ever gave. It was the same thing she had said when I told her I had gotten a job at the highest-ranked law firm in the country, and when she found out that I was nominated to deliver the speech at my high school graduation. "This is nice" was as good as it got, and I was thrilled to hear those words, especially in connection with something she had never supported like photography.

She flipped through more pictures, mostly of friends and relatives.

"When will you finish the album?" she asked.

"I'm not sure. Tushar and I are going to pool our work and create one big album rather than each doing a separate one for our events, so it's going to take longer than I had originally planned."

Tushar stood near the front of the shop, trying to give us privacy.

Mom called over to him, "Some chai would be good after all."

He nodded and scurried out the front door to the tea cart across the street. After the door closed, Mom turned to me.

"I'm glad Tushar is helping you and you are getting along, but make sure it's nothing more than that." She continued to flip through the photos.

My cheeks felt warm. "We're just friends."

Mom had paused on a picture toward the bottom of the stack. I'd forgotten it was in there. It was one I had taken of her a couple days ago when she was sitting on the hichko in the garden at dusk. Her legs were curled under her, and she had a mug in her hand. What struck me about the picture was the expression on her face—it was soft and wistful. A side of her I rarely saw. Now, as she looked at herself, that same expression crept back onto her face.

She said, "You know the rules here. It's important to follow them."

I could see that this meant a lot to her. "We're really just friends," I said.

Her jaw set when she flipped to the next photo. It was one I had taken of Tushar in the shop. His nose buried in a book. His ink-stained fingers poised to turn the page. Her skepticism was evident.

The bells over the door chimed, and Tushar hurried in with two steaming cups of chai, saving me from having to offer some lame excuse. I reached for one and began sipping the hot liquid. It burned my tongue, but I didn't care. Anything to avoid my mother's disapproving gaze and keep from having to explain myself.

Mom finished her tea and called the driver to pull the car around. Before stepping out, she called over her shoulder in a loud voice. "I forgot to tell you that Biren stopped by the bungalow today to see you. Tushar, you remember Biren from the wedding? I think you took a good photo of him and Preeti at the reception."

Tushar nodded humbly.

~

The next day, Tushar's father came into the shop to do the accounting, so Tushar and I went on a photo excursion to practice some new skills he'd taught me. It was still unseasonably hot, so I decided to cast aside my need to fit in and wore a Western-style dress. I could not handle another day of sweating through a panjabi that covered me from my neck to my ankles.

We came upon a small group of young boys in dirty slacks who were kneeling on the road watching a spinning top whirl in a frenetic circle. I knelt to photograph them, Tushar teaching me the right settings to capture the movement of the top while keeping everything else static.

"You know, since I've been here, I've wondered how different my life would have been if I'd never left India," I said when I stood.

"I'm sure it would be very different."

We continued down the road in silence.

"Do you ever wish your life was different?" I asked him.

"Why should I think that?" he asked.

I knew he had accepted his life as it was and didn't suffer the same restlessness that often consumed me as I longed for what was or what could have been.

He looked at me. "You wish your life to be different?"

In a rare moment of truth, I nodded. "All the time. I wish I could just be happy with things as they are, but I always think about what didn't go as planned, or how to change the future so it does go as planned."

"That must be very tiring, no?"

I kicked some stray rocks in my path. It was. The restlessness was exhausting. He had no idea how much so. I hadn't even realized how much so until these recent weeks in India, when I wasn't thinking about the future. It was hard not to think about the past with the pain of Alex having moved on still fresh and at the forefront of my mind when I found myself alone in bed at night, trying to fall asleep. But as devastating as that had felt in the moment, the rough edge was starting to dull, much faster than it had when we had originally separated. There was something about being in India that forced me to be more present.

"Yes," I finally said. "But I guess I've always taken for granted that I get to make choices about the future."

I watched Tushar as he continued down the road. Tushar's view on life was simple: work hard, provide for your family, and then you would be happy. He had never mapped out his future, in part because the big decisions had already been etched out for him. Like so many people who were raised in India, he had followed in his parents' footsteps. He would run the family business, so there was no soul-searching needed to discover the career that fueled his passions. He knew that he would one day marry a nice girl who met the requirements of the holy trinity—Hindu, Gujarati, and vegetarian—and she would bear him a son who also would grow up to run the family business. He knew that, as a man, he would be responsible for maintaining the household finances, and in exchange he would never clean a toilet, do his laundry, or prepare his meals. His path was in some ways quite like Hari's and Bharat's, and Virag Mama's before them. Different castes dictated different professions and neighborhoods, but beyond that, the paths were the same.

I could see that there would be some comfort in knowing your entire life was planned before you were even born. What if I didn't occupy so much of my time with my anxiety about finding my identity, purpose, and everlasting love? I could not even imagine the other thoughts that would fill that vast space. As much as I loved the thought of less anxiety, I still couldn't fully wrap my head around that life. The life I was born into and would have had but for my parents moving me halfway around the world. Now I was a product of the West, and a life without those big choices didn't seem satisfying.

I jogged to catch up to Tushar. I didn't see the sharp rock poking through the dirt on the road and stumbled as my toe clipped the edge of it. The weight of my purse and camera knocked me off balance, and I crashed to the ground.

"Ow!" I muttered as pebbles and grit pressed into my palms. There was a stinging sensation coming from my leg. I moved to a sitting position and pulled my leg toward my chest, holding my shin with both hands, applying pressure.

"I am so sorry! Are you okay?" Tushar called as he sprinted back to where I sat. He gathered my camera bag and purse and held them close, his eyes darting back and forth while he searched for looters who might have tried to take advantage of my vulnerable state.

"What are you sorry for? I'm the idiot that tripped," I said.

"You have a small cut," he said, reaching out his finger and gently touching the skin near the scrape on my leg.

My eyes followed his finger. He then lifted his gaze until it met mine, and I felt something familiar stirring within me, something I hadn't felt since those first few dates with Alex.

The moment was brief because his jaw began to drop in horror when he realized that we were in public, sharing a rather intimate moment by Indian standards. He jerked his hand away from my leg as if my skin were crawling with fire ants.

"I am so sorry," he said, stumbling backward.

"It's okay," I said, disappointed he had jumped back. "I'm fine." I stood and brushed off the dirt from my clothes.

Once he saw I was fine, he offered to carry my camera bag the rest of the way, maintaining a safe distance between us while we walked. It was as if he had heard one of my junior high teachers at our school dances telling us to always "leave room for the Holy Ghost."

As the day continued, I shifted my focus from taking photographs of people to capturing the animals roaming the city. On the surface, Tushar and I interacted the same way we always had, but there had been a shift—toward what, I did not know, but it was undeniable that a shift had occurred. Tushar represented everything I had staunchly avoided until now. On the surface, he was what my parents would have wanted for me. The holy trinity: Hindu, Gujarati, and vegetarian. Simple. Except it wasn't. It ignored a critical, unspoken element—caste.

When the sun dropped behind some buildings and the lighting was no longer good for photos, we stopped in a Vadilal shop for ice cream. I still hadn't gotten used to the iciness of the ice cream in Ahmedabad, so I stuck to fruity flavors. Here, the chocolate that I really craved tasted more like Nestlé Quik powder than the decadent chocolate to which I was now accustomed. I longed for a scoop of creamy, luscious dark chocolate but settled on a cup of lychee. Using a plastic spoon in the shape of a tiny snow shovel, I placed some into my mouth, letting the icy particles melt onto my tongue before swallowing.

I leaned back into my white plastic chair and took in the cool hues filling the sky, dulled by the ever-present haze of pollution.

"You never talk about your work as a lawyer in America."

"There's not much to tell. I don't do it anymore. End of story," I said, licking more lychee from my spoon. I felt very exposed without a camera covering most of my face. "So, what about you?" I asked.

"Me?" He looked confused.

"Yeah. You talk about your family and the business a lot, but you never talk about yourself."

"There's not much to tell." He threw my words back at me.

"Very funny," I said. "Seriously, I don't meet too many men in this town who are your age and not married. I'm surprised your parents haven't arranged something yet."

Speaking this openly was not a part of Indian culture, but the moment from earlier in the day had somehow left me feeling braver and more brazen. He squirmed at my comment, but I continued my relentless stare until he answered.

"There was someone long ago. She was beautiful, smart, and an excellent cook. But on the day we were to be wed, she disappeared," he began, his eyes boring straight into mine.

Captivated, I leaned forward. "What happened?"

"No one knows. She was in her dressing room putting on her sari one minute, and the next, she was gone. The only thing that remained was her sari strewn about the floor as if there had been a struggle. No one ever saw her again." His tone was somber, and he cast his gaze downward.

"Wow, really?" I was skeptical but tried to keep my voice even.

Tushar laughed. "No, of course not! You Americans will believe any far-fetched Hollywood tale about India!"

"I knew it!" I said, feigning annoyance but unable to mask the smile that overtook my stern expression. I flung lychee ice cream at him with the tiny spoon.

In that moment, I realized how much I needed someone I could laugh with. It was what I missed most about spending time with Carrie, Alex, or Neel before all this. With them, I could spend hours talking about stupid things, and we'd laugh until our bellies were sore. Alex and I had resolved most minor disputes with tickle fights because, with him, it had been easy to feel that carefree. I was still searching for that person in India.

"I've never seen you joke around like that."

I was seeing the lighter and freer side of Tushar, and I liked what I saw.

India had such a serious and formal aura about it, and I craved sarcastic banter.

As he collected himself, his face sobered. "The truth is that I probably would have been married when I was twenty-five, but around that time my father became very ill with cancer. He struggled with the disease for the next four years. I had to focus my energies on the store, and the years escaped from me. Today, I'm an old man." He winked at the last sentence to lighten the mood again.

I had noticed his father was rather frail. Now, I understood why. I was sure it had been difficult for him to tell me what he had about his father, so I knew not to delve further. I suspected he had shared more with me than he had with anyone else outside of his immediate family.

"Only in India would a thirty-two-year-old man call himself old. In LA, we can't seem to get the men to settle down until after they've passed forty, and even then, it's a struggle to find someone who isn't a MAPP," I said.

He looked at me quizzically.

"Middle-aged Peter Pan," I said with a chuckle.

He laughed. "California Girl, maybe that means you do not belong in California anymore."

26

When I returned to the bungalow that evening, Mom, Indira Mami, and Virag Mama were sitting in the living room with serious looks on their faces. Mom's expression was the same as when I was little and had brought home a grade that wasn't the highest-possible mark. I dutifully sat across from them and waited for them to speak.

"Preeti, we need to talk to you," Virag Mama said.

I stared ahead with an open expression and closed mouth. Even though I was family, I was still technically a guest in their home.

Virag Mama and Indira Mami exchanged a look; both seemed unsure how to proceed. Mom remained quiet, deferring to her brother because she was a guest in his home as well. Per Indian tradition, even though she had been raised there, she had lost her rights to the home when she married into Dad's family.

Indira Mami took the lead. "We are very happy you are here," she said. "But we know you are spending a lot of time with Tushar. People talk. It is not decent for an unmarried girl to be out with a boy like that."

Wow, I thought, stunned by how quickly word traveled in this city. "Oh, I'm sorry," I said. "I didn't realize that we couldn't be friends."

My apology was sincere, but only to the extent that I did not want my relatives to be the subject of gossip. I firmly believed I should be able to spend a day with Tushar—or anyone else for that matter—and not have the entire city comment on it. I missed the anonymity of LA, where I could stroll through my neighborhood without anyone speaking to me, even if they had passed me on the street a hundred times before. I also noticed the double standard that was clearly caste based, because I had been out alone with Biren on Christmas just three days earlier, but they had no cause to be alarmed about that.

"Here people gossip," Indira Mami continued. "They are looking for someone to make a mistake. We must be careful that we do not give them that chance. Our family can never be seen throwing ice cream at someone in public."

How does she know every little detail? I was shocked and annoyed that someone had bothered to report the minutiae of an innocent outing. It was such a nonissue as far as I was concerned. I would now have to assume my every action would be reported back to Mami and Mama each time I set foot outside the house. It was frustrating to think that the life I was starting to enjoy in Ahmedabad had suddenly become a fishbowl with nowhere to hide.

"We were just playing around," I said, knowing my tone sounded like that of a petulant child.

I turned to Mom, but her gaze remained fixed on her hands, primly folded in her lap. I then glanced at the closed door to Neel's bedroom and wondered if he even knew about the conversation we were having in the living room. If he did, surely he would come to my aid.

Virag Mama cleared his throat before he spoke. "Yes, but here it looks bad if people see those things. How do you think it looks for a person from our family to throw food at someone from a working-class family? Hah? On top of everything else, there are so many poor people, and it is not right to waste food, even if it is a single bite."

His words stung. Of course I saw the poverty in Ahmedabad; it was all around us. I wasn't trying to insult anyone. But I also couldn't help noticing the hypocrisy in his statement.

"I should be respectful of the lower caste, but I should not spend any time with them? What sense does that make?" I said.

Mom sat straighter. She had heard my defiant tone many times before. She perched on the edge of her seat, ready to intervene if needed.

Virag Mama's eyes widened at my statement. I stared at him, holding my ground. Hari and Bharat would never have dared question him.

"This is not America. We don't talk back here." His tone had chilled.

Mom fidgeted. She'd made that same statement to me so many times but seemed more sympathetic today.

Virag Mama opened his mouth, but Indira Mami put a hand on his arm to stop him.

She said, "An unmarried woman must protect her reputation here. It is her greatest gift to the man she marries. Your age will already make that process hard enough."

Oh God, she was serious. I had to fight to keep my jaw from dropping. Out of the corner of my eye I tried to gauge Mom's reaction. Some of the color had drained from her face. I sensed she had heard a similar statement a time or two before.

"I think that's a little extreme," I said, "but I will be more considerate of your wishes."

"We want you to be more careful, beta," Virag Mama said, his tone softening.

Indira Mami said, "Someone like Biren is more appropriate."

I had to bite my tongue to keep from calling out their bias. I sat silently until it seemed there was closure to the awkward conversation, and I could retreat to the solitude of my room.

After a few minutes, there was a knock. Mom entered and closed the door behind her.

"Are you here to yell at me?" I asked.

She sat on the bed with a small shake of her head. "Life in India can be hard, right?"

I was surprised by her supportive tone. "Sometimes. But some things are better than I remembered."

"It is these things that made me want to leave in the first place. I didn't want my children to be under this microscope . . . the way I was," Mom said.

I chewed on my lower lip while I contemplated her statement. Growing up in Illinois, I'd been more of a tomboy and had gravitated toward male friends. In fact, prior to meeting Carrie, for as long as I could remember, my best friend had always been a guy. If Mom and Dad had stayed in India, friendships with boys would have been forbidden.

"I never realized how interconnected everyone is in this city," I said.

"In Ahmedabad, everyone knows everyone and everything. That is why I wanted to stay with you kids—to make sure you did not get caught in these traps. I know it is important for you to have friends here. Be discreet when you spend time with Tushar, and be considerate of Biren. Our families are very close." She patted my leg and then said, "Dinner will be ready soon."

I couldn't handle the awkwardness of a family meal after the conversation we'd just had.

"Biren and I had talked about going out to dinner," I said. "Is that still okay?"

She smiled and nodded. I, again, ignored the hypocrisy and texted Biren that it was an emergency and he needed to meet me for dinner.

27

Biren sauntered up to me in jeans and a blue plaid button-down shirt, and it was hard to ignore how attractive he was with his broad shoulders and trim body. Maybe my family was right, and it wouldn't hurt to consider him as something other than a friend. It would certainly be simpler that way.

"So, what's the emergency?" he said.

"Family drama," I said, shaking my head. "I needed to get out of there for a bit. Sometimes that huge house feels very small with everyone in it."

He laughed. "I'm sure it does. Privacy is hard to come by."

I nodded.

He held open the door to the dosa restaurant he had chosen and gestured for me to pass.

"That's a brilliant top." He complimented the flowing red tunic I wore over a pair of skinny jeans.

"Thanks. You don't look so bad yourself," I said, already feeling lighter with the easy banter.

The smells of dosa cooking with ghee and spicy sambar wafting through the crowded restaurant were heavenly. My stomach growled the second we sat down. We ordered our food, him opting for a masala dosa and me going for a classic paper one. They arrived quickly, and the waiters showed up with pitchers of sambar and trays of chutneys in a colorful array of red, white, and green. We dived into our food, and the conversation with my family felt much further away.

He was a perfect biodata match, and I wondered if this could feel as comfortable and familiar as I had with Alex. Neel and Dipti had turned a biodata match into a Western love affair, so I knew it was possible to have both. Biren was the guy my parents and relatives wanted me to end up with, probably had since we were little kids. He was what was expected of me, and I enjoyed spending time with him. Perhaps a common background could take the place of the nebulous spark that growing up in America had led me to believe was love. Perhaps the spark would come later.

"What are Aussie girls like?" I said, trying to sound nonchalant.

He shrugged. "Same as any other girls, really."

I'd tried to get information out of him about his dating history, but it seemed he didn't have much of one, or what he did have, he wasn't willing to share with me.

As we continued to talk and laugh, I couldn't help but think about how easily I'd been able to open up to him from the start. His family was great, and would welcome me without reservation, just as mine would him. A classic "suggestion marriage."

The restaurant was not too far from Lakshmi, so I suggested walking home rather than hailing a ricksha. I was in no rush to get back to the bungalow and the judging eyes. The cool night air felt refreshing against my skin. When we got to the entrance of my subdivision, two cows were standing in front of it, sniffing through some garbage lying along the outer wall.

We stood outside, casually chatting. I'm not sure if it was the darkness, or the random cows, or the fact that I'd just had a great conversation with him, or just that for the first time in weeks we were alone with no one watching us, but I looked at him, captivated by his full lips. I rose to my tiptoes and leaned in to kiss him. Maybe learning Alex had moved on was the last thing I needed to finally leave that pain behind and move toward something good, toward someone like Biren.

What I hadn't expected was that his eyes would bulge out and he would stumble backward. The cows were startled by the commotion and moved away from the entrance, ambling down the road.

"Oh, jeez." I took a step back. "I'm sorry. It's been a weird—"

"No, no. It's not—"

"—day. I shouldn't have—"

"—your fault."

We both took a breath. Then he said, "Let me explain."

I moved toward the subdivision so I could retreat to the safety of the house. "You really don't have to. I'm sorry! I just thought, I mean, it seems like we have a lot in common, but—"

He reached over and grabbed my wrist, forcing me to face him.

"Preeti, I'm gay."

28

I slapped my palm against my forehead. "I am an idiot."

It was as if the clouds had parted and sun was streaming into my mind. How could I have ignored it? It explained why he avoided talking about dating and had only vague answers to give. Why, whenever the aunties had talked about setting him up at the wedding, he deflected and changed the subject or excused himself to take care of some task. Maybe I had needed to believe, however briefly, that I could live the life my parents and relatives wanted for me. That Neel and Dipti's story could be mine.

I looked at him and laughed. The kind of laugh that came from my gut and shook my entire body. The kind I hadn't had in months. The kind that had the power to release the months of tension I'd been carrying.

He seemed amused, rather than horrified. "I'm glad you think that's funny."

I waved my hands. "No, no. I don't at all. I just think I'm a giant idiot." My stomach hurt from the laughter, and I had to put my hands on my knees. "God, if you could have seen the look on your face as I moved toward you!" I barely got the words out before dissolving into another fit.

"I'm sorry, but I thought you knew. It took me by surprise when it became clear you didn't!"

"Why would I have known?"

"You're from California. Don't you lot think *everyone* is gay?"

He had a point.

After collecting ourselves, we looked at each other anew. There was an openness and honesty that immediately replaced the pressure of knowing my family wanted us to be married. Obviously, that would never happen. Knowing that would make our friendship much more natural.

"I'm really sorry. I hope you weren't too traumatized."

"Just don't do it again, and we're good."

I extended my hand to shake his. "Deal."

Turning serious, he said, "I'm sure you can imagine that I haven't told anyone, and you can't either."

I nodded solemnly. "I get it. I wish I'd realized sooner. But I know you ultimately have to share something so personal on your own time-line, and I'm glad you felt comfortable sharing it with me now. Does your family know?"

He shook his head. "They'd be so ashamed. And they would blame themselves for moving me to Australia. They and their friends think being gay is a Western influence that wouldn't otherwise exist."

"Really? Your father seems so understanding. And he helps so many marginalized people through his charity work."

Even in the darkness, I could see his expression cloud over. "It's easy for him to deal with a problem he's completely detached from. I've tried to tell him before, but it's almost like he suspects and always finds an excuse to change the subject. If I say the words out loud, then he can't ignore them."

It was hard for me to reconcile these two sides of Anand Uncle: one that had an open heart to strangers in need but then could not find that same compassion for his own son. But Biren certainly knew him better than I did.

"What does that mean for you? You have to tell your family someday, right?" I said.

"No, I can't tell them." He ran his fingers through his hair. "I will have to keep telling them that I haven't found the right 'girl' yet. That's an easier situation for them to handle than the truth. Better to be seen as 'too picky' than as gay. And anything else is too dangerous. It's far too risky to be open about sexuality here."

"Biren, can you live like that?"

"I have to. Even though being gay isn't technically against the law anymore, it's still not accepted. And often the police have taken the matter into their own hands. You hear rumors that when they catch someone who's gay, they beat him or . . . sometimes they do much worse."

I saw fear flicker across his face. "Why not go back to Australia or move to America? Someplace that will be more accepting so you don't have to live a lie?"

He sighed. "It's not that easy. This is where I want to live. It's home. Even though I could secretly date or whatever in Australia, it never felt like home. And I was still hiding from my parents and their social circle the few times I tried to date. That never felt right to me. Besides, the type of guy I'd want to end up with is someone like me—someone with my Hindu background and culture. Someone who wants a life here as much as I do."

"How can you be so loyal to a culture that doesn't accept that part of you?"

"I can't stop being Hindu or Gujarati any more than I can stop being gay. It sounds crazy, but that's the type of guy I want to end up with. I just have to accept that that type of guy will be just as secretive about his identity as I've been, so I may never find him."

And I thought I had an uphill battle trying to find my place in the world! My heart went out to Biren. Because of the cultural phobia surrounding anything other than heterosexuality, his life in India was far more difficult than anything I had ever been through. Dealing with something like that in a country that was so closed minded had to be unimaginable. No wonder we'd developed a close friendship so quickly. He'd needed someone in India to accept him just as badly as I had.

"Have you met that type of guy here?" I asked.

His smile gave him away.

My eyebrows rose. "Oh, do tell!"

He looked shy, and it was very endearing.

He began to shift in an adorably shy way. "Obviously, we're just friends. That's all it can be, but he's a fun bloke to be around."

I leaned closer to Biren and lowered my voice. "Does he know you're gay?"

He nodded. "Yeah." He chuckled. "Said he could sense it a kilometer away."

"Clearly he's more perceptive than me!" I joked. "So, he's open about it?"

"Not in the way you're thinking, but more than I am. He's fairly active in the underground gay scene here and has had relationships before. His parents know, but they aren't advertising it outside of the family."

"How do you know your parents wouldn't feel the same way?"

He cast me a disapproving look. "Because I do. My parents aren't as progressive as his. Our family is in the public eye because of my father's work. My parents aren't equipped to handle a scandal like this."

I could see he was getting agitated thinking about his parents, so I switched gears to learn more about this guy who had Biren so smitten that he was willing to admit his sexuality to someone.

"When do I get to meet him?"

He raised his eyebrows. "I'm not sure. You know I can't be open about it."

"Well, that's why you can take me along. I'll be the buffer, and it won't be the two of you delving into some clandestine romance in a darkly lit alley. It will just be a group of friends going out."

He thought about it, and I could see that he liked the idea of spending more time with this man, and any acceptable excuse would do. The next day was Saturday, and people our age would be out and about anyway, so he said he would set something up.

"I can't wait," I said, moving closer. He took a step back as I moved toward him. "I promise I won't try to kiss you again—I'm just giving you a hug."

He laughed and pulled me toward him. "It feels good to have said all of that out loud."

"If there is ever anything I can do for you, I'm here. I hope you know that."

"The only thing I need from you is to stay quiet."

29

I woke up the next morning feeling heavy with the things Biren had told me. Knowing how much of his life he was sacrificing for his family made me feel like I had to try to repair the ruptures in mine as best I could. Things between Neel and me had been strained for days now, and that unsettled me more than anything that had come before. But he and I would work through things. We were family. We had to. That's what I had convinced myself. But a family through marriage was not the same as blood and genetics and history. I felt like his relationship with Dipti was at a tenuous point and the longer they stayed apart, the less likely they were to come back together. I didn't think he'd ever be himself again until Dipti forgave him, and I had to try to convince her to let him back in.

I rang the doorbell to her family's house later that morning and waited for their servant to open it. Once I was shown to Dipti's room, I saw her as I had left her before: lying in bed with a notebook on her lap. On the side table next to her was a thick stack of pages that had been ripped from the notebook, and I knew those were all letters to Uma.

"Did Neel send you?" she asked, not looking up from her letter.

"No," I said, taking a seat in the chair next to her bed, where countless of her relatives must have been keeping vigil over her during this past week. "He would actually be really mad if he knew I was here, so I'd appreciate if you didn't tell him."

She raised an eyebrow and looked up at me. "Secrets between siblings? Who could dare imagine such a thing with you two?" she said snidely.

"We're going through a bit of a rough patch," I confessed, my eyes trained on her to watch her reaction.

She put her pen down next to her. It wasn't capped, and the blue ink slowly seeped into the rajai beneath her.

"About what?"

I shook my head. "I'm not really sure. Maybe about you . . . I mean the situation with you. Maybe about more." I sighed. "Maybe about a lot more. It's hard to say."

"Well, I guess that's fair," she said.

"Why do you say that?"

"Because I've lost count of the number of fights he and I have had about you or your family. It's probably time the tables were turned and you had one about me."

I met her eyes. "You're right. It's probably fair."

"What about me sparked this?"

I was so used to thinking several steps ahead and being careful with what I said—it had been my assimilation and legal training after all—but I knew in this situation, transparency was the only way to move forward.

"When he wanted to go back home and go back to work and leave you here, I told him he couldn't do that. That it wasn't fair to you, and you might never forgive him."

Her eyes narrowed. "You told him to stay? Why would you do that?"

I sighed and slumped in my chair. "I may not say this often, but you guys are good together."

"Since when did you become so supportive?" she said, an unmistakable edge to her tone.

Her words stung. I'm sure Dipti had sensed from the very beginning that I didn't understand why Neel had chosen her, but it was something she and I had never spoken about openly. We were always cordial to each other, but there was a difference between cordial and comfortable.

"I'm sorry," I said, my voice heavy.

And I was. For keeping my distance. For resenting her for taking Neel away from me. For not realizing she might have needed me. For having a long face at her baby shower. For all the pain she felt at losing the baby. For the distance that was growing between Neel and her. For not realizing what a strong person she was to be able to put one foot in front of the other with all that had happened.

"It's okay." She sounded deflated. "I shouldn't have said that."

I gingerly touched her arm. "No, you were right to say it. And you would have been right to say it years earlier. I saw you as the person who took Neel away from me, and I couldn't get past that. It wasn't right of me."

"You know, when I first met Neel, one of the things I loved most was that he came from a family. Two parents, a sister, a childhood home. It was what I had always wanted after I lost my mother."

I swallowed the lump that had formed in my throat. "Even after you saw our dysfunctional mess?"

"Every family is dysfunctional in its own way."

"Maybe you're right, but sometimes it seems like we're on the far end of the spectrum."

Without any malice left in her voice, she said, "I don't blame you, by the way. For not accepting me when Neel first introduced me. You two grew up very close. I know you felt like I was encroaching on that. The funny thing was that I wanted to be as close to you as Neel was. I wanted to know what it felt like to have a sister."

"I am really sorry." I hung my head. "It's no secret that Mom and I have always butted heads. Then you swooped in, and it looked so easy for you to get along with her." I sighed. "It made me realize she's not difficult with everyone—just with me."

"It's because I had to try harder than you. Look at the baby shower. Do you think I liked being tucked into a sari and forcing polite conversation with all of her friends?" she said. "I was so jealous that you got to hide behind your camera."

It had never dawned on me that Dipti had been putting on an act when it came to appeasing my mother. She had made it all look so natural. "You should have told her that. Or me. I would've told her for you."

She shook her head. "I don't have the benefit of the unconditional love that comes from being her actual daughter, like you do. If I had talked back to her, she'd remember it forever, so I held my tongue. And it's not as though I hated doing those things. For me, it's more important to feel like I have family than to argue about little things."

"Why are you telling me this now?"

"So far in life I've lost my mother and my daughter. I don't want to lose my only sister too."

I hesitated a moment, my mind reeling from the power of her simple statement.

"I'm sorry I haven't been better. I hate to admit it, but I was jealous, and it was easier to ignore you."

She smiled ruefully. "Let's agree to forget the past and focus on the future."

"Does that mean you'll come back home?" I asked. "Neel needs you. We all do. And if you let us, we can be there for you and get through this as a family."

She glanced around the room. "I'm not sure if I'm ready yet."

I nodded but heard less resolve in her voice than on my past visit. "Okay. But when you are, please know I'll be there for you. Not like the past, but the way it should always have been."

She managed a small smile for a fleeting second. "Okay."

I sat for a few more moments in silence with her and longed for her and Neel to make it through this awful ordeal by learning to lean on each other and come out even stronger together.

Watching them go through this had taught me so much about them and about relationships in general. Maybe most important of all, I was learning how much I still had to learn.

~

When I went to Happy Snaps after leaving Dipti, I wasn't sure what to expect. It was too embarrassing to tell Tushar that my family didn't want me associating with him in public.

I took a deep breath and pasted on a smile that Carrie would have immediately known was fake before I walked through the door. The chimes echoed in the small shop. When Tushar looked at me, I could tell he had received the same lecture from his family.

"Good morning, Preeti," he said, turning the page in his book. "I should stay in front today, but please let me know if you need help with anything."

He had resumed his polite, formal demeanor from when we first met. My heart sank when I realized we were going to have to rebuild the openness upon which I'd come to depend. I couldn't stand the thought of losing that.

I marched up to him and grabbed the book from his hands. Especially after my talk with Dipti, I couldn't go back to fake conversations.

"Did you have fun yesterday?"

He looked startled. "Excuse me?"

"I asked if you had fun yesterday," I said sternly, as if cross-examining him.

He nodded, looking amused by my straightforward manner.

"Good." I smiled. "So did I. We should be able to hang out without throwing the societal balance off its axis. We like spending time together, and there's nothing wrong with that, is there?"

He shook his head, a smile creeping onto his face.

I extended my hand to shake his. "Then it's agreed. We're friends, and no one can change that. We will respect our families and not flaunt it, but within these walls"—I gestured around the shop—"I want it to be like it was twenty-four hours ago. Joking, laughing, all of it!"

He clasped my hand. "Yes, madam."

I smiled, knowing we were okay.

"You were quite a good lawyer, I suspect," he said.

"I wasn't bad."

"Certainly better than you are at photography."

I pretended to bop him upside the head with his book before setting it onto the counter. With a coy smile, I said, "Fine, wise guy, why don't you teach me your skills?"

"To be truthful, I saw some of your photos from yesterday when we were walking the streets. They are quite unique."

"Really?" I felt my cheeks warm at his praise.

He nodded. "They offer a different perspective. One that we Indians would not see."

I focused on his words. *We Indians.*

He must have seen my face change, because he quickly backtracked. "You know I mean we resident Indians. You are Indian, too, of course."

"I know what you meant," I said.

And while he'd meant nothing by it, it still stung. I didn't know what it felt like to walk on the street and feel like I belonged as much as the people passing by me. Not since I was a seven-year-old kid living in India, and I could hardly remember that girl now. Maybe Neel and Dipti had worked together because they understood the other's loneliness. Alex could never understand that part of me, and I had just assumed it was because we had different ethnic backgrounds, but I now realized it was more than that. Tushar couldn't have understood it either, and he was as Indian as they came. But he was an Indian who had always belonged in India. No one questioned his place in this country like they did mine.

30

Shortly after sunset, Biren and I walked along the stalls making up the perimeter of the Law Garden on our way to meet his crush. I hadn't been to the area since my last trip to India but knew that the colorful lights and merriment were something I wanted to try to capture on film, especially now that Tushar had taught me some better settings to use for night photography.

"My friend from work will meet us near that corner," Biren said.

Law Garden was a small and crowded public park where people often came to shop or eat at the hawker stalls that lined its perimeter. It was nothing like the grandeur of Grant Park back in Chicago, but large by Indian standards. The smell of frying oil filled the air rather than the scent of nature. My family had spent many hot summer evenings here when we had been visiting from America. Tonight it looked no different than it had fifteen or twenty years ago. There were families walking around talking and laughing while licking shaved-ice popsicles. NRI kids were still sporting Christmas sweatshirts even though the holiday had just passed.

"So, you're still calling him your friend?" I said.

"Isn't that what you're calling Tushar?" he shot back.

"Touché," I said.

He laughed. "Anyway, that's what he is. We've never crossed that boundary. Besides, he's more into this scene than I am. I'm not sure if he's single or even interested in me as anything other than a friend."

"Well, you won't know unless you try! I'll see what I can find out."

"You Americans can't ever stop prying, can you?" His tone was playful, so I knew he wasn't bothered.

"I just want you to be happy, and there must be something about this guy if you were willing to share this part of yourself with him," I said.

Biren's lips curled into a lopsided grin. His dark eyes shone with that glimmer of possibility that people felt at the beginning of a new relationship. It was the same look I'd seen on Alex's face in those early months, and the same look I was sure I had reciprocated. It was the look I'd probably have if Tushar and I grew closer than we were. It was a look that meant the same thing in every country and every culture.

He stopped and faced me. "Don't go getting any ideas. This isn't America. People like me don't ride off into the sunset. Samarth is someone I feel connected to and whom I can be myself with. That's all."

How could he minimize it so easily? It was no small feat to find that connection with anyone, and even more difficult to find it with someone you were attracted to.

Ahead of us, a man in slacks and a gray sweater waved in our direction. He was several inches shorter than Biren, but then again, most people in India were. His hair was combed away from his face, revealing premature white hairs along his temples that gave him a more distinguished look. His hazel eyes stood out because they were in stark contrast to the sea of dark-brown-eyed people around us.

"He's not bad on the eyes either," I whispered before we were within earshot of Samarth.

Samarth was a doctor who frequented Biren's pharmacy. They were both very coy about how their friendship had developed from there.

Biren had warned me that Samarth was into the underground gay scene near Law Garden, so we might end up there.

Biren made the introductions, the two of them shifting nervously in each other's company, but in that bashful way that suggested Biren was wrong and the feelings were mutual.

"I've actually got some friends getting together behind the garden. Maybe we can go meet them?" Samarth suggested.

He led us through the park, past a dark corner where I'd noticed most of the people around us were men in their twenties and thirties, to a dimly lit street behind. I wondered if the families roaming around Law Garden knew parts of the garden and the roads behind it doubled as a gay meeting point. That thought had certainly never crossed my mind before tonight.

There were around a hundred men leaning against the buildings or sitting in rickety chairs spitting out tobacco from paan and sipping chai or Thums Up. It was all so civilized. It wasn't that I had expected a full-blown orgy in the streets, but this common, everyday sight wasn't what I had envisioned for a gay cruising area. People were just talking and laughing, acting like people did in any average bar in Los Angeles. The only thing that stood out was that I was the only woman around.

Samarth approached two guys and introduced us. They seemed skeptical of me, especially with the large camera I had around my neck and its bag slung over my shoulder, but Samarth explained I was not only Biren's friend from America, but from *California*. Their eyes shone as they heard the word, and I realized that to a gay man living in secret in Ahmedabad, California was his version of moksha.

Samarth seemed to know most of the people behind the Law Garden and joked and laughed with the guys we ran into. Biren's expression fell as each guy gave Samarth a familiar hug. His feelings for Samarth were plainly written on his face, but Samarth's lifestyle was likely very different from the one that Biren had chosen. Biren was too reserved to roam the scene and flirt in the easy and natural way that Samarth did.

Out of the corner of my eye, hidden by the shadows, I saw two men locked in an embrace. It was so unfair that the shadows of dark alleys, late at night, were the only places they could show their affection. Biren had noticed it, too, and seemed uncomfortable, because he was now actively avoiding looking in that direction.

"So, you are a journalist?" one of Samarth's friends asked cautiously, gesturing at my camera.

I toyed with the straps that hung around my neck and shook my head. "No, just an amateur photographer." I held his gaze while I removed the camera from my neck and capped the lens, about to return it to its case.

The man nodded. He struck me as the ringleader of the group that had gathered tonight. If I could get his approval, then the others would trust me as well.

After a few moments, he said, "You cannot show anyone's face. Even if you publish something in America, with the internet, those snaps can get back here quickly. It is not safe to be open here."

"Oh, no." I held up my hands. "I'm sorry. I wasn't planning on taking any photos here. Just some of the Law Garden that I took earlier. It had been so many years since I had seen it, so I wanted to remember it." I shoved my camera in the bag, not bothering to secure the latch.

The man turned around and nodded to the people who stood at a distance behind him. They seemed to relax and went back to whatever they were doing before we'd arrived.

While I wasn't taking any pictures, I wished I could. I mentally framed shots I felt would tell an important story. On my left were two men kissing in the shadows. It would have been a powerful message to frame a shot where the light caught what I considered to be the most important part—both men wore gold wedding bands. Both men had wives and possibly children at home. I could frame the shot so that their faces were indiscernible and there would have been no way to distinguish them from the other Indians running around the streets in frayed jeans and cotton shirts.

I heard a commotion behind me. People began to scream and scatter. I looked over my shoulder and saw six men in khaki-colored uniforms with matching hats on their heads. They had narrowed eyes and nightsticks in their hands. Police. My pulse quickened and my palms grew sweaty. In America, especially after September 11, I'd known to avoid interactions with the police at all costs, and that same philosophy seemed true half a world away. Someone jostled me as he ran past, and I dropped my bag on the ground, the camera tumbling out of it. Before I could reach it, someone grabbed my wrist and tried to pull me away. Biren.

"What the—"

"It's a raid. Come on! Run!"

The police were smirking and yelling things in Hindi. I couldn't understand what they were saying. We began scanning the crowd.

"Where's Samarth?" Biren asked, eyes darting around us. I saw nightsticks rising before they came crashing down. Screams of pain traveled through the cool night air.

Biren began dragging me toward the shadows. "We have to go!"

"Wait! My camera." I started to turn back toward the melee, not wanting to lose the gift I had cherished most from my parents for nearly twenty years.

It was only fifteen feet away and had somehow not yet been trampled by the men darting in every direction. Biren glanced from the camera to me. A pair of cops was heading in our direction.

He pushed me away from them. "I'll get it," he said.

I grabbed onto his arm. "No, I can do this. They're not going to hurt a woman."

I moved as quickly as my legs would allow and snapped up the camera and case by their straps. I began to run back to Biren. His eyes were wide, fear emanating from them. When I was within his reach, I took his hand and we began to run. We'd only taken a few steps when we were both jerked backward by someone grabbing our shirts. We were now face to face with a cop whose thick black mustache was unable to hide his obvious smirk.

"Let us go! We haven't done anything wrong!" Biren demanded as he struggled to push the officer away.

My mind swirled, trying to think of how to get out of this situation.

"He's my fiancé," I said loudly. "Leave us alone!"

The policeman's grip on my arm was painful, my skin smarting at the way he twisted it to pull me closer to him.

"Isn't she a pretty NRI," he sneered at me, licking his lips like a lion about to descend upon its prey. "Except she's a liar. You have no engagement ring." His steely gaze was fixed on my naked left hand. "A pretty girl like you shouldn't be here with these outcasts."

The cruel look in his eyes made my pulse stop for a second. His hand was now gripping my upper arm, his fingers grazing my breast, and I had never felt so uncomfortable or violated. Biren pushed the officer, forcing him to release his grip on my shirt.

Seeing that I was free, Biren said, "Go!"

Acting on instinct, I did as he said and bolted away before the cop could reach for me again. When I turned back, I saw Biren struggling to get away. He towered over the officer, but I saw another one heading toward him. I heard Biren say in clear, loud English, "Do you know who I am? My father is the president of the energy company. He's best friends with the police commissioner. You had better let me go before he finds out how you've been harassing innocent citizens."

Smart, I thought. He was letting the officers know that he was foreign and educated and from an important family, trying to scare them with the ramifications of not letting him go.

"Is that right?" I heard one of them scoff, and my heart skipped a beat.

I would have known how to deal with cops in America, but my legal training was useless in this country, in which I didn't know the laws or ramifications. In America, I would have known to pull out my cell phone and start filming and streaming the video on social media. That would do us no good here.

The one holding him looked in my direction. "What is wrong with your pretty friend? Is she a deviant too? Maybe she likes girls?" He licked his lips in a manner that made my blood run cold.

Biren tried to shrug him off and caught my eye. "Get out of here!" he mouthed to me.

I didn't want to leave him there but had no idea what to do. I scanned the crowd but didn't see Samarth. I knew no one else whom I could turn to for help. I turned and ran toward the crowded expanse of Law Garden.

After making sure I wasn't being followed, I exited from the place we had entered. I was now on the regular roads around the Law Garden, again seeing families with ice cream who had no idea what had just happened. Everything appeared normal even though nothing was. The smell of fireworks hung heavy in the air. Nearby some local children held sparklers, laughing as they danced around the sparks, both fearful of and exhilarated by them.

31

I called Biren's cell phone, but it rang and rang until his voice mail picked up. I kept trying, and eventually it began going straight to voice mail. I wandered around, desperate to find Samarth and Biren. But I never did. Too scared to go back to the street where the raid had been and not knowing what else to do, I eventually hailed a ricksha and went back to Lakshmi, clutching my phone in the hopes Biren would call me soon to tell me he was okay.

By the time I got home, it was after midnight. All the lights were off, so I slunk in as quietly as I could and went upstairs to my room. I closed the door, sat on the bed, pulled my knees to my chest, and continued to try Biren's cell again and again.

My camera, which had once filled me with such joy and had reminded me of a time in my childhood when my parents seemed like they understood me, now seemed to mock me. My fingers grazed the new scratches that had formed when it fell during the raid. Had those few seconds when I went back to get it been the difference? If I had left it there, would both Biren and I have gotten away?

I kept calling until the sun rose around six in the morning. Still nothing. I had to find him. I put on my champals and walked the ten minutes between our houses. I stood outside his gate, waiting for some sign of life from within. I didn't want to disturb his entire family, but I needed to know Biren was safe.

The morning air was cold against my skin, but I didn't care. I must have been standing outside his gate for over an hour. Finally, I saw a servant emerge from the house with some dirty dishes, a signal that someone in the family was awake.

I rang the doorbell, and its cheerful melody rang throughout the interior. The servant opened the door and stepped aside for me to enter.

Anand Uncle was sitting at the dining table with a newspaper. "This is very early for a visit, no?" he said, his eyes kind.

It was hard for me to picture him as someone who wouldn't accept his son's sexuality, but I knew better than anyone how different parents could act with outsiders compared to immediate family.

"I'm sorry. There was something I needed to speak to Biren about."

"Ah, a belated Merry Christmas. Here, it's easy to forget."

I shifted my weight from side to side, relieved Anand Uncle wasn't acting different than any other day. That must mean Biren was fine. "Right, yes. I hope your family had a nice Christmas as well. Can I go up and see him? I promise I'll just be a minute."

His father looked skeptical about sending me up to Biren's room alone. "I think he is still sleeping. It seems he got home very late last night. But you can try."

I felt his eyes on me as I raced up the stairs to reach the upstairs landing. I knocked on his bedroom door, softly so his mother wouldn't hear and come out as well. I doubted she'd be as okay with me trying to talk to Biren in his bedroom.

"I don't want any breakfast, Mum," I heard from behind the door.

"Hey," I whispered. "It's not your mom. Can I come in?"

The door slowly creaked open, and I gasped.

"What happened?" I managed to eke out the words.

Biren had a large cut above his eyebrow and looked like he'd taken some punches—or, God forbid, nightstick blows—to other parts of his body. He walked stiffly and very gingerly lowered himself to the bed.

I went to his side. "You're hurt! This is my fault! What can I do?" Seeing him like this made me cringe.

The light I normally saw in his eyes when he spoke was not there this morning. His expression was vacant. I reached out to touch his forearm, but he flinched and jerked his hand away.

"I'm fine," he said in a monotone.

"You're not fine. Look at you! What happened?"

"I'm fine," he repeated, jaw clenched. Staring straight ahead, he said, "If my mother asks you, last night when we were out, some young kids tried to steal your camera, and I fought to get it back. That's how this happened, okay?"

"Biren, you should report this to someone! Police can't run around beating people up on the streets for no reason."

He turned to me. I saw a hardness on his face I had never seen before. "This is not America. You don't report bad behavior by one cop to another cop. That is asking for more trouble."

He was right. I was thinking too much like an American lawyer. "What did they do?"

Biren's eyes narrowed. "You can see it on my face. He punched me. Then I ran away and came home. That's it."

Everything about his demeanor screamed there was more. "And Samarth. What happened to him? Have you talked to him?"

Pain flashed across Biren's face. "He's fine too." He turned to stare out the window. "You should go now. I hear Mum, and she won't want to find you in my room."

~

It was clear that Biren needed some time to himself, so I made my way down the stairs.

"That was fast," Anand Uncle said.

I startled at his voice. He was still at the dining table with the newspaper spread out before him and a steaming cup of chai next to him.

"Is Biren on his way down?" he said.

I shook my head. "I think he's not feeling well."

"You want to stay for chai and nasta?"

"I should really be going," I said, feeling claustrophobic within these walls.

"Of course, of course," he said jovially. "You know, Biren said you are staying in India for a bit, so I should really like to get your thoughts on some immigration work I do with my charity. When you have time, of course, but I think your help would be valuable."

I nodded absently. "Sure, Uncle. I'd be happy to help." I forced a smile before leaving their bungalow.

After walking aimlessly for a couple hours, I went to the only place that made sense.

Tushar's face lit up when I walked into Happy Snaps. "How was your night out?" he called out.

"Okay," I said, managing a small smile so he wouldn't know something was wrong.

"No work for you today?" he asked.

"Huh?"

"No camera."

He was right. I hadn't bothered to bring my camera with me. There was no way I could have worked today. After what had happened last night, I wasn't feeling particularly inspired or creative.

"No, just came by to say hi."

My voice was not that convincing, but his face lit up just the same. I had to keep up the pretense because there was nothing about last night that I'd be able to share with him.

"What are you doing?" I asked.

He was working at the computer and had dozens of photographs up on the screen. "Trying to finalize the photos from Hari's reception."

232

I sat next to him and watched him quickly scroll over the small images, occasionally finding one he wanted to see in full size.

In my best nonchalant voice, I asked him, "Have you ever been behind the Law Garden at night?"

He shook his head. "Why do you ask?"

"I was at Law Garden with Biren last night. You know, to get some ice cream and meet his friends, but then we saw a commotion behind it with a lot of cops."

He nodded knowingly. "Oh, yes. Maybe you saw the area where the gay men spend time. Police are always trying to catch people there."

"Catch them for what?"

He continued, "They don't talk about it, but I've heard sometimes people go just to teach them a lesson."

I felt nauseous. I feared the answer but asked the question. "What do you mean?"

"I've heard the police sometimes go to show them why what they are doing is wrong." His tone was neutral as he reported his knowledge on the issue, and it was hard for me to know where he stood, but I knew how sensitive this issue was in India, and now wasn't the time to get into an in-depth discussion of his personal feelings on the subject.

As I processed Tushar's explanation of the raids, I thought back to when Biren had first told me he was gay. He'd said that if the police found out, he could be beaten or something much worse. Panic swelled within me as I contemplated what that meant and thought about how he had looked that morning. His body aching, his steps so careful, his spirit broken.

I remained calm on the outside while a little voice inside me screamed. I went to the small bathroom in the back of the shop. I pulled the chain to turn on the light, took one look at myself in the small mirror with the crack in the corner, and leaned over the sink to vomit.

32

When I got back to the bungalow, I saw the door to Neel's room was slightly ajar. Things had been stilted since our fight, but I had to see him. I knocked softly before pushing the door open and then closing it behind us.

I saw the half-full suitcase on the bed. "Are you going back home?"

He shook his head. "Dipti and I talked yesterday, and we agreed I should spend a few days with her at her family's place," he said. "Maybe you were right after all, and staying was best, and this is another step in the right direction."

"What changed her mind?" I asked.

"She didn't say. But she did say you had gone to see her."

He looked at me pointedly, and I worried yet another thing had gone wrong in the last twenty-four hours and I'd messed something up between them too.

"Seems I owe you a thank-you for something because she said as she thought about that conversation, she realized we needed to find a way to the other side of this."

He smiled softly. I could see he was acting as if everything were okay, but it was understandable under the circumstances. *Fake it till you make it* had been our mantra when we first moved to Chicago and were trying to make friends in school. Old habits died hard.

"I also owe you an apology." He raked his hand through his hair.

I sat in the chair across from the bed, knowing we needed this conversation before we moved to the next one.

"It's okay," I said. "You've been going—"

"No." He shook his head. "It's not. I've never been that cruel with you."

"No, you haven't," I agreed. After a long pause, I said, "What hurt most was that I could tell you meant what you said."

He came to me, shaking his head. "It's not your fault that we wanted to protect you. You were the youngest. It was our job to protect you, and it wasn't right for me to throw that back at you. I shouldn't have blamed you for decisions that I made. Sometimes I resented having to carry the knowledge on my own. I couldn't let Mom and Dad know that what I saw was affecting me, and we normally shared things with each other, but I didn't want you to have the burden either, so I buried so much of it."

"I think we all take on a lot of burdens in this family by trying to protect each other," I said, thinking about my conversations with Mom as well.

He half grinned. "Yeah, maybe we do."

"It's going to be a hard habit to kick," I said. "I do it too. Our good intentions have caused a lot of pain, and we need to stop making decisions for each other."

Neel nodded. "I'm always going to be here for you, Pree. No matter what happens with Dipti. She doesn't replace you. I hope you know that."

I smiled. "I think you picked a great wife. And the reality is that she does need to be your number one priority. That's how a marriage works. You shouldn't feel torn between us. It's what I would want from my husband if I ever get married."

"Thanks. But I'm going to work on sharing the emotional stuff with you and Dipti. You were right when you said that I don't do that.

We've all been conditioned to focus on making sure the family is okay and the bills are paid. The amount of stuff we have all repressed cannot be healthy."

"No, but we have finally found something that we all have in common."

Neel laughed. "Guess so. Where have you been hiding out this week? I knew you were probably avoiding me, but I wasn't sure where you had gone."

"I've been spending a lot of time with Biren," I said, my eyes avoiding his gaze.

"That must make everyone happy. If you marry him, the families could unite in a powerful matrimonial union," he said with a smile.

My mood instantly turned somber. While I knew Biren didn't want me to tell anyone about him being gay, Neel could be trusted, and telling him would not put Biren in any kind of danger.

"I need to tell you something private about him," I said, and then told him what happened last night at the Law Garden.

"Is he okay?" Neel asked after I finished.

"I'm not sure. He's distant. I think he was really hurt and is trying to pretend nothing happened."

"Emotionally or physically?"

I took a deep breath. "Both."

"I can't even imagine how lonely he must feel," he said.

"I know. Gives my problems a healthy dose of perspective. I wish I knew how to help him."

"I'm not sure if you can. Guys like to have space. So just give him that, and he'll know where to find you when he's ready."

Giving people space wasn't my forte, but I suspected Neel was right, and I was grateful for his advice.

33

Tonight was New Year's Eve, but it seemed years away from when Biren and I had talked about spending it together at Swiss Cottage. He had not responded to my texts or calls after I'd seen him the day before. When I called his house, his mother said he was at work. Neel had been at Dipti's since yesterday, but his loss was felt instantly by me. I'd never spent a day in India not under the same roof as him.

Knowing Biren needed space, I accepted Tushar's invitation to spend the holiday at Happy Snaps. The photography shop was the only place we could ring in the New Year together without worrying about gossip getting back to our families. I was grateful for the respite even if it had to be in a controlled environment.

I had a bottle of wine that Neel and Dipti had brought in when they arrived for the wedding. Prohibition was in full effect in the state of Gujarat, apart from a small liquor shop at the airport. NRIs could purchase a liquor license upon arrival and buy two bottles of alcohol for personal consumption. Thankfully, my brother and Dipti had bought the maximum allotment when they'd arrived.

Alcohol was to be consumed discreetly, if at all. It was as though I were fifteen years old again when I told Mom, Indira Mami, and Virag Mama that I was going to work through the evening to make sure Hari and Laila's album was ready. I felt smug satisfaction as I stepped out of the house with my camera bag containing the hidden bottle of wine.

The bag rested securely on my lap as the ricksha honked its way through the busy streets. Children with sparklers lit small fireworks that sizzled and erupted strips of confetti. The singed smell of burnt paper hung heavy in the air. Animals on the road hardly flinched at the chaos. For them it was business as usual. I pulled my shawl tighter around my shoulders to guard against the chill.

I had been dreading this night. As much as I believed I was strong and independent, I was self-conscious about being thirty, unemployed, and single. I was anxious about starting a new year with such uncertainty in my personal and professional life, but I was also trying to embrace the feeling. With nothing planned, it meant that anything was possible.

Tushar raced to open the door to the shop while I was still unfolding colorful rupees to pay the ricksha driver. Tushar wore a purple button-down shirt tucked into his black slacks. His pants hung loosely on his thin frame; it seemed the thin cloth belt was the only thing keeping them above his hips. His hair was greased into place with castor oil, the scent more pronounced than usual.

I wondered if I should have dressed up more for the occasion. Because we were just staying in the shop, I had worn my favorite pair of jeans and a long-sleeved red tunic. My family thought I was working, so anything fancier might have aroused suspicion.

We didn't have a wine opener, so I used the handle of a spoon to push the cork into the bottle.

He made a sour face as he sipped from the mug he normally used for chai. "You actually find this taste pleasing?"

I laughed. "Not at first, but you get used to it. Eventually, you can't live without it."

"Your parents know you drink this?"

"Yeah. When I was younger, I was too scared to tell them, but what are they going to do now?" I hadn't had any alcohol since arriving in India, so it affected me quickly. My cheeks began to warm before I finished my first mug.

"Do your parents drink?" he asked.

I had been taking a sip and nearly choked when he asked the question. I wiped my mouth with my forearm before answering. "My parents may have left Gujarat, but Gujarat didn't leave them! We didn't keep a drop of alcohol in our house. They wouldn't even eat food that was cooked with alcohol!"

Tushar raised his eyebrow. "People in America put alcohol in food?"

"Sure. Most of the alcohol burns off." I leaned in closer and lowered my voice in conspiracy. "In fact, I've never told my parents that the mushroom risotto I once made for them had white wine in it. They loved it, so I figured some things were better left unknown."

He shook his head at me—something he did at least once whenever we spent time together. Our lives were so different. He often commented that I was much more outspoken than anyone he had met before.

This was his first taste of alcohol, so, not surprisingly, Tushar was a lightweight. After half a mug of the Jacob's Creek Shiraz, he was back to the friendly banter we'd had that day at the ice cream shop.

"Tell me what you normally do for New Year's Eve," I said.

"We do typical things. Go to dinner parties."

"And what happens at midnight?"

His cheeks reddened, but I wasn't sure if it was from embarrassment or the alcohol. Either way, it was endearing.

"Everyone just says congratulations or 'Happy New Year,'" he said.

I poured more of the cherished wine into my mug. The smell of tangy, spicy grapes warmed me. I breathed in deeply to savor the aroma, unsure when I would have the chance to taste wine again.

"My parents think I'm at a dinner party with my friends," he confessed after he set his empty mug on the wooden table. We had spent many hours sitting around that table examining prints or talking about the books he was reading. Tushar reached for the bottle.

"You've started lying to your parents? How very American of you," I said with a wink.

"Would you rather I go see my friends?" he shot back.

I grabbed his forearm even though he didn't make any move to leave. "It's eleven forty-five. With the Ahmedabad traffic, you're stuck here with me unless you want to be in a ricksha when the clock strikes midnight."

He shrugged. "Western New Year's Eve isn't a big deal to me. It's not like I'd be missing the real one," he said with a wink.

We began to tell each other stories about past New Year's Eves on both the Indian and American calendars and dissolved into fits of wine-induced laughter. Neither of us kept an eye on the clock, so we missed counting down to midnight. We didn't care. It was enough to be with someone and enjoy the company. When I stood to leave around one in the morning, I was emboldened by the wine, so I went to Tushar and hugged him.

"It may not be the Indian way to say Happy New Year, but we Americans have to at least give each other a hug," I said.

Tushar stood stiffly at first but eventually relaxed and squeezed me back. I sank into him before he began to pull away. Our eyes locked, arms still loosely around each other, neither fully letting go. My lips parted. I willed him to bend to meet my mouth. His eyes searched mine before he finally released me.

"It's late. Your family may worry," he said.

I cast my eyes downward and nodded.

34

On New Year's Day, I awoke with an all-too-familiar red wine headache. After my monthlong forced detox since arriving in India, my body was struggling to process it.

"Worth it," I mumbled to myself as I lay in bed with my eyes closed, thinking about how nice it had been to spend time with Tushar and just be two adults talking about our lives.

I felt a bit guilty that he had lied to his parents. It was the type of innocent lie I had told my parents countless times, but Tushar was different, and this type of lie had different stakes for him. But then another side of me appreciated that he had done it for me because I knew the list of people he would have lied for was very short. It was increasingly difficult for me to navigate the waters of a society that did not date in the way I understood. Meaning, they didn't date at all. I thought of my parents and realized I could not have done what they each had done—marry a total stranger. People had serious expectations at such an early stage, and the whole process of getting to know someone was circumvented entirely.

Once my headache cleared, I sent Biren an email saying I knew he needed space but would be there whenever he needed someone to talk to or listen. I checked in with him every day, and he would occasionally send a short response, so I knew he was seeing my messages even if not responding to them all. Neel and Dipti were still fighting a lot, but at least now they were fighting with each other under the same roof and not on their own. There was a certain comfort in that.

A couple days into the new year, Carrie called me and said her case had settled, and she was going to get a ticket and arrive in India on January 10. I could hardly contain my excitement at seeing her in such a short time.

~

Tushar and I didn't speak of the moment we'd shared on New Year's Eve and carried on putting the wedding album together with the utmost professionalism. It seemed we were both trying to heed our families' wishes and keep our relationship platonic. There was so much I needed to share with Carrie when she arrived.

Spotting Carrie coming out of the Ahmedabad airport was easy—she was the only white person amid the sea of brown. Even with her red hair pulled into a ponytail, she was impossible to miss. It was probably the first time in her life she had experienced being a minority. She emerged from the terminal with a look of utter confusion and raised her hand to shield her eyes from the sun.

Men were approaching her, offering to carry her bags or serve as her driver. She kept saying, "No, thank you," not realizing she'd need to be much more assertive if she was going to make it through her India trip. Her pale skin made her an easy mark. Children ran up to her and stopped inches away as if an invisible shield had risen. They shyly looked at her. Those more daring reached out to touch her skin and then giggled as they ran back to hide behind their mothers, covering themselves with dupattas as if that made them invisible.

I stood on the hood of Virag Mama's Fiat and waved wildly until she saw me. Relief registered on her face, and she wheeled her suitcase in my direction. I jumped off the car and gave my best friend a fierce hug while the people around stared openly at us and tried to decipher the context in which this white woman was in Ahmedabad.

"It is *so* good to see you! I can't believe you're here!"

"You and me both," Carrie said as she released me and glanced around her unfamiliar surroundings. "People here are really not into personal space, are they? I've had so many strangers touch me between the customs line and here."

"They're touching you because they've never seen a white person in the flesh before. Be glad you aren't a blonde. People would be begging for a strand of your hair."

Virag Mama had been standing a respectable distance away so we could greet each other privately. I introduced the two. He looked mildly startled when Carrie extended her hand to shake his. She looked at me, her eyes asking if she had done something wrong. I shrugged, not knowing if she had. It was custom for me, as an Indian, to touch an elder's feet upon meeting them, but I had no idea how Carrie, as a foreigner, was supposed to behave.

Our driver and Virag Mama took Carrie's suitcase and hoisted it onto the roof with a low grunt. Then the driver tied it down with yellow string. Carrie's small leather satchel went onto the passenger seat.

"Guess people here are also not into trunk space," Carrie said, gesturing toward the dozens of others who were undergoing the same exercise of tying luggage to the tops of their cars.

I grinned. "There are over one point three billion people in this country. Space is scarce." I held the door open for her to slide into the back seat with me.

Carrie felt the seat around her. "No seat belts?"

I shook my head and laughed. Carrie's expression during the drive was priceless. She gripped the edge of the seat as we swerved around animals and lorries. She flinched with every blast of a horn, and there were many. Her renegade driving style on the 405 was tame in comparison to this. After a few days, she would tune out that sound like everyone else did. As nervous as she seemed about her surroundings, I knew she'd ultimately be glad to have seen India, and I could not have been more delighted to have her sitting next to me.

Her relief was evident as we pulled into the driveway of Lakshmi. The bungalow was calm and inviting, providing a respite from the commotion she had seen on the streets between the airport and home.

Upon our entrance, a pair of guest champals waited by the door. Indira Mami must have left them out for Carrie. She slipped into the house shoes, familiar with the routine of removing her shoes before entering my apartment in Los Angeles.

I tried to rush through introductions with the other family members, but Indira Mami insisted that Carrie have something to eat or drink before sleeping.

"The food on those flights is so terrible. You must be quite hungry," Indira Mami said, bringing out a plate of khari biscuits and a hot pot of chai. Before setting them down, she looked at the traditional Indian snacks and hesitated. "We also have bread and butter if you prefer some toast. Or juice? Would you like orange juice?" Carrie was the first white person to ever set foot in Lakshmi, and Indira Mami seemed unsure of how to act around her.

I sat next to Carrie. "This is fine, Indira Mami. She'll like this."

Indira Mami and Mom joined us at the large dining table. Both poured some tea from the teacup into the saucer to cool it more quickly. Then they slurped from the saucer. Carrie looked relieved to see me drinking directly from the teacup and followed suit.

By the time we got upstairs, the servants had pulled another cot into the room I was sleeping in, and the two beds filled the space. I had to crawl over Carrie's bed to get to mine, but that small room was as close to privacy as we were going to get in this country. Carrie sank onto the bed. If the hard density of the mattress jolted her, she didn't show it. She stretched her long, pale legs and closed her eyes. I sat across from her.

Without opening her eyes, Carrie said, "Jared asked why you quit."

"What did you tell him?"

"The truth. That I didn't know." She rolled onto her side to face me and opened her eyes. "You going to tell me what this midlife crisis is all about?"

I remained silent. Not sure what to say.

"Does it stem from the fact that Alex moved on?"

I felt as if a heavy rock had been placed on my chest. On some level I knew I had thrown myself into life in India to distract from my broken personal life, but that was not the only reason. My time in India had forced me to face emotions that I had buried very deep inside me for a long time. How could I explain to Carrie what it felt like to be an Indian person at a white law firm? To be an Indian person anywhere in America?

"Thanks for coming out here," I said, deflecting.

She held my gaze, not letting me have a pass.

"You know the way you felt coming out of the airport today? Everyone staring at you because you look different?" I sighed before saying, "I've felt like that most days of my life. Around the clock. Without a break. And especially at that firm."

Her gaze dropped to the floor. It was obvious that she was white and I was Indian, but we'd never talked about that during our friendship. I had always avoided talking about race and ethnicity with white Americans, whether it was colleagues, boyfriends, teachers, or friends. I knew it made them uncomfortable, and I had been conditioned to make white people feel comfortable. Assimilation required that above all else, and I had done everything possible to assimilate.

"I didn't realize you felt different there," she said softly. "I've always thought of us as the same."

I managed a half smile. "I know. But we never were. I had to be that reliable Indian workhorse. I had to be the highest biller in our class to prove that I deserved to be there. I had to bite my tongue when

Jared said and did things I disagreed with. Speaking up was a luxury I've never had."

"I disagree with Jared all the time," she said. "He handles it well. As well as can be for a power-hungry narcissist."

"From you. But you are a member of his club. I'm not. I can't draw any attention to myself, so I do everything possible to blend in."

Her face fell. "I didn't realize you felt that way."

"I know," I said. "It's too hard to say these things to white people."

"Do you feel that way with me?"

I pondered her words. "I think I feel that way with everyone who is white. The degree varies, but I have sought acceptance from white people since the day I moved to Chicago."

"I'm so sorry if I did anything to make you feel that way."

"It's the world we live in. I'm only now realizing how much it has affected me. It affected my career choices, my relationship with my family, my friendships, and my romantic choices."

"You mean with Alex?"

I nodded. "I thought a lot about what you said about him."

"I'm sorry if I was harsh," she said.

"It was harsh," I said evenly, "but I have thought a lot about why I was with him."

She looked at me, urging me to continue.

"He was my only serious relationship, but even before that, I was only attracted to white guys," I said. "And I'm trying to figure out why. Was I rebelling against my parents, or was I trying to blend into American society?"

"Maybe both?" she offered.

"I keep asking myself whether I'd still have wanted him if he had all of the same qualities but was Indian."

"And?"

"And I think I give white people more slack. That's the group whose acceptance I needed to succeed . . . in school, at work, in my personal life. If he'd been an Indian guy picking up random shifts for a caterer and trying to write screenplays, I'd have thought he was lazy," I admitted. "I gave him passes that I wouldn't have given people who weren't white."

"I never knew you felt that way. I always thought you were color blind, just like I am."

I looked at her, knowing she meant well. "Only white people say they're color blind like it's a good thing. I've known what color I and everyone around me were since the day I moved to America. When you're not at the top of a social hierarchy, you notice everything about the ones who are. So when a white person says they are color blind, it makes me feel like they are treating me as if I'm *white* rather than what I am. Like I'm not going to be demoted for being brown. It's not the same as saying my brownness is equal to your whiteness."

Carrie met my gaze, her eyes showing that she was thinking deeply about what I had just said. "I hadn't thought about it that way."

I smiled at her. "I know. The greatest privilege of being born at the top is that you never have to think about how to get there."

I could see the wheels churning in her head as my words sank in. "Looks like I need to do some thinking. A lot of thinking."

"Being here has made me reconnect with Indian culture in a way I haven't since I was a little girl. I'd been so determined to be American that I forgot what being Indian even meant."

"You're right about what you said earlier. The way I felt at the airport was the first time in my life that I've ever been so overwhelmed by what I looked like. I can't imagine that you've felt that since you were seven."

"It's exhausting."

"I can only imagine. But I'm glad you said something. I'm sure it wasn't easy."

I smiled at her. "You're the first person I've ever said anything like that to. And you're also the person who made me start thinking about these things and not sweeping them under the rug, so I'm grateful for what you said about Alex. Even though it was harsh. I needed to hear it."

She smiled at me. "I'm glad you are seeing these things. And I'm really glad you aren't seeing Alex as the be-all and end-all of your life. He doesn't deserve that."

She turned to her back and faced the ceiling, and I could see her reflecting on what we'd said.

I turned to her and said, "I know this has been kind of a crisis year for me, and you've been there to help me through it, but I hope you also know that if there's something you want to talk about, I'm here for you. Whatever it is . . ."

She didn't respond, nor did I expect her to. She had always been slow to share the personal things in her life, even to me. But I knew when she was ready, I was the person she would tell.

I stared out the window as her breathing slowed to a rhythmic pattern, the jet lag creeping up on her. I was grateful that, for once, the dogs behind the house were quiet, and Carrie would be able to rest. The exhaustion on her face when she arrived seemed to be from something more than the journey. She was asking why I had run halfway around the world, but I wondered what had caused her to do the same.

35

The next day Carrie woke up early. It would take her a couple days to adjust to the time difference. We waited until dawn and quietly left the bungalow while everyone else was still asleep. I had my camera with me, it having become a habit for me to carry it in case I happened upon something interesting I wanted to make sure I remembered. During my time here, I'd learned that my memories of the country had gotten distorted by how long I had been away from it, and I wanted to be able to bring myself back to these moments, to this culture, no matter where in the world I was or how much time had passed.

"We'll buy you some shoes as soon as the shops open," I said.

Carrie looked down at her flip-flops, standard-issue California gear. "What's wrong with these?"

"Trust me. You don't want to be traipsing around in open-toed shoes all day. The streets are filthy. There's a ton of debris that could cut your feet. Not to mention animal dung all over the place."

She shuddered. "Yeah, let's avoid animal shit and Indian hospitals."

"Agreed." I pulled the heavy front door closed, and we stepped onto the road leading out of the subdivision.

As soon as we emerged from the gate, Carrie gasped. She stared at the shantytown across the street. The inhabitants had a direct line of sight to the posh living quarters within my family's upper-caste neighborhood. "That's pretty fucked up," she whispered into my ear as she looked back and forth between the stark socioeconomic lines.

"I know. Space is a scarcity. It's not like back in LA, where there are entire areas of the city for the poor, rich, et cetera. Here, everything is mixed together. You can't pretend the poor don't exist."

I considered how this scene would appear to someone who hadn't grown up seeing it. For me, straddling the two cultures had been a way of life, and both seemed normal or abnormal depending on the context, but I could appreciate how jarring each would be for someone who hadn't previously experienced it. Tushar would likely look at America in the same wide-eyed way that Carrie was now experiencing India.

There was more activity than usual for this early hour of the morning. Men along the side of the streets dyed giant spools of string into bright pinks and oranges. The string was then coated with a paste of rice flour and ground glass to make it abrasive enough to cut kites from the sky. Nearby, vendors had set up stalls where they were selling vibrant paper kites—patangs—with contrasting colored circles on them, all in preparation for the Uttarayan holiday.

"You picked a great time to be here," I said to Carrie as we trudged along the side of the road. "The annual kite-flying festival is in three days. You'll love it. It's a citywide competition where you try to be the last kite standing."

It seemed as if an electric current flowed through the air as the city prepared for the festival. Smiles were wider, eyes shone brighter, and no one seemed to mind the flash from my camera as I documented the process. Children stood on flat rooftops, flying colorful kites and practicing cutting others with razor-sharp string. Their shrieks of laughter filled the air. People were too distracted to stare at Carrie as much as they normally would have upon seeing a white woman in the city. Even the cows on the street managed to stay out of people's way while they prepared.

"It looks like you're getting pretty comfortable behind that lens," Carrie said after I framed a shot of a little girl swinging a kite around her body as if it were a lasso.

"Yeah, it's been fun to think creatively after so many years of being a lawbot."

"You seem happy doing it."

"I am." I realized that as different and unexpected as my life was from where it had been a few months ago, I was content for the first time in a long while. It was amazing what time and a change of place and perspective could accomplish.

~

The next day, Carrie and I hailed a ricksha and made our way toward Happy Snaps. I had not seen Tushar since Carrie had arrived. Inside, we found him tying bright-orange string to a royal-blue kite with a yellow circle on it. The paper was so thin it seemed like a strong wind could have ripped right through it, but I knew looks were deceiving. Indians had turned kite making into a science many generations ago, and not much had changed over time.

"You too?" I asked with a smile on my face.

"Uttarayan is my favorite day," he said as he stuck his thumb in his mouth to suck the drop of blood that had emerged from the latest string-induced cut.

It had been many years since I'd flown a kite, but I still remembered the cuts from the string when we flew kites as kids in India. Those sharp pricks made needles seem tame.

"I see your friend has arrived," he said. His eyes had the same shiny reverence as the eyes of the children who had wanted to touch Carrie's skin at the airport.

Introductions were made, and I gave Carrie a tour of the shop, which really meant showing her the darkroom and some of the prints I had put together for Hari's wedding album. When we emerged from the back room, Tushar was still working on his kite.

"Need help?" I asked.

His head was bent low while he focused on creating the perfect knot. "You will be cut," he murmured, the end of the string dangling from his mouth.

"I'm not such a delicate flower," I said, rolling up my sleeves and sitting at the counter.

Carrie raised an eyebrow.

Tushar shrugged and pointed to another kite on the floor near his feet. This one was purple with a white circle on it. I picked it up and watched the way he worked the string so I could mimic his method.

Carrie pulled up another stool. "Okay, I can't just watch you two work on this. Toss me one of those."

Tushar passed Carrie an orange-and-pink kite and a spool of string. She watched Tushar as he meticulously made knots.

"Where do you plan to celebrate?" he asked.

I pulled string off a third spool, this one neon pink. "Ow!" I said, sticking my index finger in my mouth. The metallic taste of blood mixed with my saliva. I hadn't even tied my first knot before cutting myself.

Tushar laughed and shook his head. Carrie joined in until a second later, when she pricked her finger on the spool.

"Karma," I said jokingly, before turning my attention back to Tushar. "I don't know. Neel and Dipti are going to spend it with her family. Carrie and I will probably just do whatever my cousins are doing. Or maybe Biren has some plans."

Tushar looked up, horrified. "You have not planned this day?" His eyes grew wide.

Clearly, this was his version of Fourth of July, Christmas, and his birthday all rolled into one.

"You must come with me, then," he said. "Both of you. Each year, we meet at my kaka's house. The location is good. Lots of nearby kites to cut."

"Cut?" Carrie asked.

Tushar turned toward me, astonished. "You have not told her about the festival?"

"She just got here! Give the girl a minute to adjust," I said in protest.

Tushar faced Carrie. "You are in for an exciting time. Ahmedabad is the kite capital! You see, kite flying used to be a sport for kings. But now it is something *everyone* enjoys."

The way he emphasized *everyone* made me conscious again of our caste- and class-based differences.

"What's the cutting you were talking about?" Carrie asked.

Tushar had a glimmer in his eye as he spoke. "This string, you see, is special. Very sharp. Glass particles are glued onto it, so when you are flying kites, you can cut the strings of other kites. The goal is to be the last kite in the air."

"Oh, so it's like *The Kite Runner*," Carrie said.

Tushar slapped his palm to his forehead. "Oy! Americans!"

His tone was exasperated. This was the most animated I had ever heard him. I couldn't help but smile as this lighter, more playful side emerged.

"Okay, it is *similar* to the novel, but there is a great significance in India. It is the day of the year when the sun travels north, marking the decline of winter. It is the day that signals the awakening of the gods from their deep slumber," Tushar said.

"That's interesting." Carrie turned to me. "Why didn't you tell me any of that?"

I shrugged. "Because I didn't know it."

"So, you will join us then?" Tushar asked again.

After the ice cream shop debacle, I hesitated and wondered how my family would react.

Tushar looked at me. "This is the one day no one cares."

Carrie's face registered confusion at his comment. I gave her a look to convey that I would fill her in later.

To Tushar, I smiled and said, "We're in."

36

Tushar had been right. The camaraderie of Uttarayan seemed to transcend caste boundaries. Virag Mama drove Carrie and me to Tushar's kaka's house without any warnings or disapproving looks. It was only three miles away from Lakshmi, but with the traffic on the roads it took nearly forty minutes. These days were public holidays, and it seemed everyone in the city was rushing to get somewhere for the festivities.

When we pulled up to the house, Virag Mama nodded with approval. "This is an excellent location for cutting."

I looked up, and my jaw dropped a little. The morning sky was a kaleidoscope of swaying, colorful diamonds. I had never been one for kites, but the laughter floating from each rooftop and the streets below was infectious. I was eager to launch my kite into the rainbow overhead.

"That's awesome!" Carrie typically gave off a disinterested vibe, but today her face had a youthful exuberance I had never seen before. "Let's do this!"

Virag Mama waved as he maneuvered back onto the congested street. "Cut a lot of kites. Make the family proud!"

I smiled at Virag Mama's comments. Today really did put a pause on caste-based norms. All anyone seemed to care about was the kite festival. I could have spent time in public with a beggar if I had wanted, and I wondered if anyone would have looked twice.

I told Virag Mama we would take a ricksha back when we were done and grabbed the turquoise-blue kite and pink spool Bharat had given me the day before. Carrie held her own pink-and-orange kite—the very one she had tied herself in Happy Snaps.

The doorbell made a loud, hollow sound like a gong. A little boy who couldn't have been more than five years old opened the door holding a gooey piece of tamarind candy between his fingers. Before I could tell him who I was, I heard footsteps running behind him, and the door opened wider, revealing Tushar's enthusiastic face.

"Come in! We're already on the roof," he said, stepping aside so Carrie and I could enter.

"Don't you look very American?" I pointed at his jeans. It was the first time I'd seen him in anything other than the formal slacks he always wore to Happy Snaps.

He laughed. "It's important to be comfortable for cutting."

The little boy grabbed for the kite I was holding.

"No, Jayesh. This is not for you," Tushar said in a stern but kind voice.

The boy pouted momentarily but then stuffed the candy in his mouth, his smile returning.

The house was small, much smaller than Lakshmi and far simpler in its decor. The living room was set up with mattresses on the floor and takias against the wall as backrests. They did not have the Western-style furniture that Virag Mama had at Lakshmi. We went straight to the stairs and made our way up.

As in most of the houses in Ahmedabad, the staircase led up to a flat roof where people could gather. The roof provided a giant outdoor space with a three-foot-high wall around the perimeter. About fifteen of Tushar's relatives and family friends were sitting in brightly colored folding chairs. Some had spools of string at their feet and kites flying in the sky; others were sipping chai and munching on nasta.

Tushar's mother rose from her chair to greet us.

"We are glad to see you again. It is wonderful to meet your friend from America. Would you like a Thums Up?" she said, offering Carrie and me chilled glass bottles.

"Thank you, Kanta Auntie," I said, taking one, the outside moist from condensation.

Carrie nodded and mumbled a soft thank-you as well.

I noticed Carrie grew more subdued around Tushar's family, but it was also the first time I was seeing her this far outside her comfort zone. I sensed that after our conversation, she was taking in the feeling of being an outsider and really trying to understand it for the first time.

I took a swig from the Thums Up bottle. The cola was much sweeter than its American counterpart, and the carbonation burned my throat.

We accepted our plates of nasta and began munching on the snacks.

"Whoa!" Carrie began sucking down her soda after taking a bite.

I saw that she had bitten into one of the fried jalapeno peppers.

"You're going to want to taste everything carefully. Some of it is pretty spicy," I said.

Carrie finished off her soda. "Your warning is a little late."

After getting Carrie a lassi to soothe her tongue, Tushar introduced us to the rest of his family. They were very welcoming, and all seemed to know in advance who Carrie and I were.

Tushar, Carrie, and I stood near the edge of the roof, chatting and pointing out unique kites in the sky.

Carrie pointed to a string of kites that looked like Chinese lanterns. It seemed no one was trying to cut those. "What are those box-shaped ones that are all on the same string?"

Tushar's gaze followed her finger. "Those kites have small electric candles in them. When the sun sets, the lights will look like stars."

"People don't try to cut them?" Carrie asked.

Tushar gestured toward the hazy sky. "You see all of this pollution? We would do anything to see stars even if they are not real."

Seeing them unlocked some memories of beautifully lit box kites, and I couldn't wait until nightfall to see them again and have the benefit of supplementing my mental images with actual photos.

Jayesh snuck up behind Tushar and began tugging at his jeans. Tushar leaned down so Jayesh could whisper something into his ear.

"You can ask her yourself," Tushar said to him, rising back to his full height.

Jayesh held Tushar's hand and looked at the ground. He shuffled his feet while Carrie and I watched, amused.

"Go ahead," Tushar prodded.

Jayesh raised his head. He pointed at Carrie and said, "Can I touch your hair?"

I stifled my laughter. Carrie hated people touching her, especially children.

"Oh, um, yeah, sure," she said, awkwardly kneeling until she was at his eye level.

Jayesh reached out his hand. "Why is it the color of the Thums Up label?"

Carrie chuckled. "Because I'm Irish and never had a chance to have pretty dark hair like yours."

He pondered her answer and broke into a shy smile. He nodded before scurrying off to his mother and hiding in the folds of her sari.

Tushar, Carrie, and I broke into laughter as soon as Jayesh was out of earshot.

"I am sorry," Tushar said. "He is not used to seeing people who look like you."

Carrie shrugged it off. "I get it. Not a lot of red hair and freckles around here."

She became much more comfortable and relaxed as we chatted while watching cut kites flutter to the ground. Children in the streets chased after them, their laughter floating to the rooftop.

"California Girl, do you know how to fly a kite?" Tushar asked me, picking up a spool of string. His eyes shimmered. I wasn't sure if it was from the sunlight or his sheer excitement. I had never seen him radiate such joy.

Carrie, never one to miss an opportunity to tease someone, jumped in before I could answer. "That's cute. You have a nickname for me already."

Tushar's cheeks reddened.

"It can't be that hard," I said, playfully grabbing the spool from him. "You can do it, right?"

His eyebrows shot upward. "Let's hope you fly kites better than you take photos."

I slapped his arm. "I can't believe you went there."

My eyes darted to his parents, making sure I hadn't been disrespectful by touching him. Thankfully, they seemed more interested in the kites flying overhead. It seemed that on Uttarayan societal formalities were abandoned.

With an expert flick of his wrist, Tushar's orange kite caught the wind and began soaring upward. As it ascended, he released tension on the string, allowing the kite to glide up through the crowded sky.

Never one to be outdone, I confidently dangled my kite from my fingers and flicked my wrist the way I had seen him do. But rather than flying up to join Tushar's kite, mine fell to the floor with a faint tapping sound as it landed against the cement rooftop.

Tushar and Carrie laughed, and after a second, I couldn't help but join in.

"Now do you want help?" he asked.

Defeated, I nodded. Tushar handed his spool to Carrie so she could take over flying the kite. He showed me how to dangle the kite from my fingertips, flick it up to catch the wind, and immediately release the spool. After a few attempts and some more pointers, my turquoise kite was sailing into the sea overhead, the thin paper making a flapping sound against the gusts of the wind. My palms began to burn from the friction of the wooden spool handles rotating in my hands as more and more string released.

"Pull it back!" Tushar yelled. He used his hand to shade his eyes from the sun as he followed my kite into the air.

I held the spool in my left hand and wrapped my right fingers around the glass-laced string to stop my kite from traveling any farther. The string made tiny cuts in the pads of my fingers, but I didn't care. As the wind floated through my hair and the sun kissed my face, the only tension I felt was that on the kite string.

"Careful!" Tushar called, reaching out and jerking my spool toward him. "Someone is trying to cut you."

Sure enough, a bright-red kite was closing in on mine. Tushar yanked the string with a few sharp jerks. The kite caught a breeze, and he maneuvered it out of harm's way.

He laughed. "If you take your eyes off for even a second, someone will come. Let me show you how to go after those people before they can come to you!"

He taught us the tricks of kite cutting—releasing the string as fast as the spool would allow when two strings were tangled, or pulling it in quickly. As he showed us his skills, I saw kite after kite spiral downward from the sky and into the arms of children running along the streets collecting the fallen soldiers.

Jayesh brought Tushar a yellow kite to launch into the air, so all three of us now had warriors in the sky.

I saw Tushar's kite, so I stealthily steered mine in his direction.

"What is this? You try to cut your teacher's kite?" His eyes shone as he said the words.

Our strings were now intertwined high above the building. "You taught me well."

I tried to cut his kite using the release method he'd taught me earlier, but he guided his kite to the safety of higher air. He then looped his string back and was in prime position to cut mine. I tugged on my string, frantically trying to move my kite away from the danger zone. Out of the corner of my eye I saw him glance at me and then ease up on his string, allowing my kite to cut his. We watched his yellow kite swirl headfirst back toward earth.

"Got it!" I shouted.

"You have learned well," he said.

We both ignored the fact that he had let me win.

I noticed Carrie staring at us, a question in her eyes.

37

After a traditional dinner of undhiyu, Carrie and I took a ricksha back to Lakshmi. Box-lantern kites lit the night sky, soft glowing steps leading to the heavens. Fireworks crackled around us, and sparks fell on the road as we swerved through the streets. The air was heavier than usual, thick with the scents of incense and burnt paper. Street vendors added the aromas of fresh roasted peanuts and sugary fried jelabi to the mix. Scraps of fallen kites littered the road like confetti, fluttering around with the light airiness of snowflakes as cars and rickshas cruised past.

When we arrived back at Lakshmi, my relatives were still on the roof. Two lines of neon-pink string stretched upward. Bharat was still flying kites despite the darkness. Carrie and I joined my family on the roof and rehashed stories of our day at Tushar's. Virag Mama was impressed Carrie had caught on to kite cutting so quickly and ended up with twelve kite war victories on her first attempt.

Exhausted, we retreated to our room after half an hour of small talk with the family. As soon as I flicked on the dim yellow light overhead and closed the door to our small bedroom, Carrie turned to me.

"Now I know why you wanted to stay here!" she said.

"It's not what you think."

Carrie kicked off her house champals and sat on the bed. "When you told me your relatives freaked out because you were friends with a boy from a lower caste, you didn't mention that you were *friends* in the Indian-mom sense."

I dropped onto the mattress and folded my legs under me. "Nothing has happened. Really. Can you imagine? I'd be going from a guy like Alex who my parents didn't approve of to someone *all* of my relatives wouldn't approve of."

"From where I'm sitting your parents have wanted nothing more than for you to marry an Indian guy, and it seems like there's one who's interested in you—who you actually like—so what's the problem?"

"The damn caste system." I shook my head. "Tushar's family is from a lower working-level caste—farmers, animal herders, et cetera. People from his caste work for my family, not date them. It would be taboo. For both of us."

"You don't believe in any of that stuff. Or about doing what Indian society expects. You were living with a white guy a few months ago."

"I know. I think it's bullshit. People are people. But my relatives believe in that. And more importantly, so does Tushar. He's never left India and doesn't want to. He has to play by these rules. It's not like someone's going to pat him on the back because he was able to 'date up.' His family would be worried about jeopardizing their working relationship with my family and about their reputation in the community." I sighed, the frustration clear in my own ears. "It's too complicated."

"Does it have to be?" she said simply.

I pondered her question. "If I were only thinking about myself, then no. But if I'm thinking about Tushar, his family, my family, et cetera, then yes. And here, I need to be. It's a collectivist culture for a reason, and I can't waltz in and spread my American individualist attitude around without thinking about the repercussions."

"That's an interesting way of thinking about it. Guess I've never had to think about anything other than an American individualist attitude, but I suppose I will add that to my growing list of things to reflect on."

She looked lost in thought before adding, "I'm really glad I came out here."

"Me too. I couldn't believe you did, though. This isn't exactly your scene."

"No, but when you suspect that your best friend has gone crazy, you make exceptions."

I raised my eyebrow. "You know I'm fine, right?"

"I do now. Having seen you here for a few days, I'd even say you're better than fine."

"And what about you?" I said. "Are you also fine?"

She sighed. "I'm fine," she said unconvincingly.

We sat in silence for a few moments. The light from the full moon shone through the small window overhead. It was propped open, so we could hear the Uttarayan celebrations continuing at the nearby homes. The sky still had kites swaying in the wind. Dogs barked wildly at the commotion.

Carrie broke the silence and said, "My dad had an affair."

I whipped my head to face her. Carrie's expression was somber. She clenched the bedsheets in her hand so tightly that her knuckles were white.

Mr. and Mrs. Bennett had served as surrogate parents to me during these past few years. I was convinced their marriage was everything my parents' marriage wasn't—happy, balanced, successful. If my mind was reeling from the news, I couldn't imagine what Carrie was going through. Guilt instantly surged through me as I registered that I had been halfway around the world when my best friend discovered this and needed me most.

"When did you find out?"

"Three weeks ago. Merry Christmas to me!" she said sardonically.

"He told you?"

"No. My mother did."

"I'm so sorry." I cringed at the thought of Mrs. Bennett having to explain such a thing to her daughter. At least that was something I'd never have to worry about with my parents. They'd be way too worried about the karmic ramifications of such an act.

Carrie released the bedsheets and folded her arms across her chest. "She's not leaving him. She's not even going to tell him she knows."

"Are you going to say something to your dad?"

"I don't think I can. It's my mom's decision to make, right? I want to slap him, though. It was with the human resources lady at his company. Ugh, how cliché. Just like all the disgusting partners we know who are banging their assistants on the side." She shook her head. "It was killing me to be there and pretend life was normal."

I sat next to her and put my arm around her shoulders. She didn't flinch when she felt someone touching her. That's when I knew how much this was affecting her.

"I would have come back if I had known what was going on," I said softly.

"Yeah, I know," she said. "I didn't want you to do that. And there was so much going on here with your family. Guess when it rains it pours." She chuckled half-heartedly. "Getting away and out of my comfort zone was good. And this is *very* far outside of my comfort zone."

I managed a small grin. "True. But you're doing great. You even impressed my mama with your kite-cutting skills. That isn't easy. He fancies himself a semiprofessional."

Carrie wiped her nose.

A few moments later, she said, "I'll get over this. I have no choice. I know that. But you don't expect your parents who are in their sixties to suddenly have marital problems after so many years together. They seemed so damned happy and normal."

I thought about my own parents. I couldn't recall a time when they had seemed as happy as the Bennetts. My parents accepted each other's company, but that seemed to be the extent of their feelings toward one another. I'd grown up never knowing anything different, and I didn't think they even aspired toward anything more. The result of growing up in a culture where romantic love wasn't expected was just that—you didn't expect it, so you weren't disappointed if you didn't have it.

"Since I've been here, I've been thinking a lot about my parents' lives, and there is so much I don't know about them. I guess the same is true for everyone. We'll never know what your parents' relationship is really like because they'll always try to shelter you from the bad."

She nodded slowly. "At least we get to pick our friends."

I gave her a hug. "Me too. Friends are the family you choose, right?"

After a few moments, she laughed and playfully pushed me off. "All right, enough human contact for one day!"

I squeezed her tighter before letting go.

That night I couldn't fall asleep. Carrie was emotionally spent and fell into a deep slumber. I lay in bed for a long time, thinking about what she had said and about how she had been carrying the burden alone for a few weeks. I thought about love and the role it played in relationships. Arranged marriages were based on loyalty, commitment, and shared family values. I'd always thought that wasn't enough by itself. That happiness required Western love. Now, I wondered if maybe the Indian way was enough. I felt like everything I knew—or thought I knew—was being tested.

38

Carrie was still asleep when I woke up the next morning, so I quietly crept out of the room, wanting her to get as much rest as possible from the burden she'd been carrying. I made my way across the street to the vendors and began perusing the candies and confections. In a straw basket that the sales boy handed me, I collected an assortment of Milka and Cadbury chocolate bars, Smarties, sugar-coated fennel seeds, and tamarind candy. It wasn't the sour gummies or licorice ropes that Carrie sustained herself with typically but was the closest Ahmedabad could offer to give her a taste of home. Carrie lived off candy, and in her short time in Ahmedabad, her sugar intake was the lowest I'd ever seen.

I noticed two young children loitering nearby, watching me, their clothes smudged with dirt and their expressions wishful as I filled my basket. I looked down and felt guilty that I could easily put whatever I wanted into it and have it billed to my family's monthly account. I grabbed four more chocolate bars before letting the sales boy tally my items and add it to the ledger. I stepped out of the shop and handed the older of the two children the four chocolate bars. His eyes bulged as he took them from me. His little sister looked wide eyed as he handed her one. I wondered what these children's stories were. How had they ended up in the life that they now led? My childhood challenges in America paled in comparison to what so many children in India dealt with for much of their lives. I considered whether these were the types of families Anand Uncle's foundation helped.

When I returned to the bungalow, Carrie was sitting up in bed and scrolling through her phone.

"Sleep okay?" I asked.

She nodded. "Surprisingly so. Felt like I was in a coma."

I sat on the bed next to her. "Unburdening that extra weight may have helped. When it comes to emotional stuff, better out than in, right?"

She looked at me sheepishly. "Not sure any of us are good at that. Maybe that's what makes us good lawyers," she said. "Being dead inside seems like an asset to the trade."

"Maybe," I said, laughing. "But I'm hoping to become less good at that. Never too late to learn to be human. Maybe we can encourage each other to share the stuff that we are so used to burying."

She looked at me. "Sharing isn't my forte."

"Nor is it mine. But I hear this whole life thing gets harder the deeper we go into adulthood, so now feels like the right time to make a change. Pretty sure life isn't done handing us shit yet."

She laughed. "Doesn't seem like it."

"But before we have to tackle the next challenge," I said, dumping the contents of the plastic bag onto the bed between us, an impressive and colorful array of candy and confections that would have rivaled any great trick-or-treat haul, "I got you a breakfast of champions!"

Her eyes lit up as she reached for a purple Dairy Milk bar. "Perfect timing. I was worried my emotions were a symptom of the withdrawal I was having! This should lock everything back up nice and tight."

I swatted her playfully before going to get myself some khari biscuits. A breakfast of sugar was Carrie's thing, but definitely not mine. As I walked toward the stairs, I found the door to my mother's room slightly ajar, and I poked my head in to ask her if she wanted me to bring her chai or biscuits on my way back. She sat on the bed, sifting through some photos. The box next to her was different from the ones I'd seen in Indira Mami's locked cabinet.

"What are those?" I asked, joining her.

Her lips curled into a nostalgic smile, as if by holding the photo she could transport herself back to that moment. "Indira Mami found these pictures of you and Biren from when you were little. When we lived in this house." She handed one to me. "Isn't this funny?"

It was an image of Biren and me when we were five years old. It was the infamous photo of us wearing matching little girls' chaniya cholis, mine red, his yellow. We both beamed into the camera, him a head taller than me even then. Even at that time, our parents had joked about our arranged marriage, and I couldn't help but wonder if he'd known at that young age that he was gay.

"Why were you looking for this?" I asked.

"Oh, he didn't tell you himself?"

"What?"

"Biren's mother called us yesterday. They found a girl for him, and he agreed to be married. His mother wanted some childhood photos of him to show at the engagement party."

I felt like I'd been slapped in the face. *No, he didn't mention anything. Because he knew I would think it was crazy.*

My mother continued rummaging through the pictures, avoiding eye contact with me. "Seems you waited too late," she said pointedly, even though I could tell she was trying to sound neutral.

Still reeling from the shock, all I could manage was, "This is nuts! Are you kidding?"

"What's so crazy about a nice-looking, educated boy from a good family getting married?"

"He doesn't want to marry her," I said through gritted teeth.

"How should you know, hah? Have you met her? Do you know anything about her?"

"I don't need to know anything about her."

268

Mom sighed. "Preeti, if you are upset, you have no one to blame but yourself. You cannot wait forever and expect everyone else to do the same."

"I'm not jealous!" I said, frustrated she thought that was the issue.

"Then be civilized and be happy for him," she said in the tone she reserved for when she thought I was throwing a tantrum for no reason.

"I can't be happy that he's throwing away his life because of the pressures of this damned culture!"

"Simply because you choose to be alone does not mean something is wrong with the rest of us, hah. This culture has a rather successful marriage rate."

"Sure, no one divorces, but how many people are happy? Let's start with you." The words flew out of my mouth before I could stop them. It was like being in court again, and I was arguing on instinct without worrying about how the listener would feel.

Her face hardened. "Biren will probably be happier with this girl than you will be if you keep living like this and end up alone."

I threw up my hands. "You wouldn't understand."

"What is there to understand, yaar?" she said. "He's getting married, and that's final."

I struggled internally, wanting to tell her and make her understand, but I knew it wasn't my place. Especially now that he was getting married. These were not matters that were taken lightly in Ahmedabad. This wasn't a "cold feet" culture, so announcements were almost as good as nuptials. That was also what made the engagement photo I had seen of my mother such a big deal. Something like that would have been a huge scandal. I knew if Biren was engaged to this girl, they would be married, and that would become his life.

My mother handed the photograph to me along with some others. "You should take these to him."

~

Biren's father answered the door, his smile from ear to ear. "You have heard the news?"

I pasted on a smile. "Yes, Uncle."

He clapped my back, his excitement unbridled. "My son is getting married! It is about time, no?"

I nodded politely.

"Sorry, I am getting ahead of myself. Can I offer you some chai? Nasta? Mithai?"

He moved into the house and gestured for me to follow him.

"My mother asked me to give this to Auntie," I said, handing him the envelope with the photographs.

"She is out sharing the news with her ladies' circle. She is so happy." He went to place the envelope on a ledge near the kitchen and then turned around as if he'd just remembered something.

"You know, the lawyer in New York who I was working with has taken her maternity leave. I simply cannot follow all of the different laws and things that are asked of us for the application paperwork. Could you find some time to help me this week?"

"Of course, Uncle. I'm sorry I haven't followed up sooner. I'm not an expert in this area, but I would love to help you, and I can ask friends back in the States who are more experienced for the things I cannot figure out on my own. I think the work would help me as much as it would help you!"

He clapped his hands together. "Great! It is settled then! I would pay you, of course."

Before I could protest the payment, he called out for Biren to come and greet me. Jobs for someone with my background were so simple in India. That he knew my family was enough and took the place of the multiple days of job interviews that I had undergone to get my job at FLF.

Once Biren came downstairs, we had a few pleasantries with his father before going outside, where we could get more privacy.

"What are you doing?" I asked, once we were alone in the garden outside his house.

His eyes still had a hollow look to them, and I wondered if they'd ever get back their sheen.

"My parents have been suggesting girls to me for quite a long while. It's time I grow up and move to the next chapter."

Next chapter. His words were familiar; Hari had used the same ones when he and I had spoken about his arranged marriage when I had first arrived.

"Biren, this is a prison sentence for you," I said gently. "What about Samarth?"

"What about him?" he said too quickly. After a pause, his voice softened, and he said, "We haven't spoken much since that night. We both agreed the risk was too high to pursue anything."

After making sure none of his family members were watching us, I put my hand on his arm. "I know what happened that night was bad. *Really* bad. But do you really want to give up your chance to ever be happy? To find someone worth taking that risk for?"

He scoffed. "That's what you don't understand. This is India. People like me don't have that kind of chance, so I'm not giving up anything." His eyes flashed with anger. "You run around here thinking about love and ignoring the caste system, but the rest of us don't have that luxury. We have to grow up and be adults."

I flinched. When I'd learned he was gay, I'd wanted to help him find a way to be happy. He was so amazing and deserved at least that much, but I hadn't appreciated the trade-offs that came with it for him.

"I'm sorry," I said, feeling the weight of the words.

"The best I can hope for is a normal life where people don't look at me differently, one where I don't bring any shame upon the family. Getting married will accomplish both."

"You have nothing to be ashamed of," I whispered.

His hard expression crumbled, and his eyes glistened. "You should have seen my mother's face when I told her I was ready to accept her last suggestion. She was moved to tears. I'm an only child, her only son, and it is up to me to carry on this family's good name."

He glanced at the house. We could see his father directing their servant to tidy things inside. I moved my hand and slid a few inches away from him so we wouldn't be close enough to arouse any suspicion. After all, he would soon be a married man.

Tears now shone in his eyes. The first sign of genuine emotion I'd seen from him in weeks. "I love my family. In life, everyone makes sacrifices. This is mine."

"Are you sure? Are you really sure you can't have both?" I asked.

He stared into the distance. "No one gets to have everything they want in life. That's true no matter where you are. Every day we make choices."

"But isn't this a huge thing to give up?"

His expression softened a bit. "I thought about it a lot. I've always thought about it a lot. You and I have spent time in the West, and over there, romantic love is everything. It is worth sacrificing every single thing in your life and seems to be the great path to happiness, right?"

I nodded, thinking of the conclusion I had come to that, if I had to choose, Alex was more important than my family.

"But what if there are more paths?" he said. "Our parents never dreamed of romantic love in the way the West teaches us. Our parents' generation was focused on love of family. They found happiness a different way. Even our generation for those raised here, right? Think of Hari and Laila. My parents don't have burning passion for each other like a Hollywood movie, but they support each other and have developed a relationship that will last for their entire lives. They know they will have each other until one of them dies. How often does that happen in America? A lifelong partner means something different here, and maybe it can be something better."

I pondered Biren's words. He was right. The Western notion of romantic love was not a universal truth, god-given right, necessity, or prerequisite to happiness in many other parts of the world. There were many cultures, like the Hindu one, that prized familial love above all else, and that was the path to happiness. I thought about my choices thus far in life. I had chosen Western values, including Western notions of love, and had not contemplated anything different. But could I say that I was fully happy with where I was in life right now? I assumed all immigrants to the West adopted those views like I had, but seeing Biren, who had flirted with those values and ultimately decided to come back to his Indian roots, was novel for me. I saw how earnestly he wanted to have a close relationship with his parents, and how not having that would make him less happy than not having a romantic partner.

"You're right," I said. "Every life involves sacrifice. I have always had my blinders on, and while I hoped I would never have to choose, I knew I'd choose a romantic partner over my family. It's what I've done in the past, and it's what I've become accustomed to." I smiled at him. "But it's not the only way. Having a safe, healthy, happy life surrounded by your family and friends sounds pretty great too. May even have less drama overall. My quest for romantic love hasn't led anywhere great so far . . ."

His eyes met mine, and I saw both the appreciation for the support and the apprehension at the unknown that he was moving into.

"She could end up being your best friend," I said.

He nodded. "She could . . ."

"I mean, not better than me," I said.

A small laugh escaped his lips, and it lifted my spirit. I hadn't heard him laugh since the night of the raid. It would take time, but I hoped he would be okay. I hoped this new person in his life would be the support he needed in whatever path he chose.

"If she's awful, divorce isn't great, but at least it's not as taboo as it once was," he said.

"Also true," I said. "You have more options than our parents had forty years ago. And if at any point you change your mind, whether before or after the wedding, that's fine too. I'm here for you on any path you choose."

Walking back from Biren's house, I wondered how many of the people I passed were living a secret life. How many had been pressured—or scared—into a marriage, career, or lifestyle? Or were they more like my parents and Biren and had made the choices that were right for them? It was likely a combination of the two. No culture was perfect, and no culture had a guaranteed path to eternal bliss. Certain Western values, like romantic love, seemed too deeply ingrained in me to be on Biren's path, but during my time in India, I was finding more appreciation for the nuances between the different types of relationships around me. Had we never moved to America, the reality was that I would not have developed this desire for the Hollywood romance either. I'd have been like Hari and Laila, or my parents before them. I realized how much I was now a product of the place in which I had been raised. I couldn't change that aspect of myself any more than I could have changed my caste or skin color, and I didn't even know that I would want to change that part of me despite the heartaches I'd suffered in the past.

39

When I returned to Lakshmi after seeing Biren, I was surprised to find Dipti's father's car parked in the driveway. It had been over a week since I had seen Neel, and I was excited to tell him about Uttarayan and the first few days of Carrie's trip. I bounded into the house and found Neel, Dipti, and her father sitting in our living room with my mother, Virag Mama, and Indira Mami. They were all having chai served in tiny Corelle mugs that my mother had brought over from America. Indira Mami used those mugs only on special occasions like engagements, weddings, or when guests were visiting from the States and she wanted to impress them. I'd never seen them used when it was just family in the room.

"What's going on?" I said, flipping off my champals and heading toward the couch to sit next to Neel.

Mom motioned for Gautam to bring a mug of chai for me, and he silently scampered off to the kitchen.

Neel looked at Dipti and smiled at her before turning to me and saying, "We are ready to go home."

Relief washed over his face, and it was the most calm and happy I'd seen him since arriving in India. Dipti managed a small smile as well. My mother, Virag Mama, and Indira Mami were beaming.

"That's great news!" I said, knowing that while they had a long road ahead of them, the saga that had unfolded while in India was coming to an end.

Neel's smile grew wider, and he touched Dipti's arm. I could see she was still conflicted about leaving the country where her daughter had died. Uma would always be remembered, but I was glad Dipti had chosen her life with Neel over the death of her baby. They would be okay, and seeing them begin the journey ahead filled me with such peace. I felt that no matter how uncertain my future was at the moment, life would unfold as it should.

"When are you heading back?" I asked.

"As soon as we can pack up and get tickets," Neel said. "Planning for the day after tomorrow."

Mom clapped her hands. "This is wonderful! Looks like we can all go home now!"

She was right. We had all stayed for Dipti and Neel, and now that they were heading back, there was no reason for any of us to linger on. It was time to get back to our lives. It was time for her to get back to my father and resume their normal routines. And it was time for me to go back to Los Angeles and figure out what my life would look like going forward. I could fly back with Carrie. It was logical. It made sense. While I had begrudgingly stayed in India because Neel needed me, as I thought about leaving, I realized that part of me had needed India. I had gotten used to my life over the past month. Going to Happy Snaps, reconnecting with photography, getting over Alex, developing a friendship with Biren. I was excited about working with Anand Uncle. All those things had happened seamlessly without me even realizing. I had felt comfortable and present in this country for the first time since I was a little girl. I hadn't been worried about the day-to-day grind or the corporate ladder or figuring out what my future should be. I had stopped being conscious of my skin, and even a few weeks of that had been liberating beyond words. When I had stopped looking for answers, it seemed I had found some. But then my thoughts went to Tushar, and I realized some questions remained. My stomach sank. After a couple days, I might never see him again. I wasn't sure what that meant for me or for him, but I knew I would miss him.

I went upstairs and found Carrie in the small room we were sharing. She had made an impressive dent in the candy stash I had left her with earlier in the day. She was pecking away at the keyboard on her work laptop, so I knew the Warden had sent her some "urgent" task that only she could do from her vacation halfway around the world even though there were hundreds of lawyers in the Los Angeles office.

"Looks like I'm heading back with you," I said, flopping onto the bed.

She stopped and looked up at me. "Really?"

I nodded. "Neel and Dipti are ready to go home. So that means there's nothing keeping me here either."

She glanced at her computer. Two new emails had come in during our small exchange, each with the telltale red exclamation point that had once made me jump to the ready like Pavlov's dogs. She held up a finger gesturing for me to wait while she sent off hurried responses.

"You don't seem that excited to head back," she said.

"No, I am." My voice trailed off, and I fidgeted with the rajai on the bed.

"That's convincing." She laughed and then said, "Are you sure there's nothing keeping you here?"

"Of course. I've never spent a day in India without my mom and Neel. It makes sense for all of us to go back together. That was always the plan."

She shrugged. "Plans change."

Sure, sometimes they did. But I had always been someone who stuck to the plan, and that was how I survived. Fit in with the American kids after we immigrated. Get a job in which I didn't have to worry about financial instability. Commit to Alex because I had said I would, even if it meant losing my family. I wasn't one to deviate from the plan.

Carrie looked at me in the way that only a best friend could—with compassion, understanding, and pity all blended together.

"Go talk to him," she said.

I made a move as if I was about to object, but then stopped myself. She was right.

I was about to fly down the stairs and out the door and hail a ricksha when I heard Dipti call out to me. She was in the room she and Neel had shared before she'd moved out and was collecting her clothes that she had brought for the wedding but never worn.

I leaned against the doorframe and tried to keep the angst out of my voice. "Do you need help with something?"

She shook her head. "I wanted to say thank you."

"For what?" I asked.

"For not giving up. On me, and on Neel."

I moved closer to her. "There's nothing to thank me for."

Dipti managed a half smile. "I doubt any of that was easy for you."

"It was easier than you think," I said. "I've seen what you and Neel have through such a different lens while we've been here. I was too stubborn to see it before, but I see it now. You'll always have my support."

I tried to be present in what she was saying and not let my mind wander to where I needed to be.

"Are you okay?" Dipti asked. "You seem . . . I don't know . . . jittery."

I tried to calm my nerves. "I'm fine. Just didn't realize we were going to be leaving so soon, so trying to wrap some things up."

"You mean with that photographer?"

I froze and looked at her.

She laughed. "Come on, I'm grief stricken, not daft! What wedding album could possibly take this long to put together or require a late-night session on New Year's Eve!?"

I wrung my hands together.

"Don't worry. I haven't shared my suspicions with anyone. People have been so distracted by other things that you've managed to stay under the radar."

"Thank you," I said, the tension subsiding a little.

"It will be our secret. I hope you get whatever answers you need."

As I rushed down the stairs, I knew Dipti would eventually be okay. That *they* would be okay, and it propelled me forward as I bounded out of the bungalow.

The ricksha ambled through the traffic at the same pace as the lackadaisical animals crowding the streets. The horns from the cars and the people yelling from the cycles and lorries were deafening. I willed the sea of traffic to part and let me continue on my way to Happy Snaps, but the ricksha moved as if it were slogging through wet cement.

All I cared about was getting to the shop. I hardly noticed the exhaust around me or the swirling dirt that normally irritated my eyes. Thirty-five minutes later, I threw some rupees at the driver and nearly tripped over my feet as I scrambled out of the seat.

The little bell above the doorway chimed when I went barreling through. Tushar was at the counter tending to a customer, so I tried to collect myself. He looked at me with curiosity blended with irritation at my raucous entrance. It did not help that the elderly lady in his shop made a show of clearing her throat, annoyed by the NRI girl who had just bounded into the shop as if she owned the place.

Slipping behind the counter, I waited while Tushar rang up the woman's order. She seemed to move more slowly than a cow in traffic, counting out her coins on the counter to pay for the prints. I began tapping my foot. Tushar shot me a warning glance. I mouthed the word *sorry* to him and put my hand on my knee to control the bouncing.

"What is wrong with you?" Tushar asked when the bell to the front door chimed after the woman left.

"Me?" I felt my cheeks flush, suddenly shy.

"Why are you acting so strangely?"

"I . . . I . . ." I felt myself getting flustered. I had wanted to talk to Tushar, but now that I was standing here facing him, I wasn't sure how to begin. I crossed my arms over my chest, unsure of what to say.

I felt silly, like a high school girl who couldn't string together a sentence in front of a boy she liked but with whom she also knew things would never work out. We would not be the first people who flirted with dismissing the caste system, but it had persisted for thousands of years, and it was clear that it would continue to exist for thousands more. I started to turn away.

My skin tingled when Tushar touched my shoulder. "What is wrong?"

His hand on my shoulder made me feel tainted, dirty, against the purity of his worried expression. A reminder that above all the other obstacles that would be in our way, I was *damaged* in the Indian sense. Even someone of a lower caste wouldn't want me, knowing I'd dated other men.

I was torn, and then before I could stop them, the words tumbled out of me. "I came to say goodbye."

"Goodbye?" He stared at me blankly.

Yes, this was the right thing. To just leave and not think again of the moments we had shared. Nothing could come of them anyway.

I forced a smile onto my face. "Yes, Neel and Dipti are ready to go home, so we're all heading back."

"I see." His face dropped, showing concern, and something more—much more. I felt the same current between us that I had on New Year's Eve and Uttarayan.

In an overly polite tone, I said, "I just wanted to come here in person and—and thank you for everything you've done for me while I've been here. I've learned so much from you."

"I suppose it's easy for you to just go back home then," he said.

His face turned to stone, and he looked hurt. I could see he felt like he had been a mere distraction to me, something to pass the time before I returned to my real life. I wanted to correct him, but what could I say? It was best for both of us to move on and back into the social circles in which we belonged, to play the roles we were born to play.

"I guess there's nothing left to keep me here," I said, intently watching his reaction.

Even though all logic told me to just say goodbye and leave, I still longed to know what was really going through his mind. But what had I expected from Tushar? To tell me to stay the way I had tried to get Alex to stay when he first brought up New York? Did I even want that? We both knew the caste system would never let us be anything more than what we were. He was the only son in his family. It would shame them if he didn't abide by the customs. That was why he'd become my closest friend here and nothing more, right?

He looked me in the eyes, and I held his gaze. His lips pressed together as if he wanted to say something more. I leaned forward, urging him to voice whatever he was thinking. I wanted—no, *needed*—to hear it.

The familiar ring of the bell above the door sounded, followed by champals clomping against the floor. A customer.

Whatever moment we had was lost. He shook his head, wiping away the remnants of whatever thoughts he had been having.

"You will be happy back at home," he said.

He sounded so distant. Tears stung my eyes, but I couldn't let him see them.

I nodded half-heartedly. Then I dashed out of Happy Snaps. Among the throngs of people sauntering along the street around me, I'd never felt so alone. But it was clearer than ever that there was nothing left for me in India and it was time for me to go back to Los Angeles.

~

I walked around the city for a couple hours, taking in the sights that had felt so foreign upon my arrival but now felt comfortable and familiar. I wanted to breathe in the smells, memorize the sounds and buildings, because I wasn't sure when I would be there again. By the time I returned to the house, I knew I wanted to talk to my mother about what had happened with Alex while I'd been in India. I'd been thinking about my conversation with Biren, and it had opened my eyes to the choices of my parents. I wanted to clear the air between my mother and me so we could pave a path forward. She deserved to know that I now thought perhaps she had been right all along, and I wished I hadn't shunned everything Indian in favor of everything American. I wanted to balance the Eastern and Western cultures in which I had been raised, and not have to choose one to the exclusion of the other. It would be a new chapter for both of us, but I was ready to turn the page and hoped she was too.

Gravel crunched underneath my feet as I opened the gate to the driveway. Fluorescent lighting shone through the windows of the living room and parlor area. An unfamiliar black Maruti was parked in the driveway. It was too old and worn to be a relative's car. Mentally exhausted, I opened the front door with every intention of saying a polite hello, sneaking past the guests, and pulling my mother aside.

I was taken aback upon seeing Tushar in the living room sitting with Mom, Virag Mama, and Indira Mami. Carrie sat on a corner of the sofa looking uncomfortable. The mood was tense.

"Tushar? What are you doing here?" I asked.

His eyes glistened with hope before he shifted his gaze toward his lap. His expression was much softer than when I had seen him earlier. Everyone else was focused on me. Mom's expression was weary, and her lips were set into a thin line. Virag Mama looked angry. The smell of cardamom and cinnamon from the chai hung in the air.

Mom gestured for me to sit. My instincts told me to back out of the room and pretend that I had never walked in, but obediently, I did as she indicated and sat between my mother and Carrie.

"Do you know why Tushar is here?" Mom asked.

I scanned Tushar's face for an answer, but he offered nothing. I wondered if his parents had somehow found out about the wine Tushar and I had smuggled into the shop on New Year's Eve. Perhaps the old lady in the shop had complained about the way I'd been acting earlier. I thought about Tushar's father being angry with him because of something I had done and felt sick. I slowly shook my head.

"He has come to ask our permission," Virag Mama said matter-of-factly.

"Ask permission?" I said. "For what?" I could not have sounded more American as the words flew out of my mouth.

Out of the corner of my eye I could see that Carrie wanted to slap some sense into me.

The tips of Tushar's ears looked red, like they were burning up. I searched his face. Then I realized what was happening. *No, it can't be.* It didn't make any sense. My father's words rang in my ears like the repetitive ding-dong of a bell tower chiming twelve o'clock: *First you marry, then you date, then you fall in love. First you marry, then you date, then you fall in love. First you marry . . .*

Tushar's face was expectant, and mine softened in response. I didn't think he was in love with me, but I could see he wanted to be someday, and for him, that was enough. It was probably more than he had expected from the woman he would marry.

For me, this was a far cry from wanting a kiss on New Year's Eve or even in his shop a couple hours earlier. A marriage proposal came after time spent together and feelings of love had formed. None of that had happened for us. This was a crush! Crushes hardly ever led to marriage in America. With him sitting in my family's living room, I knew I was not ready for this—not even close. Regardless of whatever feelings I was or wasn't having for him, I'd never thought he'd be willing to break out of the caste system, and I would never have asked him to. Especially after seeing everything Biren had gone through, I realized how deeply ingrained this culture was in those who were raised here.

I felt helpless as I stared at the room full of people who, in turn, were staring at Tushar and me. I hated being forced to consider this with my relatives sitting there. This tradition that allowed families to be present for what should be a very private and intimate moment in a couple's life was totally impractical.

A couple? What was I thinking? We could hardly call ourselves that. We had never kissed or displayed any intimacy toward one another. I reminded myself that this was a crush. Could I ever agree to a marriage proposal without having dated? I turned to my right, where my mother remained quiet. I realized this was exactly what she had done when she had agreed to marry my father—except she hadn't even developed a crush—and now appreciated how terrifying it must have been for her.

Surprisingly, given the forces working against Tushar and me, I did not find myself saying no. It scared me that I was actually thinking about his proposal rather than dismissing it instantly. I stared at Tushar, trying to find some meaning in his eyes, something to show whether he genuinely cared for me so much that it was worth going against society, or whether he was just worried that he might feel that way after I returned home and this was the best way to keep me in the country.

"Tushar, maybe you and I can talk in the other room," I said.

Indira Mami and Virag Mama immediately tensed at the impropriety of my suggestion.

Mom was used to seeing far more improper things from me, so she didn't balk. "Let them talk for a few moments," she said.

I squeezed her hand to thank her.

Tushar and I went to the room that had been Nana's bedroom. It now served mostly as a prayer room. The adults probably felt more comfortable knowing we'd be under the watchful eyes of Bhagwan. After closing the door, I waited for Tushar to offer me some explanation.

"I know this must seem odd to you," he said.

"Odd doesn't even begin to describe it. I just saw you, and you said nothing to me."

His face looked sunken and gaunt under the harsh yellow light of the single bulb dangling from the ceiling. The smell of sandalwood from a burnt stick of incense lingered in the air. A small clock sat on a table, ticking off each second.

He avoided my eyes. "I'm sorry. After you walked out of the shop, I realized I could not let you go to America. Not without considering me."

I threw up my hands. "A marriage proposal is a hell of a lot more than asking for consideration."

"You know the way our culture works."

Our culture. He said it so matter-of-factly. Was I part of this culture now? Did he now see me as the same as him and not NRI? It was so confusing when I was on the inside and when I wasn't.

"You hardly know me," I said.

"I know you are different from girls I've met here. I know you have a good heart."

I sighed. "I'm different because I wasn't raised here."

"Of course, I know you are American," he said. "But you are Indian too."

I looked at him. "You make it sound so easy."

"What?"

"Like I belong to two places. Like I can be both Indian and American."

"Is it not true?"

I shook my head. "Everyone wants it to be that simple. That immigrants have two homes and can seamlessly pass between them. I don't feel that way. I feel adrift. Like I'm an outsider wherever I go."

He moved closer to me. "You are not an outsider to me."

"Why didn't you tell me any of this before? When we were alone and could have discussed it privately?"

Tushar was clearly hurt by my tone.

I dropped onto the bed. "Sorry." I stared at the tiles. After a long silence, I said, "How could we ever agree to marry without dating?"

"I know that will be hard for you, but that is the way here. I can convince my parents to have a long engagement so you can get used to the idea. We can try to get some months maybe?"

"Oh Bhagwan, your parents! Do they even know you're here?"

He ran his fingers through his hair. "Not yet, but I think they will suspect."

"Fantastic. So, you're ready for both of our parents to disown us? And then what? We'd live here in Ahmedabad? I'd never fit in here long term!"

Tushar pointed to the dupatta I had been twirling between my fingers. "You already belong here."

I looked down at the blue panjabi top I was wearing over my jeans. Matching bangles on my right arm, a yellow-gold watch on my left. He was right. If I didn't say a word, then I might have passed for a local. Certainly, more than when I had first arrived. But that was the problem. I was still American, regardless of what people saw. Or at least part of me still was and always would be, and that was more American than he was used to.

"How long have you been thinking about this?" I asked. "You had the chance to kiss me on New Year's Eve, and you didn't even try."

"I never thought something like this was possible. As you said, there will be many challenges, but from you I learned to follow my heart."

I sighed. "I didn't mean you should go against your family. Our situations are different. Rebelling against your parents isn't who you are."

Before he could respond, we heard the sputtering sound of an engine nearing the house, and then the gong sound of the doorbell. I opened the bedroom door and peered out.

"Who could be calling now?" Indira Mami shook her head as she shuffled toward the foyer, her champals making a soft clipping noise against the marble.

"Maybe the driver?" Virag Mama offered.

Our family's driver often slept in the car outside Lakshmi if we needed him to work early in the morning.

When Indira Mami greeted the visitors at the door, it was clear that it was not the driver.

40

Tushar's parents exchanged their polite namastes with Indira Mami before coming into the living room.

Tushar leaped forward. "We must go," he urged them.

They glared at him. Bowing to my uncle, Tushar's father said, "Sahib, we are very sorry for our son's behavior. Tushar is acting against our wishes. We did not mean to disrespect your family."

"What is the meaning of all this?" Virag Mama said to him. "We have been nothing but kind to your family for so many years, and this is how you repay us?"

Tushar's father and mother bowed again. "Sahib, we are here to stop this. With your blessing, we will make sure no one will ever know of this unfortunate incident."

Virag Mama continued, "You know how this will look. She is unmarried. The only girl on this side of the family. What will this do to her reputation? To ours? How can we handle this type of scandal?"

His parents' eyes were cast downward.

My mother intervened. "Leave them, Virag. This is between the children, not us."

My heart leaped at her defending me and encouraging us to make our own decision. It was what I had always wanted from her, but in this moment, I just wanted to diffuse the tension for Tushar.

"Of course this is about our family! This is not your precious America," Virag Mama said to her. "You may have forgotten, but we do things differently here."

I could see my mother start to boil at her younger brother getting in the way of her parenting of her child. I had seen that resolute look on her face many times over my lifetime, including when I had misbehaved, when I had gotten a lower-than-expected grade in school, and when she had found out about Alex. When my mother got that look on her face, she would not back down.

"No, it's not. Because in America they would have dated and could have found out they were making a mistake *before* the marriage," she said.

Virag Mama's eyes grew wide. "You permitted her to *date* in America?" It was an accusation rather than a question.

"Perhaps we all should have done that! Then it would not have been too late to know if we married the wrong person." She looked pointedly at him and Indira Mami.

Tushar's parents scrutinized every inch of me, as if determining if I was a papaya that was ripe.

Tushar's mother stared at her son. "Tushar, this was bad enough when we learned your plan. You did not tell us she was one of those damaged girls from America! Let's go right now."

In an instant, I had gone from being too good for their son to being unacceptable because they now knew I wasn't pure.

My mother stepped toward his. "It is not appropriate to come into our house and insult my daughter."

I couldn't believe she had said that. We had gotten to the point where my mother was willing to defend me, without worrying what people outside our family would think, even when she didn't agree. I had waited my entire life for that.

Tushar's mother lowered her voice. "Madam, we know your past. I do not know why your family does not abide by our customs, but our family's reputation is still pure. I do not want to cause you trouble, but I do not want my son to marry someone with these values."

"It's not as if we are trying to arrange their marriage," my mother said to his.

Virag Mama wagged his finger. "Not arranged. We do not approve of this." He swept his arm wide around the room. "Any of this."

Tushar whispered to me, "Do not confuse your past with your future. Think about what I said. I'm willing to take the risk if you are." Then, louder, he called out, "We are leaving."

He ushered his parents out the door and, before closing it behind him, cast me a small smile. One that had the hope and possibility of a life I had never before wanted and had never even considered. A life that was not part of my plan, my mother's plan, or anyone else's.

41

The next morning, I texted Tushar and asked him to meet me at Happy Snaps before it opened so we could talk. I had spent the night talking to Carrie about his proposal, and then when she had fallen asleep, I had stared at the ceiling thinking some more about it. He was asking me to do what my parents had done, Virag Mama and Indira Mami, their parents before them, Biren. What would have seemed completely crazy a couple months ago seemed less so now. I understood better that a Hollywood romance wasn't the only path to marriage or even happiness. There were many paths, and it was a matter of choice.

When I opened the door to Happy Snaps and heard the familiar chimes, I realized how much this place, and Tushar, had given me. Tushar was behind the counter, bags under his eyes, and I knew he had not slept either.

"Hi," I said, shy for the first time around him.

"Hi," he said, running his fingers through his hair nervously.

"How were your parents?" I said.

He shook his head. "As expected."

I nodded, making my way toward him. "What you did yesterday . . ."

He met my gaze, his eyes searching mine.

"It was really brave," I said. "I know it wasn't easy for you."

He shrugged as if it was no big deal. "You would fight the same for something you want, no?"

I nodded. "I've spent my whole life fighting for the things I want. The truth is that fighting all the time is exhausting." I went closer to him, until we were just a couple feet apart from each other. "I don't want you to have to go through that."

His face fell as he realized what my answer was.

"Tushar, you have taught me so much about myself in these weeks we have spent together. And I have loved getting to know you. But what I've learned most is that I'm still trying to figure out who I am and what I want. You've already done that work, and it's not fair of me to pull you along while I go through this process."

"But that's what the marriage is for, no? A partner to help you with those things?"

I smiled at him wistfully. "Some things need to be done on my own. I don't know if I can give up the type of love I grew up dreaming about. That part of me is still very Western. It might change—I've seen how differently people think about marriage here—but it also might not. If we lived in a different time and place, maybe we would date and see how we feel about each other after a year. But we don't. And that is not possible. For me, if we get to know each other after getting engaged, and if it isn't what I want, I don't think I can go through with it out of a sense of duty or familial love. Not yet. Maybe not ever. And a broken engagement will have a more lasting impact on you than it will for me. I can go back to Los Angeles and pretend it never happened. But you . . . this is your home. I cannot be responsible for taking that away from you."

"You don't think you can love me that way?" he asked.

My eyes glistened. "I don't know. But I'm not ready to agree to marry someone before I know if I am in love with him. And that's just not the order in which things are done here. You shouldn't have to change for me."

He let my words sink in. "So, your answer is no."

Softly, I said, "It has to be. If I don't know who I am yet, then there's no way you could know who you are marrying."

We weren't together, and had never dated, but it was a breakup all the same. Emotions had been on the line. For him, more than they ever had before.

"So, that's it now? You will go back home?"

That was another thing I had thought about while lying awake last night. My time in India wasn't done yet. I needed to understand India today and continue to update the memories I had from my youth. I couldn't escape the parts of me that were Indian any more than I could the parts of me that were American, and I needed to be in India to find those missing pieces.

"I'm actually going to stay a little while longer after my family leaves."

His eyebrows shot up.

"Anand Uncle has been asking me to help him with the foundation. He needs an American lawyer, and I think it would be good for me to do some legal work that is meaningful and see how that feels."

"How long will you stay?" he said.

"I'm not sure, but at least a few months. Certainly through Biren's wedding so I can help him with anything he needs. I don't think India will be my permanent home, but I'd like to understand that part of myself better before I go back. And it sounds like the work with Anand Uncle can be done from both places, so I can be trained here and then continue it when I go back. Working a job with reasonable hours will also give me the chance to continue with photography. I want to do more with everything I've learned from you."

"You'll still come here?" He gestured to the shop around him.

"Only if you want me to," I said. "I'd like if we can be friends, but I understand if that's not possible. I want you to be happy." I met his gaze. "I'm so sorry for any pain or hardship I've caused you. With your family too. I did not realize how hard it would be for me to navigate that part of the culture in Ahmedabad."

"Your way is certainly different from ours," he said.

Ours. I was back to being the NRI. "I'm so sorry. I wish I could offer you more, but please know I never wanted anything bad to happen to you. And everything will be fine between our parents. I'll make sure of it with Virag Mama."

He offered me a half smile. "Thank you. My parents will be happy to hear that. As for me, I think it will take a little time before we can be friends. You are learning this culture, but through you, I've learned a little about another way to live as well. I'll need to think myself about those differences too."

"You can read some books about it," I said, trying to lighten the mood.

He laughed. "Yes, you are right. I will probably read some books about America and not go there."

"I'm not sure you need to," I said. "You're already home."

I looked at him, his gray shirt tucked into his black slacks, the smell of castor oil in his hair, and tried to freeze that moment in my memory. He had helped me see myself, my family, and the world differently, and what words were enough to convey gratitude for that? I didn't know if we'd ever be friends, or if I'd ever see him again after this, but I hoped I would. I hoped that he would grow the store until he could afford a larger home for his parents. More than anything, I hoped he would find the right wife, partner, and life that he deserved to have.

~

When I returned to Lakshmi, I saw my mother in the garden on the bench swing, gently rocking it back and forth. The warm weather had given way to cooler temperatures. A wool shawl was pulled tightly around her shoulders to keep away the chill. She was deep in thought, and I approached her carefully. Dried grass crackled beneath my champals. She motioned for me to sit, and I did. My legs were stretched out ahead of me, taking over the rocking motion, so she could curl hers onto the swing and relax. I recalled how on past trips I had been too short to reach the ground and needed someone else to sit with me to move it. We both stared ahead of us at the lavish home we had once lived in and the flowers and greenery surrounding it.

Finally, she said, "I was engaged before I met your father."

I turned toward her. She continued to stare into the distance, silent. I opened my mouth, but no sound came out. It was probably best because, even though I'd been steeling myself for this conversation, now that it was here, I didn't know what to say.

"You're not surprised?" Mom asked.

"I found a photo a few weeks ago, and I suspected."

She nodded carefully. "I had a life before you kids. Before this marriage." Her jaw was set, firm.

From her tone, I could not tell whether she regretted the life she had chosen—the one that included my father, Neel, and me. I steadily rocked the swing while I waited for her to continue.

"He was supposed to be a good man. A doctor. We met in college. He proposed after. It was going to be a real love marriage," she said, a wistful smile crossing her lips. "The first in our family."

"What happened?"

"His family had more money than us and did not approve. Before our wedding, they convinced him to marry someone more appropriate."

Now I understood the forlorn look in her eyes. My mother had once been in Tushar's shoes. She also felt like she had been in mine when I was dating Alex.

"Preeti, life is not easy when people who are different choose to marry. At least for me, we still looked the same. Even though the families did not approve, we still had the same skin color. Our caste difference was slight and not obvious, and not as great as between Tushar and you." She turned toward me and put her hand on my thigh. "In India people notice those things. If you are with Tushar, they will always know he is lower caste when they compare his dark skin with your wheatish complexion. And if you date people like Alex in America, people there will always think white is better."

She had revealed a depth I had never known in her. Even though I disagreed with her logic, I understood that for all those years, right or wrong, she was trying to keep me from the fate she had suffered.

"Do you think the world has changed since that time?" I asked.

She sighed. "Who can know? What Tushar did yesterday would not have happened when I was your age, so some things have changed. I worry that if you marry Tushar, you will still have the same difficulties that were there forty years ago, so then how much has really changed?" After pausing for a moment, she said, "And with Alex, do you think that the differences did not matter?"

I smiled ruefully. "If you had asked me before this trip if our different cultures were a factor, I'd have said no. But I think that was naive. Race, caste, whatever you call it, is always a factor."

She raised her eyebrows.

I continued, "I think on a subconscious level, I believed Alex was the final step in my assimilation into America. Being with him made me think that I had made it. That I had transcended all of the disadvantage that came with being Indian if I ended up with someone like him."

"You mean, if you ended up with someone who *looked* like him. Someone white."

I slowly nodded. "But I did love him. I was willing to give up everything for him and for that love."

In the distance, we could hear the chaos from the Ahmedabad streets, but within the garden walls, it felt serene and calm.

"I have to tell you something about him." I took a deep breath, knowing we could have no more secrets between us. "After Hari's wedding, I called Alex, and I was ready to go back to him."

She raised an eyebrow.

"I thought love was enough, and I knew it meant I would lose you and Dad, but I saw him as my future and had to choose him. But then I learned he had moved on to someone else, and what I thought we had wasn't really that strong after all." My voice caught in my throat. "I am so glad that he had moved on because now I know he wasn't worth losing my family over. He wasn't worth losing you. If that is the price of love or assimilation, then it's too high. I'm just so ashamed that I couldn't come to that conclusion earlier."

My puffy eyes met her composed ones, marking a generational divide: I had never learned to bury my emotions the way my mother had—and I didn't want to.

"Come here, beta," she said, putting her arm around my shoulders and pulling me closer.

It seemed she was beginning to understand she had to let me be my own person, and then I would learn life's lessons in my own way. I stared ahead as tears flowed down my cheeks and dripped onto her shawl. These tears were more solemn, somehow older, than the ones I had shed in the past. They were the type my mother had shed on the few occasions when I had seen her cry: the day her own mother passed away, the day my father lost his job, and the day of Uma's funeral.

"It was hard to watch you making such a big mistake," she said.

I sniffled and cleared my throat. "Despite how things turned out, I don't think of Alex as a mistake. I learned from that relationship; learned so much about myself. Sometimes you have to let me make my own choices even if you think they're wrong."

"It's hard for you to understand unless you have children. It is my job to protect you. I wanted your life to end up better than mine—for you to find a respectable man who will not cause the society to gossip about you. Someone who will take care of and protect you when your father and I no longer can. That is our job as your parents."

The swing creaked while we both processed what the other had said. A warm breeze blew through the garden. Mom moved her arm from around my shoulders and adjusted her shawl.

"If we had stayed in India and you and Neel had been raised here, the family would have found someone more suitable for you." She played with her yellow-gold wedding ring, twisting it around her finger in an endless loop. "That was the life I was brought up in. I had no choices. Marriage was a business contract between the families. Love was never a factor. And when it was, it ended up poorly." She faced me. "But you were right earlier. We are different people, and these are different times." The swing creaked softly as it moved back and forth. "Have you decided to accept Tushar's proposal?"

"Would it matter to you if I did?"

Her mouth set into a line. "It may not be easy for us, but we will try."

It was honest and was the best she could offer. It was more than I'd ever gotten from her before, and I knew I had to accept that.

After a few moments, I said, "I told him no."

She raised her eyebrow. "How did he handle it?"

"Like the respectable man he was raised to be."

She nodded.

As I thought about Tushar and what he would have given up for me, I understood how my mother had felt about Alex. She thought the sacrifices were too great, and now I realized she had been right. I couldn't let Tushar make the same mistake I once had. His family and culture were too important to risk for something and *someone* who was so unknown to him. I could not put him in the same position my mother had been in and end up with a broken engagement.

"Marrying Tushar would not be fair to him," I said. "I need to understand myself before I can marry another person. Any other person."

She looked at me. Understanding oneself and one's identity didn't factor into marriage decisions in India, especially when she'd been getting married, so my words were a novel concept.

"How did you learn that your engagement was broken?"

A wry laugh escaped her lips. "When I heard he was engaged to someone else ten days after ours had been decided."

I gazed at her. "He didn't even tell you himself? How awful! What a coward. I'm sorry that happened to you."

"We cannot control other people," she said. "But yes, he was exactly that!"

"I went to Happy Snaps and told Tushar in person," I said. "With the apology he deserves for any problems he will face with his family because of me. He did nothing wrong, and I needed him to know that."

A smile warmed my mother's face. Even though I'd always assumed she wanted to see me married at any cost, I now sensed I had made the decision she'd quietly preferred. "I'm proud of you for recognizing that."

"You were right too. I was naive to think love alone is enough. A sense of culture and family are important as well. Those things never go away, even if you try to ignore them. I realize they are a part of who I am, and even if my future partner doesn't have the same background, he has to respect and appreciate mine just as I would his. You can't trade in your culture for another. A leopard doesn't change its spots, as Monali Auntie would say."

We both stared ahead, lost in our thoughts.

After several minutes, she said, "I didn't realize how hard it would be on you kids."

"What?" I asked.

She sighed. "Going to America."

I stared at her.

"I had never left India before it. Everything I knew of America was from television. I could not have known." Her face fell as she said the words. "I thought we were doing the right thing." Her voice broke. "Especially for you."

"I don't think you did the wrong thing," I offered, not able to imagine a different life than the one I'd had. I reflected on my life and experiences up to that point, and a moment of clarity shone through. "I don't think you realized that I couldn't be both a traditional Indian girl like you were used to seeing here, and a successful American. I had to choose one. In America, they are mutually exclusive. And I saw how much we struggled as a family for money when we first arrived, and I knew I had to choose professional success. That meant I had to immerse myself in that world if I had any hope of surviving. Everything in my life has been about making sure I could do that and be able to help our family. All I ever wanted was for you and Dad to not have to worry about money and us the way you did when we were little."

She pondered my words, her expression changing as if a fog was lifting for her as well. "We've all made a lot of sacrifices for this family. I did not know that the Great Melting Pot forces immigrants to make that choice. That it would force you to make it."

"It didn't feel like a sacrifice to me. It felt like the only choice. It's the same one I would go back and make again if I had to." I'd realized that the only way I could succeed in the way that I wanted to for my family and the way I felt they needed me to was to distance myself from the values that my parents held so dear. America didn't allow immigrants who retained their home cultures to be accepted as American. The only way to be convincing in the workplace was to transition into American values and customs and hold them as your own.

She let my words sink in. "Maybe we were both naive. We cannot understand what we do not know."

"Do you ever wonder what your life would have been like if your first engagement had gone through?" I asked. "If you'd stayed here and never left India?"

"There is no need to worry for me. My life is as it should be." She turned to me and put her hand on my leg. "If that marriage had gone through, I would not have you and Neel. And maybe that man and I wouldn't even have developed the deep friendship that I have with your father. Chetan and I did okay in the end. It's not Hollywood love, but we love our kids and respect each other. That is what marriage should be. At least, for us."

I smiled, basking in the warmth of the moment.

She patted my leg. "We should stop idling. Things will get hectic as we rush to pack to go home."

I felt heavy as she mentioned the flight.

"There's something else I want to talk to you about," I said. "I'm not ready to go back. I want to stay in India longer. I've been gone for so long, and I really need to understand this part of me again."

She raised her eyebrows. "You've never been here without me."

"I know, but it's time I discover my own India."

"What about your job? What will you do for work?"

"Anand Uncle asked me to help with the foundation. The lawyer he works with is on maternity leave. I think it would be nice to help other immigrant families get set up. Give them the help we never got. And I can keep working on my photography while I'm here. This is the most creative and inspired I've ever felt."

"You'll just stay here?" she asked. "Maybe I should stay with you then . . ."

I shook my head. "You've protected me long enough. I need to take this next step on my own."

I looked at her face, trying to read her expression, but it was impossible to do so. I hoped she could understand this latest decision.

After several minutes, I said, "Mom, are we going to be okay?"

Without even a moment's hesitation, she said, "Yes. Preeti, we both made mistakes before, but we are starting to understand each other. I understand you need to do this for yourself. I may not understand why, but I see that it matters to you. Following tradition is what I have always known, but it may not be the answer for you."

I replayed Mom's words while inhaling the floral scents of jasmine and roses from our garden. For the first time, the silence between us was comforting, relaxed. In the background were the sounds of honking cars, barking dogs, and vendors blowing whistles. I smiled when I heard laughter from children strolling along the road outside the subdivision.

It had taken me this long to realize how lucky I was. My mother and I had butted heads for as long as I could remember, but it had never stopped me from chasing happiness and had never stopped her from loving me. Even though we disagreed, I didn't have to hide who I was from her, like so many other Indian kids did with their parents. Mom didn't understand all my decisions, but she was trying to understand the ones that mattered, and I needed to do the same for her.

The smells of freshly ground cumin, chili powder, and cloves from the nearby spice shop wafted over to us. It was the very shop where I had captured one of my best photographs: a man around my age, leaning over a large mortar and pestle, his forehead furrowed and sweat beads dancing atop his brow, crushing dried red chilies into a fine powder.

Mom took my hand and said, "Preeti, I'm proud of the woman you have become."

I was so shocked to hear the words that I'd been searching for since I was a little girl. A tear formed in my eye, and I realized this was the only thing I needed from her.

As I watched a monkey hop onto the garden wall from a nearby tree, I realized that for the first time in thirty years, she had given me her blessing to live as I chose and deviate from the plan she had mapped out for me. I had been striving toward that moving target for most of my life. I had been searching for my identity and sense of belonging everywhere other than the one place I had needed to. I had convinced myself that I needed to know who I was without my family and culture getting in the way. But that had been an impossible goal. My family and culture were the backbone of my identity, and I'd never be whole without either. And I had to accept that I would never fully belong to India or America. Being adrift was the plight of any immigrant, and it was foolish to think that I could somehow circumvent that. But I now felt like I belonged in the only place that mattered. I inched closer and rested my head on my mother's shoulder as the hichko swayed back and forth, the scent of jasmine all around us.

ACKNOWLEDGMENTS

My journey to publication has been long and winding, and there are many people to whom I owe my deepest gratitude. First is my agent, Lauren Abramo, who championed my authentic voice and story from the start, and without whom I would not have come so far in this journey. Second is my editor, Alicia Clancy, who seamlessly picked up where Lauren left off and pushed me to an even deeper and more genuine place with this story. I am eternally grateful to these talented women who helped make my lifelong dream come true.

This book would also not be possible without the wonderful team at Lake Union who helped guide this new writer from story to book. A huge thanks to Danielle Marshall, Gabe Dumpit, Rosanna Brockley, Nicole Burns-Ascue, Susan Stokes, Riam Griswold, Heather Buzila, Micaela Alcaino, and Christina L.

Special thanks to the talented instructors at the UCLA Extension Writers' Program who began guiding me on this path over a decade ago, especially Claire Carmichael, Deirdre Shaw, and the late Linda Palmer.

Thank you to the amazingly talented writer Julie Buxbaum, who led me to the UCLA Extension Writers' Program all those years ago, and whose advice on everything from writing to agents to publishing has been invaluable. Thank you for showing me what was possible.

A special thank-you to author, generous spirit, and all-around badass human Jennifer Pastiloff. Your words and positive energy found me at exactly the right time and helped propel me to this finish line. Publishing this book was the goal on my sticky note in Ojai, so thank you for helping to send some magic my way.

A huge thank-you to April Spurlock, my first writer friend, for her early and repeated reads of this story over the past decade, and for the many hours of discussion about my writing. Your belief in me and this story helped make this book possible. I'd also like to thank Sonam Makker and Srivitta Kengskool, whose insights helped shape this story during various stages.

Finally, there are no words to express my gratitude for the love and support of my family as I pursued this writing dream, even if they didn't understand it! Tejas, no matter what happens in life, I know my older brother is in my corner, and I am lucky to have that. Mom and Dad, the older I get, the more I appreciate the sacrifices you have made and continue to make for me. You taught me to be resilient, compassionate, and empathetic regardless of the circumstances, and those lessons have enabled me to become who I am today.

QUESTIONS FOR DISCUSSION

1. The title of this novel is based on the Indian proverb that translates as "a monkey does not know the taste of ginger." What do you think this proverb means? What related themes did you notice in the novel?

2. Throughout the story, we learn that Preeti felt the only way to assimilate into American culture was to adopt as many white traits as she could. Do you think she had other options? Do you think she made the right decision? Do you think it's possible for someone like Preeti to be accepted into white American culture while still retaining her Indian culture?

3. Preeti felt the burden of being an immigrant child and thought it was her duty to ensure her parents didn't have to struggle financially. That is part of what drove her to pursue law rather than photography. Do you think she made the right decision? Or do you think she gave up on photography too easily after it not working out for a year after college?

4. When it comes to careers, Preeti's dad says that "meaning is something reserved for the rich," and that is a "luxury"

that they, as working-class immigrants, don't have. Do you agree?

5. Preeti is reintroduced to the caste system as an adult in this story and draws parallels between her family being upper caste in India's system and middle caste in America's. She wonders why her parents would willingly stay in America after they made that realization. Why do you think her parents remained in a country in which, in many ways, they had a harder life than they would have had if they had stayed in India? Do you think it would ever be possible for Preeti to reach the highest caste in America through hard work or assimilation, or do you think societal caste systems are determined by immutable factors?

6. Preeti struggles with maintaining social customs in India when she starts to have feelings for Tushar. In the end, she does not want him to give up his culture to explore something with her when she is uncertain. Do you think she made the right decision? Should she have followed her heart even if things with Tushar might not have worked out?

7. Preeti's relationship with Neel suffers after he releases his long-harbored resentment for the things that she was sheltered from when the family immigrated to America. Do you think Neel's resentment is fair to Preeti? Do you think Preeti could have discovered these things earlier but chose not to notice them?

8. The story does not say what happens to Biren after the police raid, and he never tells Preeti. What do you think happened to Biren? How do you think it changed him?

9. Biren does not believe his family will accept his sexuality, so he feels compelled to choose between romantic love

and familial love. Do you think he made the right decision? Do you think there are circumstances in which a person cannot have both and does have to choose one? Why or why not?

10. Preeti and Carrie have a heartfelt conversation about assimilation and white privilege. Carrie realizes she did not fully see Preeti as she was and made assumptions that she and Preeti were the same. What do you think of Preeti's comments to Carrie, and what do you think of the way Carrie received those comments? Do you think their friendship will grow closer or further apart now that they've shared these thoughts? How do you think they will treat each other differently as their friendship continues?

11. The novel ends with Preeti and her mother speaking openly for the first time in their lives. How do you think their relationship will change as a result of how they understand each other now? If Preeti had known earlier in life about her mother's broken engagement, how do you think that would have impacted their relationship?

ABOUT THE AUTHOR

Photo by Ron Derhacopian

Mansi Shah is a writer who lives in Los Angeles. She was born in Toronto, Canada, was raised in the midwestern United States, and studied at universities in America, Australia, and England. When she's not writing, she's traveling and exploring different cultures near and far, experimenting on a new culinary creation, or trying to improve her tennis game. For more information, visit her online at www.mansikshah.com.